RICHAR

A Private
Revenge

SPHERE BOOKS LTD

A SPHERE BOOK

First published in Great Britain by John Murray (Publishers) Ltd 1989
Published by Sphere Books Ltd 1990

Copyright © Richard Woodman 1989

Printed and bound in Great Britain by
Richard Clay Ltd, Bungay, Suffolk

ISBN 0 7474 0596 4

Sphere Books Ltd
A Division of
Macdonald & Co (Publishers) Ltd
Orbit House, 1 New Fetter Lane, London EC4A 1AR
A member of Maxwell Macmillan Pergamon Publishing Corporation

Contents

For
J.P.B.S.

The South China Sea, 1808-9

PART ONE

The Damoclean Sword

'Seamen are neither reckoned among the living, nor the dead, their whole lives being spent in jeopardy. No sooner is one peril over, but another comes rolling on, like the waves of a fullgrown sea.'

Samuel Kelly
An Eighteenth-Century Seaman, 1786

The Typhoon

Captain Nathaniel Drinkwater gave up trying to sleep. His cot rocked and jerked so violently on its lanyards that his body was never still. He kicked the twisted blankets aside with a sudden spurt of furious annoyance.

His Britannic Majesty's frigate *Patrician* pitched violently, her bow flung into the air as if her twelve hundred tons were of no consequence, for all her massive timbers. Drinkwater was driven to consider her fabric as a sum of many small and separate parts which, God alone knew, were now subjected to stresses and strains beyond the computation of his tired brain. All that he could consider at that moment was a vivid image of his ship flying to pieces from the pounding she was now undergoing. There was something alarmingly new about this present motion, and the thought led him to conclude that he must have been dozing. Anger had been born out of this interruption of his rest. The knock at the cabin door only increased his resentment.

'Yes?' His voice was sharp and strained.

'Captain, sir, if you please, Mr Fraser's compliments and would you step on deck, sir?'

Midshipman Belchambers's face was grey with fatigue and fright, reminding Drinkwater that he was not alone in his exhaustion.

'What is it?' He raised himself on a precarious elbow and

3

quizzed the midshipman as the cot lanyards alternately slackened and snapped taut so that his awkwardly prone body was feather-light one second and leaden the next. The ship's stern was lifted rapidly as a sea slammed viciously under her transom and against her stern windows over which the dead-lights had been dropped. Water drove in round the sashes, squirting over the settee before running to join the mess slopping back and forth across the chequer-painted canvas on the deck.

Midshipman Belchambers grabbed a corner of the sideboard, his Adam's apple bobbing uncertainly above his grubby stock.

'I can't say, sir,' he gabbled and, clapping a hand over his mouth, fled from the captain's presence.

Drinkwater stared after the boy. The grey gleam of water, mixed with fragments of biscuit from the shattered china barrel, flowed in miniature torrents round the legs of the lashed table, and overturned chairs slid back and forth, back and forth . . .

'God's bones!' Drinkwater blasphemed through clenched teeth, hoisting himself carefully out of his cot and seeking a footing in his stockinged feet amid the cold swirl of the water. The shards of porcelain grated across the deck like shingle on a beach as he felt his stockings take up the water. Drinkwater's shins were already criss-crossed with bruises, his old shoulder wound ached abominably, his mouth was foul with the taste of bile and his eyes ground grittily in their sockets, sure evidence of lack of sleep.

He clung upright with difficulty, drawing on coat and cloak, despite the stuffiness of the air. Outside his cabin the marine sentry slithered towards him and they collided amid a confused and embarrassed explosion of apology and profanity. *Patrician*'s motion was unpredictably irregular, a bucking, scending, rolling caused by the seas which slammed her sides and ran below by a hundred leaky routes. A rancid stench rose from the crowded berth-deck below and was given seeming embodiment by the creaks and groans of the labouring ship. Grasping the companionway man-ropes, Drinkwater climbed carefully on deck.

He reached the quarterdeck surprised that it was full daylight. Fraser stood clinging to the starboard hammock cranes.

'What is it, Mr Fraser?'

The first lieutenant shook his head, concern etched in his drawn expression.

'I cannot tell precisely, sir . . . the confusion of the sea . . . 'tis the worst thing I've seen.'

Drinkwater was suddenly attentive and looked about him, the stupor of exhaustion flung away. Was it a matter of Scots caution, or did a shoal lurk beneath this monstrous confusion of water? He could not tell; his charts were totally inadequate and he had no precise knowledge of their whereabouts. For four days they had run before the storm without a stitch of canvas set and their topgallant masts struck. Two men had been killed getting the heavy lower yards lashed a-portlast so that *Patrician* offered as little top-hamper as possible to the fury of the wind. The decks were cluttered with lowered spars, yet the big frigate still steered downwind with the speed of a cantering horse.

On the second night of the storm the lower masts had glowed with St Elmo's fire, the corposant running hither and thither in the rigging until their baffled compass had, in the hours that followed, circled gently in a kind of bewilderment that confused Drinkwater. He had lost his old sailing master, killed in the action with the Russian line-of-battle ship *Suvorov*, and had no one to turn to for advice, as Fraser had now turned to him.

For those four days they had run square to leeward with great seas heaping up astern, their foaming crests breaking and running after the fleeing ship. They had been pooped twice, sluiced from taffrail to knightheads by an avalanche of green water that tore coils of rope from the fife-rails, swept men off their feet and dashed them into the guns. In this deluge arms had been broken, an elbow shattered and a leg snapped so cleanly that it lay like a carpenter's angle. Worst of all two men had been washed overboard. One, Midshipman Wickham, they had not seen again, the other, the marine quarter-guard, had been found clinging to the heads, his feet dragging in the water in the last extremity of distress. The experience made the ship's company more cautious and the second pooping caused less damage.

But this morning the sea no longer drove from astern and the wind no longer roared through the standing rigging to tear the slack stays of the upper masts in great bights to leeward. Nor was the air filled with salt and spray driving downwind like buckshot. Instead, the surface of the ocean rose up in heaps; waves slopped with malignant power against each other, flinging dark columns of water high into the air, from which they fell back in a vast welter of confusion.

In this lashing of the sea *Patrician* was caught helplessly, the violence of her motion whipping her truncated masts so that blocks flew about aloft with sufficient energy to brain a man sent to secure them. Abrupt enough to throw an incautious man from his feet as she lay down to a roll, *Patrician*'s hull would be thrust back by a wave running in opposition to the first. This conflict of forces assailed her simultaneously, sending wracking stresses through her straining hull while the tortured bodies of her company met the onslaught with instinctive and tiring muscular exertions.

If the air no longer boomed with the sound of the great wind, it was now filled with the huge slop and hiss of the aimless sea, and the desperate cries of exhausted birds. The deck was covered with their pathetic, flapping forms, a variety of species including brilliantly coloured land-birds.

Looking upwards Drinkwater saw the explanation for his surprise at the daylight. For the duration of the storm they had run under a low and oppressive overcast of thick scud. Now the sky was inexplicably clear and the last stars were fading against the blue of the morning, though the horizon that ringed them was still dull under a rim of encircling fractus.

'I tried a cast o' the lead, sir, but nae bottom . . .' said Fraser, suddenly thrusting out an arm. Drinkwater grasped it, and clawed his way uphill towards the starboard rail, then immediately found himself cannoned into Fraser by the frigate's lurch.

'Devil take it! Obliged, Mr Fraser . . .'

Drinkwater caught his breath and looked about him again.

6

He had, he realised now, known instinctively that this terrible motion was not due to shoal water; the extraordinary funnel of clear and windless sky stirred something else in his tired brain. He fought to clear it, buying time with a pathetic joke.

'Belchambers bid me "step" on deck, Mr Fraser. If it was your choice of phrase you could have bettered it.'

A thin, respectful grin spread briefly across the Scotsman's worried face.

'Aye, sir, 'twas ill-chosen.'

'No matter.' Drinkwater jerked his head at the sky. 'This present lull will not last. I mind some instruction on the matter, 'tis the same as a West India hurricane, though known differently in these seas. Do you look again to the breeching of the guns. I wish we had struck some of them down into the hold, but it is too late now. I'll take the deck.'

'Aye, aye, sir. We've beckets on the wheel and clapped lashings on the tiller. All she'll do is lie a-hull.'

'That's well done.'

Fraser skidded off, shouting names at the duty bosun's mate, and Drinkwater jammed his body against the starboard mizen pin-rail, feeling the sore places on his back where the ropes had abraded him earlier. He looked after his first lieutenant: poor Fraser, as first luff he should have enjoyed the privilege of being exempt from watch-keeping. But with Lieutenant Mylchrist and Mr Hill dead, only he and Quilhampton remained of the lieutenants and senior officers, though Drinkwater had written out an acting commission for Mr Midshipman Frey.

Fraser's predicament led Drinkwater's thoughts to a review of his hard-pressed command. In addition to her present plight there were other concerns that drove his mind into a remorseless circle of worry. The presence of over a hundred Russian prisoners placed strains upon the domestic arrangements of a ship and company already stretched by a long and dangerous voyage. *Patrician*'s own people were worn out with the war, transferred from one ship to another at the whim of the almighty Admiralty and now fighting for their very existence in this dismal corner of the north-west Pacific.

Captain Drinkwater stared bleakly ahead, noting the relative shift in the shrinking patch of blue sky and weighing up the chances of a glimpse of the sun before the cloud lowered over them again.

The squawks of the birds drew his thoughts inboard once more as a handful of seamen, clinging on to any handhold, strove to clear the decks of some of the hundreds of dying creatures. He watched them, trying to judge their temper for though they had fought well against a Russian battle-ship in the Pacific, their mood had been uncertain off the Horn and they had been near-mutinous off California, several of them deserting at San Francisco.

In his heart, Drinkwater knew he could expect no less. Some of them had been at sea since the turn of the century, had served as volunteers in the Peace of Amiens and had then been swept up in the turbulence of the renewed war with France.

Drinkwater cursed the chain of events that had led them to this day, for he too suffered, suffered as personally as his men, for the secret he and they had brought back from the Baltic in the late summer of 1807. That overwhelming need for secrecy had led Their Lordships to despatch him to the Pacific to head off Britain's quondam ally Russia, whose Tsar had abandoned his alliance with the Court of St James in favour of a shoddy opportunist accommodation with Napoleon Bonaparte. This allowed Tsar Alexander to meddle with Sweden and Turkey and lend his British-trained fleet to the Emperor of the French. Had Drinkwater, despite the odds, succeeded in crushing the Russian presence in the Pacific? He had fought the *Suvorov* to a standstill, as the state of his frigate testified, but his cruise to locate the *Juno* had failed. She had slipped from him, and his nature would not allow him the reasonable excuse of having the whole Pacific to search to comfort him in his failure.

Perhaps she was at Canton, perhaps not . . .

A watery gleam caught his attention to larboard. He turned and lifted his eyes. As the circle of clear sky moved over them a shredding of the cloud on its eastern rim exposed for a second a pale yellow disc. The sun!

'Mr Belchambers! My sextant and the chronometer! Upon the instant, sir!'

Transfixed, Drinkwater watched the face of the sun darken as, like dense smoke, cloud trailed across it, then lighten again. Impatiently he waited for the boy's return. The sun swam clear of cloud, hurting his eyes, and he thought its warmth struck him, though afterwards it seemed a mere illusion. Suddenly the confusion of the sea held less terrors and flashed friendly fire back at them in reflections. Amidships a man smiled and raised a low cheer. All about him there was a spontaneous outburst of relief. The watch, huddling in the lee of the boats on the booms, struggled to their feet, other seamen stopped throwing the birds overboard and even, it seemed, the birds themselves ceased their death struggles to bask in the sunlight.

Drinkwater's patience snapped. 'Where the devil's that boy?'

'Beg pardon, sir . . .'

His sentry's head was poked up the companionway level with the deck.

'Eh? What is it?' Drinkwater asked the marine.

'Begging your pardon, sir, but Mr Belchambers 'as 'ad a fall, sir.'

'What? God-damn! What about my sextant?' Drinkwater was already crossing the deck and exchanging the ineffable sweetness of sunshine for the stygian gloom of the gun-deck. Shoving aside the sentry, he entered his cabin. By the grace of God Belchambers had not reached the Hadley sextant, nestling in its baize-lined box and lashed atop his locker. Instead the boy lay amid the swirl of biscuit and china with a sprained ankle. His small, frightened face was twisted with agony.

'I . . . I'm sorry, sir . . . I acted with haste . . . *festina lente*, sir,' the boy added gamely.

'No matter, Mr Belchambers, are you all right?' Drinkwater bent over the midshipman.

'Apart from my ankle, sir . . .'

Drinkwater turned to the marine. 'Get a couple of hands to carry Mr Belchambers to his berth.'

Drinkwater reached across the midshipman who was

drawing himself up against the locker. 'You must excuse me, I have urgent matters to attend to.'

Lifting the sextant from its box he caught the strap of the chronometer case with his left hand. Sticking his elbows out for balance he gingerly made for the bottom of the companionway and shouted up for assistance.

'Here, zur, let me . . .'

Old Tregembo his coxswain shouldered past him and took the chronometer box.

'Mind how you go, damn it,' snapped Drinkwater as both men grabbed the man-rope at the same instant.

'Up you goes, zur, an' I'll follow . . .'

But it was too late. Already the sun had been swallowed by cloud and the eye of the storm was passing over them. Fractus again curtained the sky and the confusion of the sea was abating. Streaks of spume were appearing upon its surface which was heaping once more in regular ridges. The calm of the dawn had vanished. *Patrician*, with her lashed tiller and locked rudder, was paying off to lie beam on to the rising wind that came at them now from the contrary direction. Drinkwater bit off his disappointment at failing to get a sight. As the deck steadied to a roll, he crossed it swiftly and peered into the binnacle. He had at least a notion of their heading and now, as it blew with swiftly increasing strength, the direction of the gale. That brief glimpse of the sun had fed his starved seaman's instinct with a morsel of information.

The compass had steadied and the wind blew now from the west-nor'-west.

But it was precious little comfort. An hour later *Patrician* was assailed again by the violence of the storm. It no longer screamed with the malevolent harpy-shriek of a strong gale, but had risen to the mind-numbing boom of a mighty wind, and the spray tore at the very eyes in their sockets, forcing their heads away.

'It's blowing great guns, sir,' shouted Fraser as he clawed his way towards Drinkwater on completion of his rounds.

'A great wind, Mr Fraser. I mind now the captain of an Indiaman once telling me it was called *tai-fun* by the Chinese.'

CHAPTER 1

The Brig

Drinkwater closed the log-book. Knowledge of his position at last gave him a measure of contentment. The inadequacy of his chart sent a flutter of apprehension through his belly, to conflict with the realisation that he had been extraordinarily lucky. He recalled memories of talks with Captain Calvert nearly thirty years earlier, dredging up facts imparted to the impressionable young Midshipman Drinkwater by the old East India commander. Calvert had told him of the curious revolving storms of the China Seas which were comparable with the hurricanes of the West Indies or the feared cyclones of the Bay of Bengal.

From what his sextant and chronometer had revealed he was now able to make an informed guess at *Patrician*'s track in a long curve that had brought her from the Pacific Ocean into the eastern margins of the South China Sea. The typhoon's eye, or centre, that funnel of clear sky in which they had experienced the severest thrashing of the sea, had passed over them, subjecting them to the violent winds beyond. They had been fortunate that their ordeal had lasted only another two days, for though the wind remained fresh and a heavy residual swell still lifted and rolled the frigate, the sea was no longer vicious. A measure of its moderation could be gauged by the smell of smoke and salt pork that was percolating through the ship. The thought of hot food, however rudimentary, brought a glow of satisfaction to Drinkwater's spirits as surely as the knowledge of his ship's position.

In this mood Drinkwater, tired though he was, finished his self-imposed task of writing up his private journal. As he did so his cabin was suddenly filled with the delicious bitter smell of what passed for coffee aboard His Britannic Majesty's frigate *Patrician*. Drinkwater looked up.

'Coffee, sir?'

Mullender poured from the pot he had brought from the pantry and Drinkwater sipped the scalding liquid gratefully. Mullender stood, balancing himself against the heave of the ship which was pronounced here, at the stern.

'Hot food today, sir,' Mullender remarked. Such things assumed a rare importance on board a storm-damaged ship and Drinkwater looked keenly at his steward. How long had Mullender attended him? To his shame he had forgotten; and he had forgotten whether Mullender was married or had children. The man stood patiently, holding the coffee-pot, waiting for Drinkwater to ask for more, a grubby rag of a towel over his bare arm with its sparse flesh and pallid skin. Drinkwater caught the steward's eye and smiled.

'That's good news, Mullender, good news . . .'

'Aye, sir.'

Mullender's impassivity, the expressionless look to his eyes and face struck Drinkwater, and it occurred to him that he had taken Mullender so for granted that he was guilty in some way he could not quite comprehend. He held out his cup and watched the brown liquid gurgle into it.

'We have all been sorely tried, Mullender,' he said as he swallowed the second cupful.

'Aye, sir.'

Drinkwater handed the emptied cup back to the steward. 'That was most welcome, thank you.'

He watched Mullender retreat to the pantry. Was there something odd about the man's demeanour, or was he himself mildly hallucinating from the effects of exhaustion? He did not know. What was important was to secure for them all a period of rest. Wearily he rose from the table and left the cabin.

There was more to hearten him on deck, for it was one of the minor miracles of the sea-service that the sum of a ship's company's efforts could produce spectacular results from meagre resources. And *Patrician* and her people had indeed been sorely tried in the preceding months.

She had taken a buffeting entering the Pacific by way of Cape Horn the previous year; she had been deliberately sabotaged by someone in her own company and refitted on the coast of California; and she had fought two actions, the second against heavy odds. The brutal combat with the Russian line-of-battle ship *Suvorov* had left her a battered victor with the added responsibility of prisoners amongst her own disaffected crew. Now, bruised by the long passage across the North Pacific and the terrible onslaught of a typhoon, it was still possible to set her to rights, to turn out of her hold sufficient material to make good the worst ravages of the elements, to rouse out of her sail-room enough spare sails to replace her rent canvas, or hoist from her booms a permutation of spars which allowed her to carry topgallants on all three masts. It was true she was no longer the lofty sail-carrier that had left the Nore amid the equinoctial gales of the autumn of 1807, but despite shortages of powder and shot, despite a desperate depletion of her stores and victuals, she remained a King's ship, an arm of British policy in these distant waters.

'Good morning, sir.'

Lieutenant James Quilhampton touched the forecock of his battered hat, his tall, gangling frame familiarly out-at-elbows, his wooden fist by his side and a wide grin upon his face.

'Good to see a little sunshine, Mr Q,' remarked Drinkwater.

'Indeed it is, sir. Frey told me you were active with sextant and chronometer an hour since, sir. Dare I presume a longitude?'

'You may. And it crossed tolerably with yesterday's meridian altitude. If it remains clear, I shall get another at noon and be happy as a prentice-boy on pay-day.'

It was another minor miracle, Drinkwater thought, that

neither of his instruments had suffered damage in the typhoon. It was true there were two other quadrants on the ship, but the loss of the chronometer would have been catastrophic.

'We shall have to maintain a masthead look-out, Mr Q, day and night, for we have passed the outer islands and are presently amid the reefs of the China Sea.'

The two men exchanged glances. Both were thinking of the brig *Hellebore* and her wrecking on a reef in the Red Sea.

'God forbid that we should be caught twice like that,' Quilhampton said fervently, expelling his breath with a shake of his head.

Drinkwater caught the faint whiff of the lieutenant's breath and was reminded of another problem, for the unfortunate taint, increasingly common to them all, was an early sign of scurvy.

'We must wood and water, and seek fresh fruit and vegetables, Mr Q. I've a mind to beat up for the China coast. There's the Portuguese colony of Macao, or the East India Company's establishment at Canton where we may also find word of the *Juno*. It is still possible that she has escorted Russian ships there from Alaska with the season's furs.'

'Will you exchange our prisoners there, sir?' Quilhampton nodded forward to where, under a marine guard, a group of bearded Russians exercised round and round the fo'c's'le.

'If I can. They are a damned liability on board.'

'And their officers, sir?'

It was Drinkwater's turn to expel breath, a signal of exasperation borne with difficulty. 'I doubt they'll go, God damn 'em. My only consolation is that I do not have to suffer them day and night.'

The deaths of Lieutenant Mylchrist and the Master, Mr Hill, had left empty cabins aboard. Acting Lieutenant Frey had been ordered to stay in the gunroom while the cabins of the dead officers were turned over to the most senior of the Russians. At least Captain Prince Vladimir Rakitin did not have to share Drinkwater's own cabin, though he ate at his table. On such a long commission Drinkwater prized his privacy above all else.

'Talk of the devil,' muttered Quilhampton, drawing himself up as officer-of-the-watch to give the paroled prisoners formal permission to exercise on the quarterdeck.

'Good morning, Captain.'

The tall, heavily built figure of the Russian nobleman crossed the deck towards Drinkwater, staring about curiously. Rakitin was pale from his enforced confinement below decks for the duration of the typhoon.

'Good-day.'

Drinkwater was icily polite to his prisoner.

'You have refitted your ship in good time.'

Rakitin's excellent English was unnerving. The Russian had served with the Royal Navy before the Tsar had turned his coat and succumbed to Napoleon's blandishments at Tilsit. Drinkwater found this familiarity as repulsive as the man himself.

'My men know their duty, Captain,' he replied softly.

The two commanders stood side by side, united in rank, divided by hostility and yet compelled by convention to maintain a degree of amity. Considering them from the other side of the quarterdeck, Quilhampton thought them an odd pair. Tall and powerful, Rakitin's broad shoulders stretched the cloth of his high-collared uniform, an à la mode outfit that stank of Parisian fashion. Beside him, half a head shorter, his soft undress uniform coat lapels fluttering in the breeze, Captain Drinkwater balanced himself against the *Patrician*'s motion.

Quilhampton could see the inequality of Drinkwater's shoulders, the result of two wounds that even padding and the heavy bullion epaulettes could not disguise. The hair, receding slightly from the high forehead, still hung in a thick, ribboned queue down Drinkwater's back, an old-fashioned affectation that conveyed an impression of agelessness to the loyal and devoted Quilhampton. As if sensing this scrutiny Drinkwater turned, catching Quilhampton's eye. The thin scar on the left cheek showed livid after the weathering of recent weeks, and the powder burns about Drinkwater's eye puckered the soft skin to give him a curious, quizzing appearance.

'Mr Q!' Drinkwater called. 'Have the kindness to arrange for

15

Captain Rakitin's officers to attend the purser and supervise an issue of grog to their men in compliment to their labours at the pumps.'

'Aye, aye, sir.'

Rakitin turned, an expression of surprise on his face. 'My men have been pumping?' he asked.

'Yes,' replied Drinkwater smoothly, 'in order that mine might repair the ship.'

Drinkwater felt a contempt for Rakitin's ignorance of what his men had been doing. It seemed for a moment that Rakitin might protest, but he held his tongue. The Russian seamen had proved tireless and dogged workers, as conscientious at pumping as they had been serving the *Suvorov*'s guns. But indomitable as they had been in action, they had been ravaged by scurvy, reduced in numbers by sickness, and the high sea running during the battle had made it difficult for Rakitin to use his lower-deck guns. In the end *Suvorov* had been at the mercy of *Patrician*'s 24- and 18-pounder cannon which had cut up her rigging and masts, hulled her repeatedly, and swept her decks with a hail of canister and langridge. By the time Rakitin struck his colours, *Suvorov*'s powers of resistance were as shattered as her hull and when, in the moderating sea of the following day, they had taken off all those that they could, she had settled so low in the water that the fire they had started aboard her had barely caught. As for Drinkwater, he had lost more men in the rescue than in the action.

Rakitin, left to a sullen contemplation of his fate, had persuaded himself that his ship had been wantonly sacrificed by the British acting under Drinkwater's orders. The fact that Drinkwater possessed neither the resources nor the men to take the *Suvorov* as a prize did not enter into the Russian commander's bitter reflections. Aware that he had failed in his mission, Rakitin sought among his officers men of like opinion, cultivating them assiduously in this assumption, until they had convinced themselves of its accuracy. It was an understandable enough attitude, Drinkwater reflected, aware of the undercurrent of hostility. Rakitin would have to account for the loss of his ship to the Admiralty at St Petersburg, and the difference in force between a seventy-four and a frigate, albeit a heavy one, was going to be difficult to explain.

Rakitin had seized eagerly on the intelligence that the British ship had been built twenty-four years earlier as a 64-gun line-of-battle ship, insinuating this into his persuasive argument and glossing over the fact that she had been cut down to her present establishment in 1795. Somehow Rakitin had mitigated his defeat, at least in his own mind.

Despite this, Drinkwater could not deny an underlying sympathy with Rakitin's plight. He knew what it was to lose a ship. The loss of self-confidence alone could sink a man's spirits beyond revival. Nor did Drinkwater forget other matters concerning Russia; his brother Edward was serving with the Russian army, an agent of Great Britain now, nominally at least, an enemy. So Drinkwater cultivated Rakitin with an icy reserve, not knowing, in this long and bitter war, when Tsar Alexander might turn his coat again, or when some obligation towards himself might not prove of advantage.

'Our men work well together, Captain. We should not be enemies. I believe Admiral Seniavin feels this.'

'Seniavin?' Rakitin looked at Drinkwater in astonishment, his mind plucked from the narrow contemplation of his misery to the speculative castle-building that officers called 'strategy'.

'Yes,' went on Drinkwater, 'I am advised that he is opposed to the Tsar's alliance with Napoleon Bonaparte.'

'I have my orders, Captain. It is my duty to obey them,' Rakitin growled.

'But,' said Drinkwater, suddenly brightening at the prospect of a little innocent bear-baiting, 'you also have your opinion, *n'est-ce que pas?*'

Rakitin turned and drew himself up. 'The alliance with the Emperor Napoleon is one offering great advantages to Russia. It is impossible that the French should rule Europe from Paris, but Europe ruled from Paris *and* St Petersburg *must* be, he shrugged, *très formidable . . .*'

'Until the Emperor Napoleon wishes otherwise, eh?'

'Captain Drinkwater, you cannot hold out the hand of friendship to Russia. Your army abandoned ours in the Netherlands, your Nelson threatened our ships in our own Baltic Sea. You still have a fleet there blockading our coasts, you tell us we can only trade with you . . .'

'You sailed in our ships, Prince Vladimir, you learned much from us and supported us in the North Sea. We pressed gold and arms on you, even refitted your ships; was not this proof of our friendship?'

Rakitin flushed with anger and was about to launch into a tirade on Britain's perfidy when there came a cry from the masthead.

'Deck there! Sail to leeward!'

Quilhampton reacted instantaneously, leaping into the lee mizen shrouds and yelling back: 'Where away?'

'Three points on the lee bow, sir . . . looks like a vessel under jury-rig!'

Quilhampton scanned the horizon and could see nothing. He jumped to the deck and held his glass out to Midshipman Dutfield.

'Up you go, cully, and see what you make of her.'

Drinkwater and Rakitin, their interest aroused, dropped their conversation instantly and stood watching the nimble boy ascend the rigging of the main mast. Dutfield reached the top-gallant yard and threw a leg over it, hooking himself steady and releasing his two hands to raise the glass. His body arced against the sky for what seemed an eternity as everybody on deck waited for his opinion of the stranger.

They saw him lower the glass and look down, expecting any moment to hear news, but, apparently unsure, the midshipman raised the telescope again. The waist was filled with a murmur at the delay.

'Bosun's mate! Keep the men busy there!' Quilhampton ordered, adding, 'Watch your helm there, quartermaster,' as the petty officer at the con inattentively let the ship's head pay off.

At last Dutfield's voice hailed them from aloft.

18

'Brig, sir, and seen us by the colours reversed in her rigging!'
'What colours?' bellowed Drinkwater through cupped hands.
'British, sir . . .'

'Up helm a trifle, Mr Q, let's bear down on this fellow. Call all hands to stand by to reduce sail . . .'

Patrician lay hove-to, her main-topsail billowed back against the mast and her fore and main courses flogging sullenly in the buntlines as they brought the brig under their lee and prepared to hoist out a boat. Drinkwater studied the craft through his Dollond glass. She was a brig all right, and lying low in the water with both masts gone by the board. Her crew had managed to fish a yard to the stump of her foremast and had a leg-of-mutton sail hoisted, just, Drinkwater judged, giving her master command of his vessel.

'Ah, Mr Frey,' Drinkwater turned to the young man at his elbow, 'do you be kind enough to go over and offer what assistance is in our power. Find out her port of destination and her master's name. If she requires it, we can get a line aboard.'

'Aye, aye, sir.'

'And Mr Frey . . .'

'Sir?'

'Ask if she has any charts of the China coast.'

Drinkwater watched the boat bob over the swell, the oar-blades catching the brilliant sunshine, then disappearing in the deep troughs. As the boat rose again he recalled himself and turned suddenly, casting an incautious eye skywards and receiving the solar glare in his face.

'How bears the sun, Mr Q?' he asked urgently.

Quilhampton grasped Drinkwater's meaning and covered the three yards' distance to the binnacle. 'Close to the meridian, sir.'

'Damn!' With the agility of a younger man, Drinkwater made for the companionway and dropped below, startling Mullender as he fussed about the cabin. Grabbing the sextant from its lashed box and crooking it in his arm, he hastened back on deck. He flicked down the shades and clapped it to his right eye. To his relief he saw the sun was still increasing its altitude, climbing slowly to the meridian, and he waited for the ascent to slow.

'Watch the glass, there!' he called.

The quartermaster of the watch moved aft to heave the log as Quilhampton stood ready to turn the sand-glass. Forward the lookout on the knightheads walked aft and stood beside the belfry. Drinkwater caught the culmination of the sun on the meridian. He could compute their latitude exactly now and by a piece of legerdemain determine, to a reasonable accuracy, their longitude as well. Knowledge of their position would be invaluable both to himself and, he suspected, the beleaguered master of the wallowing brig.

'Eight bells!' he called, lowering the sextant. The log was streamed, the glass turned and eight bells struck. The watch was called and yet another day officially began on board the *Patrician*.

An hour later he was bent over the cabin table, comparing his calculations with the reckoning of Captain Ballantyne, Master of the Country brig *Musquito* of Calcutta. Ballantyne was a short, red-faced man in a plain blue coat and tall boots, a tired man who had wrestled gamely with the typhoon for ten days and been forced to sacrifice his masts in order to preserve his ship.

Sunlight reflected off the swell beyond the windows and danced upon the white paintwork of the cabin, filling it with flickering lights as the frigate rolled easily.

'Well, sir,' said Drinkwater straightening up, 'will you serve us as pilot? If we are to bring both our ships safely to an anchor our need of each other is mutual.'

He was aware of continuing suspicion in Ballantyne's face. The merchant shipmaster remained obviously circumspect. To Ballantyne, Drinkwater was something of an enigma, for he was no youthful popinjay like so many of the young sprigs that came out in sloops and frigates to press men like carcasses from Country ships. In fact his appearance in these eastern seas was something of a mystery to a man like Ballantyne who, in common with all the trading fraternity, liked to keep his fingers on the pulse of Government business. Drinkwater's request for a pilot and charts confirmed him in one suspicion.

'I am indeed under an obligation to you, Captain Drinkwater, and one that I would not willingly shirk, but I am surprised to find you here. Are you not part of Drury's squadron?'

It was Drinkwater's turn to show surprise. 'Drury's squadron . . . ? No sir, I am not. I am from the coast of Spanish America. Furthermore I understood Admiral Pellew to be commanding the East India station . . .'

'Pellew still commands, but Drury has a squadron at Macao . . .'

The welcome news that British men-of-war were at hand, that he might speedily obtain spare spars and canvas, perhaps fresh victuals too, besides making good other deficiencies in his own stores from Drury's ships, seemed to lift a massive burden from Drinkwater's weary shoulders.

'Then let us make for Macao, Captain Ballantyne . . .'

'No, sir! That I must urge you not to . . .'

Drinkwater was surprised and said so.

'Captain Drinkwater,' Ballantyne said as patiently as he could, 'you are clearly unacquainted with the situation in these seas. Drury has been empowered by the Governor-General of India to offer what Lord Minto is pleased to call "protection" to the Portuguese Governor at Macao. This is nothing more nor less than coercion, for the Portuguese colonists there are friendly to us, the more so since the damned French have designs on both Portugal herself and her overseas settlements. There are already stories of a French army coming overland through Persia and of an enemy squadron bound for these waters. If they take Macao then our China trade would be ended at a stroke . . .'

Ballantyne stopped, his serious expression adding emphasis to his speech. 'It would mean ruin for many of us in Country ships and the end of the East India Company.'

Drinkwater regarded this information with some cynicism. He held no brief for the India monopoly, but he acknowledged the influence of those who did. Ballantyne seemed to sense some of this indifference.

'Consider, sir,' he said, 'what the alliance between the Dutch and French has already achieved: the Sunda Strait is closed to our ships and it has been necessary to convoy the trade through the Strait of Malacca. I do not think you can be aware of the numbers of French cruisers, both privateers and men-o'-war frigates, that the French have operating out of the Mauritius. One, the *Piemontaise*, a National ship, was taken by the *San Fiorenzo* off Cape Comorin, but at appalling cost, and that is our *only* success! That damned rogue Surcouf plundered our shipping right off the Sand Heads with complete impunity . . .'

'The Sand Heads . . . ?' queried Drinkwater, aware of his ignorance and the apparent hornet's nest that he was blundering into.

'Aye, off the entrance to the Calcutta river, Captain, plumb under the noses of the Hooghly merchants and Admiral Pellew himself!' Ballantyne's tone was incredulous.

'Pellew cannot have liked that,' observed Drinkwater drily, 'he used to enjoy the boot being on the other foot.'

'You know him then?' asked Ballantyne.

'A long time ago, when he commanded the *Indefatigable*. But this does not explain your reluctance to allow me to take you to Macao. You must understand that now I have learned of a British flag-officer in the area it is my plain duty to report to him.'

'By all means do so, sir, but *after* you have towed me into the Pearl River. It will delay you perhaps a day, two at the most.'

'You have a reluctance to go to Macao, Captain Ballantyne? A commercial one, perhaps?'

Ballantyne nodded. 'Yes. I have a cargo, sir, a valuable cargo and a mortgage on the ship. Opium for the mandarins makes me damned anxious to take your offer of assistance. Mind you,' Ballantyne added forcefully, 'no salvage claim, by God, or I'll counter-claim on the basis of these charts and my services to bring you into the Pearl River . . .'

'Or Macao . . .'

Ballantyne's eyes suddenly narrowed. 'No, *not* Macao, Captain. My services are not available for Macao.'

'Very well, sir,' said Drinkwater coldly, 'then I shall order the preparations for passing the tow discontinued and make up the numbers of my complement from your ship. While being indebted to you for your elucidation of the mysteries of Oriental politics, I believe that I may find my own way to Macao . . .'

'Hold fast, sir,' Ballantyne snapped back, 'if I lose *Musquito* I am a ruined man. If I go direct to Macao with my ship in her present condition I shall not get her up to Whampoa, nor will I avoid incurring crippling tariffs payable to the Portuguese.' Ballantyne paused. 'I am willing to compensate you for your trouble; an *ex gratia* payment, perhaps . . .'

Drinkwater was indignant. 'I am not to be bribed, damn you!' he said sharply, and Ballantyne met his outrage, raising his own voice.

'An *ex gratia* payment is not a bribe, damn it, it is a legitimate payment for actual services! God damn it, Captain Drinkwater, you have my fate in your hands, sir; it is not easy for me to beg . . .'

Drinkwater considered the man before him. Exhaustion was perhaps making them both over-hasty. Above their heads and floating down through the open skylight came the noise of men heaving a hawser aft, ready to pass across to the stricken brig. Drinkwater needed a few minutes to reflect. He was desperate for those stores, yet there might be problems over having them allocated to *Patrician*, since she was not under Drury's orders. On the other hand the Honourable East India Company's ships at Canton would almost certainly hold stocks of spars and canvas which he could requisition. Judging from Ballantyne's jittery anxiety the spectre of his pressing men would be lever enough for him to have his own way.

'Has Admiral Drury power to take over the dockyard at Macao?' he asked in a more conciliatory tone.

'I think not. The last I heard was that the matter was at an impasse. Drury commands the ships, but his troops are mainly sepoys in the Company's service. *They* are under the direction of a Select Committee acting in the Company's interest. If you ask me there will be trouble with the Portuguese and, after that, trouble with the Chinese.'

'Which is why you are anxious to get your cargo to Canton?'

'Aye. I want to break bulk before the trade is stopped. There are already rumours that the Emperor at Peking wants it permanently terminated. That would not be in the interest of the Viceroy at Canton, it's his principal source of income, both by way of customs duties and chop . . .'

'Chop?' queried Drinkwater.

'*Cumshaw*, *baksheesh*, bribes . . .'

Abruptly Drinkwater made up his mind. He and his ship needed a brief respite. If he proceeded to Macao doubtless Drury, a man whose reputation he did not know and who in turn owed Drinkwater nothing, might press further duties upon him. He wanted to work his ship homewards and had no wish to have her detained in eastern waters on arduous service that would end up with half his crew dead of scurvy or malaria. He could tow the *Musquito* towards Canton as Ballantyne desired, pretending ignorance of Drury's presence and arguing his urgent need of fresh victuals. He would be certain of finding stores at the Company's depot and might recruit his ship before finding Drury. In addition he might persuade Drury to send another vessel after the *Juno*. He felt desperately tired, overwhelmed by lassitude and, in reality, only too happy to accommodate Ballantyne's entreaty. He felt that sometimes a postcaptain might play for advantage like a politician.

'Very well, Captain Ballantyne, the matter is agreed. You will pilot us into the Pearl River and provide me with charts necessary to take me to Penang. I shall take your brig under tow and endeavour to take off as much of your cargo as possible if she shows signs of foundering.'

'Damn it, thank you, sir!' Ballantyne held out his hand, his sudden smile evidence of his relief and the stress under which he had been labouring. Drinkwater wondered how much money rode upon the successful discharge of *Musquito*'s cargo. 'I will put my second officer aboard you, sir,' Ballantyne went on, 'to act as your pilot. He is as familiar as myself with the navigation of the Pearl River.'

'You have perfect confidence in him?'

'Absolute, Captain Drinkwater, and he may stand surety for my good conduct – he is my son.'

'I had not exactly wanted a hostage,' Drinkwater said wryly. 'Come,' he added, 'let us drink to our resolve.'

He summoned Mullender from the pantry and the two men sipped their wine while the companies of their ships passed a towline.

Drinkwater could only guess at what Ballantyne's son's mother had been. A Begum, perhaps, or a Rani? Or did such noble ladies refuse to cohabit with the likes of Ballantyne? With the tow passed, he stood now with the younger man as he had his father, consulting the charts. Possibly he was merely the bastard offspring of a nautch-girl, for he was clearly a man of colour. Drinkwater had yet to test his abilities, though he hoped he had inherited some of his father's skill, for Ballantyne had saved *Musquito* after a fight of ten days against the worst weather a mariner could encounter in these seas. Yet was it possible that so prosaic-looking a man could have sired so exotic a son?

Jahleel Ballantyne was taller than his father, his skin a light coffee colour, his hair jet-black and loosely flowing to his shoulders. He wore a blue broadcloth coat like his father, but his trousers were thin cotton pyjamas, baggy in the leg and caught at the waist by a wide, scarlet cummerbund from which a pair of pistol-butts protruded. His low-crowned hat sported an elaborate aigrette and the man smoked long, thin cheroots. He spoke perfect English with a clipped, slightly nasal accent, emphasising his words with eloquent movements of his hands. *Patrician* already had a crop of exotics among the inhabitants of her lower deck. Only time would tell what the wardroom would make of such an addition to its number.

'It is perhaps unnecessary to warn you, sir, of the dangers ahead, because you have many guns and are a ship of force. But we will be proceeding slowly, and we might be mistaken by the Ladrones for an India ship . . .'

'Pardon my interrupting, Mr Ballantyne, but who, or what, are the Ladrones?'

'Chinese pirates, sir. They usually take ships off the Ladrones Islands here.' Ballantyne laid the point of the dividers upon a small archipelago, one of several which lay scattered about the huge estuary of the Pearl River. 'They have numerous junks armed with cannon.'

'Don't the Chinese authorities take a dim view of these people?'

Ballantyne smiled, a peculiarly engaging smile, accompanied by a gentle rocking of his head. 'To the mandarins these people are poor fishermen . . .' he paused, seeing Drinkwater's expression of mystification. 'There is much to understand about these parts, sir.' Jahleel Ballantyne smiled again.

'Indeed, so it would seem, Mr Ballantyne.'

They were interrupted by Mullender.

'Beg pardon, sir, Mr Fraser's compliments and he says he'll have to turn Mr Chirkov out of Mr Mylchrist's cabin, sir, to accommodate . . .'

Mullender nodded in Ballantyne's direction and Drinkwater sensed an amusing antipathy to the presence of the half-caste officer.

'That will be very satisfactory.'

'Mr Chirkov won't like it, sir, he's a very particular young gentleman.'

Drinkwater turned. 'He's a prisoner-of-war, damn it, Mullender, not a maid to be cossetted over her mooning . . . my apologies, Mr Ballantyne, come, let us go on deck . . .'

Tregembo, Drinkwater's coxswain, emerged from the pantry grinning at the discomfited steward who stood in the centre of the suddenly empty cabin.

'What did you stand up for that Russian booby for?' he growled at Mullender. '*Particular* gennelmen aren't exactly the Cap'n's cup o' tea.'

Mullender shrugged, a man of proprieties more than words and deeds.

'Ain't proper . . . Count Chirkov's a gentleman . . .'

'*Count* Chirkov's a damned bugger, you old toss-pot,' said Tregembo dismissively.

'But he's a gentleman,' persisted Mullender doggedly.

New Orders

Midshipman Count Anatole Vasili Chirkov of the Imperial Russian Navy found captivity amusing rather than irksome. A proclivity for indolence helped, together with a rather fetchingly cultivated languor. Chirkov had discovered that a certain type of lady in the salons of St Petersburg found the affectation attractive, combined as it was with a biting sarcasm about the endeavours of others. It was a pretension peculiarly adapted to a rich adolescent. The conceit had also proved surprisingly useful aboard ship where, he had realised, a dearth of variety gave him a natural advantage over the dullards on board and provided him with innumerable targets. In fact, captive or not, Midshipman Count Chirkov found himself rather more popular than otherwise.

An exception to this general rule was Captain Drinkwater who proved impervious to Chirkov's charm. The Russian regretted he had not killed the British captain when he had had the chance in Lituya Bay. The momentary advantage he had enjoyed over Captain Drinkwater had enlarged itself in Chirkov's fertile imagination and he would have boasted about it, but for the fact that losing it so swiftly argued against himself. Drinkwater, Chirkov reluctantly had to admit, was no fool. But then neither was he a gentleman, for Chirkov had felt Drinkwater's contempt as long ago as their first encounter in San Francisco and was happy to shrug him off as a curiosity of the British navy. His own captain, Prince Vladimir, had more or less confirmed this, calling Drinkwater 'a tarpaulin', to be tolerated, when he could not be avoided, whilst Chirkov's present inconvenient circumstances persisted.

Chirkov, fluent in the French of his class, had had only a rudimentary knowledge of English when he had been taken prisoner. Recent association with *Patrician*'s 'young gentlemen', particularly since his transfer from a cabin to the gunroom, had brought them into a greater intimacy. Chirkov had assumed a casual ascendancy over the youthful Belchambers, and formed a loose friendship with Frey who, although rated acting lieutenant, remained accommodated in his former quarters due to the overcrowding of the ship.

Although Chirkov had some duties, they were nominal. He was supposed to supervise a division of the Russian sailors who had their hammocks slung in the cable tiers, but this irksome responsibility was easily delegated to a petty officer. This allowed him to indulge his apparently limitless capacity for doing nothing. At the present moment he was leaning on *Patrician*'s fo'c's'le rail, half-propped on the breech of the foremost larboard chase gun while Mr Comley, *Patrician*'s bosun and another amusing tarpaulin, hove a cable up outside the ship from the hawse pipe and bent it on to one of the sheet anchors.

Astern of them and, remarkably, still afloat, the brig *Musquito* stretched her towline. It had taken almost a fortnight to beat up into the mouth of the Pearl River among the blue hills and myriad islands of the Kwangtung coast. The bat-winged sails of the big fishing junks that had loomed out of the dawn mist two days earlier were here replaced by hundreds of small sampans. Under sail, fishing or being patiently sculled by short Chinese who tirelessly manipulated their long stern scull, or *yuloh*, they dotted the waters of the estuary. Ahead Chirkov could see that the banks of the river came together and pale marks against the grey-green of the distant hills betrayed the embrasures of forts.

Far above Chirkov's indolent head the lookout reported the

presence of 'sails', by which all on the quarterdeck assumed he meant he had sighted the heavy crossed yards of European vessels.

'They will be the Indiamen loading, I suppose,' remarked Drinkwater to Mr Ballantyne who stood next to him on the quarterdeck. A warm afternoon was producing a sea breeze, giving them their first favourable slant since they had picked up the tow, and under all the sail she could set, the British frigate was working slowly inshore.

This fair breeze had produced a mood of contentment in Captain Drinkwater. Ballantyne's fears of pirates had proved groundless. Though two big junks had closed with them in the morning's mist, they had sheered off when they ranged up close, and there was no evidence to suspect their motives had been sinister.

'No, sir . . . they cannot be Indiamen or Country ships,' replied Ballantyne. He raised his glass and studied the masts and spars of the distant ships at anchor. Then he lowered it and pointed ahead of them. 'See, there are the forts at the Bogue, sir, what is sometimes called the Bocca Tigris. Those are the Viceroy's war-junks, three of them anchored under the cannon of the forts. The Indiamen are inside the Narrows, beyond the Bogue at Whampoa. They should already be discharging. Some of those ships *may* be Indiamen but . . .' Again he raised his glass and stared at the anchored vessels, some two points to larboard.

'They're men-o'-war, sir,' shouted Quilhampton suddenly. He had hoisted himself into the mizen rigging and had been looking at the ships himself. 'And flying British colours . . .'

'They must be Admiral Drury's ships, sir,' said Ballantyne.

Drinkwater sensed a rivalry existing between the two young men. He turned to Fraser, standing beside the binnacle and watching anxiously as they crept into Chinese waters.

'What's your opinion, Mr Fraser?'

Fraser borrowed Quilhampton's proffered glass and clambered on to the larboard rail. At last he jumped down.

'No doubt, sir. A British seventy-four, two frigates and two sloops . . .'

'A seventy-four!' exclaimed Drinkwater, unable to contain his surprise. The presence of a powerful third-rate argued it was, at the very least, a force under a senior captain flying a commodore's broad pendant. And that meant an officer senior to Drinkwater. Now his plan to recruit his ship before reporting his presence to his seniors was impossible. He fished irritably in his tail-pocket for his Dollond glass and, stepping up on a carronade slide, half-hoped to confound the experts beside him. To his intense annoyance he found they were correct.

There was something familiar about the seventy-four. She lay with her head to the eastward, riding to a weather tide, and he had a good view of her. He was certain he had seen her before. Then he recognised her. He shut his glass with a snap and jumped down to the deck.

'She's the *Russell*, gentlemen, unless I am greatly mistaken.' But he was confident of her identity. She had been part of Onslow's division at Camperdown and had stood in the line at Copenhagen where, punished for her mistake in following the *Bellona*, she had taken the ground under the Danish guns. 'And she flies a flag at her mizen . . .'

There was no doubt in Drinkwater's mind that he had discovered the squadron under Rear-Admiral Drury.

He had his barge called away as soon as he had saluted Drury's flag, leaving Fraser to anchor *Patrician* and *Musquito*. He could only clearly identify one of the two frigates, the *Dedaigneuse*, for a fine rain had begun to fall and a damp chill filled the air so that the oarsmen bent to their task over a smooth sea, blowing the trickling rain from their mouths. Drinkwater sat wrapped in his thoughts. He watched the big two-decker loom over them as they approached, remembering her on a grey, gun-concussed October afternoon off Camperdown eleven years earlier. Eleven years! Where had the time gone? He wondered if Tregembo, sitting beside him at the tiller, entertained himself with such gloomy thoughts. Eleven years! They were both worn out in the King's Service, grown grey in the harness of duty like their ships.

'Boat ahoy!'

'*Patrician*!' Tregembo's quick response gave no indication of such day-dreaming. On board *Russell* they were already aware of *Patrician*'s identity, for they had exchanged the private signal as they approached, but Tregembo's short reply to the challenge indicated that *Patrician*'s captain sat in the boat. A few minutes later Drinkwater stood on the deck of the line-of-battle ship listening to the apologies of *Russell*'s first lieutenant who was excusing the absence of her captain.

'He is in conference with the Admiral and the other captains of the squadron, sir,' the lieutenant explained, 'and they have been joined by the Select Committee.'

'And what precisely is that, sir?' asked Drinkwater, feigning a deliberate obtuseness.

'The Select Committee?'

'Yes.'

'A body appointed by Lord Minto, the Governor-General, sir . . .'

'The Governor-General of *India*?' interrupted Drinkwater.

'Why, yes, of course, sir.' A faint note of exasperation was creeping into the lieutenant's voice. 'We have occupied Macao and are now making demands of the Chinese.'

'What the devil for? I had some notion that Macao was Portuguese territory.'

'Why, sir, we have to protect our trade.'

'To protect our interest, more like it.'

'If you say so, sir,' said the lieutenant with ill-concealed disdain. The arrival of His Britannic Majesty's frigate *Patrician* may have taken the flagship by surprise, but it was easy to see that this Captain Drinkwater was a curmudgeon of the old school. The first lieutenant did not think that such an officer would pose much of a threat to the promotion stakes on the East Indies station. Drinkwater appeared to possess the intelligence of an ape! Captain Drinkwater's next remark plucked him out of his smug reverie.

'Be so kind as to tell me the names of the squadron, if you please. I remarked the *Dedaigneuse*; who commands her?'

'Captain Dawson, sir . . .'

'Never heard of him,' snapped Drinkwater.

'A promising young officer,' replied the first lieutenant, laying too facetious an emphasis on the word 'young' and attracting a hard stare from Captain Drinkwater. The lieutenant blushed and hurried on. 'The other is the *Phaeton*, Captain Pellew . . .'

'Sir Edward's son?' asked Drinkwater.

'Yes, sir, Captain Fleetwood Pellew. She's just in from Nangasakie, been trying to discover what the Dutch send two ships to Japan for every year.'

'Is this part of protecting our trade too?' asked Drinkwater drily. 'And the sloop?'

'The *Diana*. The *Jaseur*, sloop, is cruising in the offing. The Indiamen', he went on, gesturing to two Company ships anchored inshore, 'are the *David Scott* and the *Alnwick Castle*, they were taken up to transport five hundred sepoys and some European artillery . . .'

'To occupy Macao.'

'Exactly, sir.'

'Are we at war with Portugal? Or merely doing in the East Indies what we are fighting the French for doing in Europe?'

It amused Drinkwater that such heresy silenced the lieutenant. The uneasy conversation was brought to an abrupt conclusion by a group of men spilling out on to the quarterdeck from the admiral's cabin. Three were obviously the civilians of the Select Committee, the others were the captains of the squadron. Drinkwater wondered what contribution Fleetwood Pellew could make to Admiral Drury's deliberations. He seemed little more than a boy, scarcely older than his own midshipmen.

'Captain Drinkwater?' The admiral's secretary was at his elbow. 'Admiral Drury will see you now, sir.'

'I don't like it, sir, damned if I do. Don't know why Pellew's got us into this damned scrape, running round at the behest of the Governor-General when his lordship represents the Company's fiscal interest with no thought of policy. God damn it, Drinkwater, all I've heard since I came out is '"the Company this", and "the Company that". Begin to think the sun rises and sets out of the Company's arse, God damn me if I don't!'

Drury paused, venting his spleen and clearly glad to be rid of the role of courtier.

'Help yourself to a glass.' He indicated a decanter and the sparkle of lead crystal glasses on a tray.

'Thank you, sir.'

'Well, Captain Drinkwater, where the deuce have you sprung from? When this business is over I'm to relieve Pellew, but I'm damned if my briefing mentioned you or your frigate.'

'I'm under Admiralty orders, sir, discretionary instructions concerning the deployment of a Russian line-of-battle ship . . .'

'A *Russian* battle-ship! Good God, this matter has more complications than a witch's brew!'

'She is destroyed, sir. I have her commander and her survivors aboard *Patrician*.'

'You took a line-of-battle ship with your forty?'

'Her people were much debilitated by scurvy, sir.'

'By heaven, sir, your report will make more interesting reading than most of the paper on my desk!' Drury waved his hand over the litter of correspondence before him. 'I see you brought in a brig.'

'Yes, sir. The *Musquito*; Captain Ballantyne master. She's a Country ship, damaged in the recent typhoon.'

'It missed us here. You'd better get her up the Bocca Tigris and into shelter . . .'

'Very well, sir.'

'Send your written report as soon as possible.'

'Aye, aye, sir. My ship is in want of repairs . . .'

'Is she fit for service, sir? If not you may have a week. No more.'

'A week will be ample, sir.'

'Very well. Thank you, Captain.'

It was rather an inconclusive dismissal, thought Drinkwater as he regained *Russell*'s quarterdeck. Despite his assurance to

Drury, a week seemed quite inadequate for what needed to be done. The continuing rain only added to his depression. Later he was to regard the interview as fateful. For the time being he wanted only to sleep.

Rear-Admiral Drury regarded the arrival of an additional frigate as providential. The fact was that the East Indies command was like no other in the long list of the Royal Navy's responsibilities. It had already been the victim of intrigue, formerly being divided between two officers who, admirable individually, reacted like poison when requested to co-operate. Pellew had won the contest and Troubridge had been recalled, to die when the *Blenheim* foundered through old age, rot and the use of 'devil-bolts' in her hull. Now Drury was to inherit the edifice that Pellew had erected, and Drury did not like it. Pellew was universally acknowledged as a fine seaman. As a frigate captain he had been without equal, receiving the reward of a knighthood for the destruction of a French frigate early in the war. But honours had dried up after a decade of conflict, and Pellew had ruined his reputation by shameless nepotism. His boys Fleetwood and Pownall were barely old or fitted enough to be lieutenants in charge of the deck, never mind post-captains!

Drury cursed as he bent over the papers on his desk. As for grand strategy, all that mattered to Lord Minto and the damned Selectmen was the China trade, the India trade, and the self-interest of the merchants of Madras, Bombay and Calcutta. The scum had already written to London with their opinion of no confidence in Pellew and his measures to protect their confounded commerce! Drury wished the Honourable East India Company to the devil.

It was a damned irony, Drury mused. How could anything associated with mercantile transactions be honourable? The very notion was preposterous! He snorted indignantly and while his secretary waited with the patience of a tried and beaten man, the admiral scribbled his signature on a dozen letters and notes.

But William O'Brien Drury was a pragmatist brought up in a

hard school. He had not yet inherited Pellew's command and he acknowledged the influence of India House and its Court of Directors. The Select Committeemen hung on his coat tails, eternally muttering about loss and demurrage and half a hundred other insignificant notions that were bound up with their infernal and corrupt business. It was bad enough having to coerce the Portuguese, for it *was* just conceivable that a French squadron from the Mauritius, or a Dutch squadron from Batavia might occupy Macao and strangle the Canton approaches with a blockade, but the idea of bullying the hapless Chinese was quite contrary to Admiral Drury's idea of duty!

At last he sighed, and put down his pen. He rubbed his hand wearily across his face.

'Bring me Captain Drinkwater's report when it is delivered,' he remarked to his secretary, reaching out for the neck of the decanter.

'Do you have any orders for him, sir, that I may be drafting in the interim?'

Drury thought for a moment. 'Yes, I'm going to send him to Penang with those few ships that are completing their lading. They will need an escort and I cannot spare young Pellew or Dawson. Besides,' the admiral added, 'with French cruisers about I'd rather have an experienced officer in command of a convoy than one of those young popinjays.'

'Not to mention the pirates,' muttered the secretary as he scooped up the signed letters for which he had been waiting.

Whampoa

'Steady as you go, sir.'

Drinkwater lowered his glass and nodded at Lieutenant Fraser. 'Mr Ballantyne has the con . . . sheets and braces to the Master's helm, if you please.'

'Aye, aye, sir.'

Drinkwater held Fraser's eyes, searching for a flicker of resentment. Had Fraser hesitated out of deference to Drinkwater's presence? Or was there a taint of bad blood in the air? Surely not, though God alone knew the undercurrents of discontent that ran beneath the decks of his precious command. Ballantyne was a newcomer, a cuckoo in the uncomfortable nest of *Patrician*'s wardroom.

Drinkwater dismissed the morbid train of thought. The Narrows known as the Bogue were closing in, the embrasured forts clearly visible as the breeze blew the ship steadily inshore, with the Chinese Viceroy's war-junks closing in on either quarter like huge, primordial birds of prey. The little *Musquito*, tugging and dragging at the dripping towline, rolled in their wake.

'Very well, Mr Fraser, you may send the men to quarters. In silence, if you will.'

Ballantyne turned and, to avoid his eyes, Drinkwater raised his glass again, studying the curious rig of the closing junk to larboard. He did not want the rat-a-tat-tat of the marine drummer's snare alarming the unpredictable Chinese, despite

Admiral Drury's assurances that a bold front would secure him a safe anchorage with the Indiamen above the Second Bar.

'Sir,' implored Ballantyne, 'I most earnestly entreat you not to compromise my father.'

Hissed at by Comley's mates who were deprived of their pipes at the hatchways, the watch below were pouring up from the berth-deck to take their stations at the quarterdeck guns with the low slap-slap of their bare feet.

'And I entreat *you*, Mr Ballantyne, to attend to your duty. You are a King's officer now.' Drinkwater looked quickly at Fraser, but the first lieutenant appeared to derive no satisfaction from his rebuke to the newcomer. Chastened, Ballantyne turned away. There were always problems arriving off a foreign coast, Drinkwater reflected, matters of propriety, of the correct number of guns to fire in a salute; of the number to expect in return and of the action to be taken if one did not receive them. He had gathered enough from Drury and Ballantyne himself to realise the delicacy of the balance maintained by the Honourable East India Company and the satellite shipping houses of Calcutta, Madras and Bombay in their relationship with the Celestial Empire of the Son of Heaven.

'The Emperor in Peking, sir, regards King George as a vassal chieftain,' Ballantyne had explained, highly amused, 'such is his ignorance . . .'

Drinkwater raised his telescope and studied the junk to the west of them. There would be no exchange of gun-salutes, Drury had said, not until he had concluded his negotiations with the Viceroy.

'Mr Ballantyne,' said Drinkwater, without lowering the glass, 'there is a gentleman aboard that junk who appears to be a man of some importance.'

'He's the *hoppo*, sir, the mandarin charged with the duty of collecting the customs revenue, the *chop*. I imagine he will board *Musquito* when we bring her to anchor. We should take in the fore-course now, sir . . .'

'Very well.'

'Fore clew-garnets! Rise fore-tacks and sheets!'

Drinkwater turned his attention to the forts. Brilliant-hued banners fluttered over ramparts of pale stone and he could see the muzzles of heavy cannon.

'Antique guns, sir,' reassured Ballantyne.

'What are those things beside the banners?' Drinkwater pointed to coloured shapes bobbing up and down behind the parapet.

'Tiger masks, sir, intended to intimidate us.'

'I see . . .' replied Drinkwater uncertainly.

But the Chinese cannon did not dispute their passage, though the war-junks hung on their flanks until they had passed beyond the Bogue and the First Bar. Under topsails, *Patrician* forced her ponderous way upstream against the yellow ebb of the Pearl River. To starboard the hills rolled away to the east, echoing the jagged peaks of Lin Tin Island offshore, but to larboard a flat alluvial plain stretched westwards, intersected by convoluted channels and formed from marshy and insubstantial islands that altered as the river altered. The hills to the east were bare of trees, stripped by the hand of man, terraced here and there to form fields which fell away from the walled villages on their summits.

With sharply braced yards and the jibs and spanker to assist, *Patrician* rounded a long bend, finding the main stream divided by low islands. Although the layered spire of a pagoda broke the skyline, it was the tall masts and yards of the East Indiamen that dominated the anchorage.

'Whampoa, sir, and that is Danes Island, and that is . . .' Ballantyne aired the knowledge of a dragoman while Drinkwater studied the shipping through his Dollond glass. Most of the Indiamen seemed to be discharging, though there were smaller 'Country' ships, Indian owned, loading from the mass of junks, sampans and lorchas that crowded round them. One or two of these seemed ready for sea.

An hour later *Patrician* had cast off *Musquito* and anchored beside her. From her quarterdeck Ballantyne senior waved his gratitude. Drinkwater turned to the son. The man was well pleased with himself, puffing contentedly on a cheroot.

'Well, sir, you acquitted yourself with credit. If you still wish it I shall request Admiral Drury confirm your acting warrant as master. In the meantime we shall further test your abilities in a refit.'

'I am honoured, sir, to accept.'

'In that case, Mr Ballantyne, be so good as to obtain the services of a tailor and extinguish that confounded cheroot!'

Drinkwater gestured at Ballantyne's exotic figure, and this time Fraser could not repress a smile.

'Sentry!'

Drinkwater's exasperated voice rose to a querulous pitch and he dragged himself to his weary feet. He half opened the cabin door to bawl again at the sentry.

'For God's sake, man, do your duty and keep these hawkers quiet!'

His attempt to close the door failed. Instead the mortified marine, his shako missing and his ported musket pressed impotently across his own chest, fell backwards into the captain's arms.

'Beg pardon, sir . . .'

The sight of *Patrician*'s commander, his blue, white and gold uniform marking him as a personage of supreme importance to the people of the Pearl River, only fuelled their desire to secure some patronage from him, the reason for their besieging his quarters. If Drinkwater had entertained any reservations about Ballantyne's ability to find a tailor, they were now swiftly dispelled. Ballantyne could obtain the services of a tailor, a washerwoman, a boot-maker, an ice-seller, a vendor of chickens, eggs or cabbages, a barber, a fortune-teller, a servant or a whore, though, at that moment, they all seemed to be attempting to claim the attention of Captain Drinkwater.

'Tregembo! Mullender!' Drinkwater bellowed, putting his weight behind the broad shoulders of the marine; but no reinforcements came from the pantry and Drinkwater's tired brain realised that similar scenes were being enacted throughout the ship.

'I'm sorry, sir,' mumbled the compressed bootneck.

Drinkwater grunted acceptance of the unfortunate marine's apology. Doubtless the poor fellow expected a dozen at the gratings tomorrow and would likely get them if nothing mollified Drinkwater's rising temper.

'Fire your damned musket, man!' he bellowed in the marine's grubby ear. The sudden report gained them the necessary second's initiative and the throng of supplicating Chinese was pushed beyond the doorway.

'Pass word for Mr Mount!' Drinkwater called through the closed door, leaning his back upon it and wiping his forehead. Catching his breath after the unaccustomed exertion he stared through the stern windows. It was a grey, drizzly late November day, yet the broad waters of the river swarmed with sampans and junks. Somewhere just out of sight on their larboard quarter, *Musquito* lay aground on the fringes of Danes Island. Here, where the Europeans were allowed by the Chinese authorities the concession of a place to repair and refit their ships, Captain Ballantyne was discharging his cargo of opium in order to survey his ship. Low sheds had been erected on the island, under the roofs of which the crews of the Indiamen repaired masts and spars, reminding Drinkwater of the pressing needs of his own ship.

'Sir? Sir? Are you all right?'

Drinkwater recovered himself and opened the door a trifle. The crowd outside had subsided, clearly concluding that admittance to the great man's cabin was impossible. Most had gone in search of more accessible prey.

'Mount, come in, come in. Of course I am all right, but what of the rest of the ship?'

Mount grinned. 'Taken lock, stock and barrel by boarders, sir.'

'Get your men aft, then, and clear 'em. We've got work to do!' Drinkwater noticed the crestfallen look in Mount's eyes. 'Damn it, Mount, you know as well as I do what will happen if liquor vendors get among the people. We will have a species of anarchy aboard.'

'Aye, sir, but the men know there are women available and even I have need of a new shirt . . .'

Drinkwater eyed the marine officer; Mount had served with him for five years and Drinkwater knew him for a steady, reliable man. The plea was eloquent, Drinkwater's testiness a reaction after the long weeks of lonely strain. They had a day or two . . .

'Very well, Mr Mount, clear the ship, then have the goodness to request Mr Ballantyne to arrange for two tradesmen of each kind to come aboard. He and the Purser are to issue passes, you are to put Sergeant Blixoe on the entry and double the sentinels.'

'Aye, aye, sir.'

'And send Fraser aft, I want a guard rowed round the ship. And your men are to fix bayonets and load powder only. I want no unnecessary blood shed on our account.'

'What about women, sir?'

Drinkwater stared at the marine, hesitating. He could allow women on board in accordance with the usage of the Service. It was common in Spithead where men-of-war at anchor frequently assumed a frantic and degenerate appearance, aswarm with whores who were fought over and coupled with by men denied outlet for their natural urges for months at a time. It dispensed with the awkward business of shore-leave and reduced the risk of desertion. One thing could be relied upon if women were allowed on board, and that was the exhaustion of the seamen in a violent excess of promiscuity. It had its merits, if strictly controlled.

Against it was the threat of further rumblings among the men. They were not a happy crew, compounded of volunteers, pressed men, Quota men and the sweepings of British gaols. Many of them had been at sea now for years, hardly stepping ashore except on remote beaches to wood and water the ship. The sight of women would inflame the men, denial of access to them might precipitate serious disaffection and even desertion.

Hovering over this delicate equation was the ever-present spectre of disease. Release of libidinous pressure now might result in an epidemic of clap or worse, the lues. The venereal list already bore eighteen cases of the former acquired in California in addition to the decrepit and decomposing luetic whose appearance served as a ghastly warning to them all and whose shambling figure kept *Patrician*'s heads clean. Surgeon Lallo had reported two more cases of the disease already in the second stage. How many more would be acquired here at Whampoa? He felt irresolute, exhausted.

'You may allow the tradesmen, Mount.' He hesitated, his eyes meeting those of the marine officer who remained expectantly in the cabin.

'Very well . . . women as well, but not until this evening . . .'

Mount departed and soon the frigate was filled with the shouts and squeals of disruption as his mustered marines forced the Chinese back into their boats at the point of the bayonet. If the unfortunate vendors had earlier mistaken *Patrician* for a run-of-the-mill East Indiaman, they were now learning their mistake.

For the next two days Drinkwater kept himself to himself, taking a turn on deck shortly after dawn and again in the evening. The chance to sleep undisturbed while his charge swung to her cable in a safe anchorage was too luxurious an opportunity to forego after the relentless months of service he had endured. He was overwhelmed with a soporific lethargy, dozing off over his charts like an old man, even after sleeping the clock round, eating erratically, to the despair of Mullender who had purchased fresh vegetables, and drinking little. On the first evening at anchor he had barely been able to keep awake as Captain Ballantyne eloquently expressed his gratitude and sought to introduce Drinkwater to the commanders of the East India Company's ships at Whampoa. Drinkwater excused himself, pleading the disorder of his ship, but in fact the plain truth was that he was utterly exhausted and had no stomach for socialising.

Mullender and Tregembo, his coxswain, crept in and out of the cabin while Derrick, the pressed Quaker who did duty as the captain's clerk, silently maintained the ship's books without the dozing Drinkwater ever being aware of his presence.

'Don't you wake him,' the solicitous Tregembo had said as Derrick passed through the pantry to collect the muster books.

'I am sufficiently acquainted with the virtues of silence, Friend,' replied the Quaker drily.

But their protection was broken by the still-limping Belchambers who nervously, but over-loud, tapped upon the cabin door.

'Sir . . . sir . . . Sir! If you please, sir . . . there's a boat that's brought orders from the flagship, sir.'

'Specie, Captain, my clerk will give you the details. At one per cent its carriage should compensate you a little for the inconveniences attendant upon my diverting you . . .'

It had been a long pull in the barge, though they had sailed much of it, and Drinkwater still felt a mild irritation that Drury had summoned him in person to acquaint him of something as easily conveyed in a letter.

'And the *Juno*, sir? I had hopes of finding her here.'

'Damn the *Juno*, Captain. These matters that I have in hand supersede that preoccupation. I have read your report, read it with interest, Captain Drinkwater, and not a little admiration. I think I may relieve you of the discretionary part of your orders . . .'

Drinkwater looked at the admiral; this was a different Drury. It was obvious to Drinkwater why he had been chosen to relieve Pellew: there was a clear-thinking and obviously principled mind concealed behind the ram-damn seaman's exterior. He warmed to the man, forgiving the admiral the tedium and risk of the long boat journey. He was suddenly pricked with conscience, aware that Admiral Drury might be able to answer a question that had been bothering him for months now.

'Please, do be seated, Captain, and take a glass . . .'

The admiral's servant proffered the tray and then Drury waved him out, seating himself. 'Y'r health, Captain Drinkwater.'

'Your servant, sir.' The fine *bual* reminded Drinkwater of a long dead Welsh commander, and also of the question that begged resolution.

'Sir, forgive the presumption, but I am anxious to know the fate of Lord Dungarth. You will be aware from my orders that I have some knowledge of his Lordship's office . . .'

Dungarth was the obscure head of the British Admiralty's Secret Department, the very centre of its intelligence network and a man who, along with the formidable figure of John Barrow, the Second Secretary, was instrumental in forming Admiralty policy. Drinkwater had known him since he had been a midshipman, even held him as his patron and friend. The last news he had had of the earl was that he had been blown up by an explosive device which had destroyed his carriage somewhere near Blackheath.

'You heard . . .'

'By the hand of Rear-Admiral White, sir . . . an old messmate.'

'Dicky White, eh?' smiled Drury. 'Had the sense to hang up his sword and take his seat in Parliament for a Pocket Borough . . .' Drury sipped his madeira. 'As for Dungarth, he still breathed when last I heard . . . what, eight months ago.'

'But the prognosis . . . ?'

'Was not good.'

Drinkwater nodded and they sat in silence for a moment. 'You had some expectation of preferment by his hand, did you?' asked Drury.

Drinkwater smiled ruefully. 'I fear I am a little long in the tooth to entertain such thoughts, sir.'

'We are of one mind, Captain.'

'I beg your pardon, sir . . . ? Drinkwater looked up in surprise. Drury was mocking him!

'I am aware that you are an officer of experience, Captain. I have here', Drury patted a folded bundle of papers, 'your written orders which, loosely summarised, instruct you to take under convoy those ships ready to proceed. Our presence here in force has disrupted the trade and most of the India ships will not be ready. The Viceroy in Canton has been ordered by his Emperor to evict us from Macao and halt all intercourse with us. This interdict is contrary to the private ambitions of the Viceroy and will inconvenience him in the collection of his revenues. The Son of Heaven at Peking will expect the same tribute from his proconsul in Canton irrespective of its origin. I have come here to stop the French or Dutch from seizing Macao and ruining our trade, but I am also hounded by a mercenary pack of Selectmen to compel the Viceroy to continue trade through Canton and Whampoa and disobey the Emperor. The Indiamen have only just begun to break their outward bulk. There are fourteen large Indiamen, fifteen large Bombay vessels, six from Bengal, five from Penang and a brace from Negapatam and Madras. They have all yet to load. A boom and a fleet of war-junks could seal them above the Bogue and they could be forcibly discharged without any payment for their lading.

'Such a threat has the Selectmen quivering in their boots! That's why I want you to get out whatever specie the Chinese merchants have already collected, and, together with the two Indiamen and eight or nine Country ships that *have* managed to load, see them safe to Penang. If you ain't doing a service to the merchants, you'll be doing one for old Sir Edward.'

'I see, sir. And you think my grey hairs will help me . . .'

'Damn it, Drinkwater, you've *seen* these boy captains! What the hell use d'you think Fleetwood Pellew is without I have a steady first luff to stay his impetuous helm. Such arrant nepotism will ruin the Service, to say nothing of prohibiting the promotion of worthy men who must be shackled in subordinate stations. Between us, magnificent seaman though he be, Pellew's made a ninny of himself on behalf of those two bucks of his.' Drury paused to drain his glass. 'All these young blades think about is prize money; prize money before duty . . .

'Have you heard about young Rainier? No? Last year he was a snot-nosed midshipman; pulled the strings of influence and got himself command of a sloop; begged a cruise off the Commander-in-Chief and went a-skulking in the San

Bernardino Strait. Took the Spanish Register ship *San Raphael*, pocketed fifty thousand sterling and sent Sir Edward his share of twenty-six. Yes, that stings, don't it, eh?

'And Fleetwood; sent up to Nangasakie to reconnoitre? Reconnoitre, my arse! Old Daddy Pellew wanted another slice of eighth-pie. Young Fleetwood, the valiant captor of Batavia, was to take one of the two Dutch ships that visit those parts every year and relieve them of the silk or spices, or whatever they go up there for and buy off the Mikado.

'That's why I want *you* to see these ships safe to Penang, Captain. There are several powerful French frigates working out of the Ile de France. Surcouf has raided the doorstep of Calcutta with impunity in a letter-of-marque called the *Revenant* that sails like a witch; word has it that he's at the Mauritius now, but he's quite likely to take another look into the Hooghly or the Malacca Strait.'

'I see, sir . . .'

'Apart from the French National frigates, their privateers and the Dutch ships of war, you've pirates . . . oh yes, sir, pirates. The Ladrones are infested with 'em and they'll take Country ships, knowing them lighter armed than the Company's regular vessels. Get south of the Paracels reefs and you can forget the Ladrones. What you'll have to worry about then are the Sea-Dyaks from Borneo. Fall into a calm and they'll paddle their *praus* up under your transom and cut out whatever they fancy . . . that's why I want a man who knows his duty, Captain Drinkwater, so your one per cent will be well earned if you get a chest or two of silver dollars to India safely.'

Drinkwater put out his hand for the packet of orders. Already his head was formulating the likely signals for his convoy. How the devil could he extend comprehensive protection with a single ship?

'Will you send a sloop with me in support, sir?'

'I doubt I can spare one,' Drury said bluntly. 'When will you be ready for sea?'

'You promised me a week, sir, of which five days yet remain.'

'Very well. And now to a more immediate business . . .'

'Sir?' Drinkwater frowned, puzzled.

'I want to hoist my flag in *Patrician*, Captain Drinkwater, just for a day or two.'

The Dragon's Roar

Captain Drinkwater looked across the strip of grey water between his barge and that of the *Dedaigneuse*, and met Dawson's eye. He smiled encouragingly at the young post-captain. Dawson smiled back, a trifle apprehensively.

The two captains' barges were leading a flotilla of the squadron's boats, their crews bending to their oars and leaving millions of concentric circles expanding in their wakes to mark the dip, dip, dip of the blades. In each boat sat a small detachment of marines, muskets gleaming between their knees.

Dawson was in command, for Drury had ordered him to proceed the twelve miles upstream from Whampoa to obtain stores (in particular liquor) from the European factories at Canton and to determine the whereabouts of the specie. Drinkwater, out of a sense of curiosity and the realisation that his presence aboard *Patrician* was frustrating Fraser in his attempts to refit the ship, had volunteered his own services and those of a midshipman and his barge. The whiff of action had persuaded Mount to come with a file of his marines and Drury himself had, at the last minute, hailed Dawson's passing boat and climbed aboard. Perhaps it was the admiral's presence that rattled Dawson.

Or perhaps it was the situation that was rapidly deteriorating and that promised trouble ahead of them, that caused the young captain's anxiety. Drinkwater did not know.

To be truthful, he did not much care. The whole sorry business seemed utterly incomprehensible and as distant from his pursuit of Russian warships and defeating the French as if he were engaged at single-stick practice on Hadley Common.

The fact was that he was a mended man; his physical collapse had given him time to recover his faculties and his vigour. He wanted to be off with the convoy, to get out of the Pearl River and headed, if not for home, then for the staging post of Penang. He had vague thoughts of persuading Pellew to take ship in *Patrician* when he handed over the chief command to Drury, as a guarantee of their destination. That, he thought, would make a fine Christmas gift to his ship's company. But the silver specie had yet to come down from Canton and *Patrician* was not ready to proceed; so when Drury announced his intention of sending Dawson upstream with the squadron's boats, Drinkwater had found the suggestion of adventure irresistible.

And so, judging by their efforts, had his men. They were all volunteers, all save Tregembo, who followed his captain out of affection, though he would never admit it was more than duty. Drinkwater looked at the men closely as they plied their oars. They looked well enough on their diet of, what had they christened it? Ah yes, he recalled the crude jest, the coarse synonymous phrase for coition, bird's nest pie.

'River's more or less deserted, sir,' remarked Acting Lieutenant Frey beside him.

It was true. Though sampans and a few small junks moved up and down the river, the normal volume of traffic with which they had become familiar was no longer visible.

'I suppose they know what we're up to, Mr Frey.'

'I suppose so, sir.'

It was all an appalling tangle, Drinkwater mused. At Macao an affronted Portuguese population were suffering the occupation of the Company's sepoys, anxious to see the British gone. In the European 'factories' at Canton an increasingly beleaguered group of merchant agents were anxious to get out of China at least *some* of the huge deficit owed by the native merchants. The mandarins and Viceroy, organs of the Imperial civil service, had to maintain their own 'face' and power, while at the same time obeying the orders of the Emperor in Peking who, celestially indifferent to the fate of Canton, wanted all contact with the *fan kwei*, the barbarian 'red-devils', broken off. Meanwhile at Whampoa the ship-masters and the Select Committee wanted to use Drury's armament to force the Chinese to pay up and the Viceroy to permit trading to continue. Drury, declaring the whole thing a 'complex, crooked, left-handed, winding mode of proceeding', had himself joined the boat operation to stop the matter getting entirely out of hand.

Beside Drinkwater, Frey suddenly craned his neck and stared ahead. Drinkwater followed his gaze. The roofs of Canton were coming into view. The tall, narrow-fronted buildings of the factories, marked by the flag-poles and the flaunting foreign colours, lay downstream from the more distant pagodas and the yellow walls of the city which rose from a higgledy-piggledy mass of scratch-built housing clustered about its buttresses.

'Canton . . .', muttered Frey, speaking without knowing it. Drinkwater smiled inwardly. He must remember to call in the midshipmen's journals in a week or two, and see what Mr Frey's skill with brush and water-colour made of the scene.

'Boats ahead, sir!' The call came from the barge's bow. Drinkwater stood up, steadying his knee against a thwart. In the next boat Dawson did the same.

They were strung across the river, lying to a boom of ropes, eight or nine heavy junks, and just below them, sampans which appeared to be full of armed men, men with what looked like medieval hauberks of heavy cloth or leather over their robes, and small metal caps with horsehair plumes.

'They've got bows and arrows, sir!' reported the bowman, and the sailors and marines burst out laughing with good-natured contempt.

Drinkwater, appraising the cordon of junks, judged the passage of the river effectively barred, unless they were going to break Drury's injunction not to open fire. He cast a quick look at either bank. There were cavalry drawn up and though they would be seriously hampered by the multitude of people that stood curiously along the margin of the river, the entire mass was a formidable barrier to their progress.

'Easy there, Mr Frey, easy . . .'

'Pull easy, lads . . .'

The oarsmen slackened their efforts and Drinkwater heard Drury hailing him.

'Cap'n Drinkwater! I'm pushing on ahead . . . do you hang back in my support. My interpreter tells me one of the junks bears an admiral.'

'Very well, sir. And good luck.'

Drury waved his hand and sat down again. Drinkwater saw him lean forward and exchange remarks with the interpreter. Dawson's face was set grimly.

'Oars, Mr Frey.' He turned and waved to the boats astern. As Dawson's barge pulled forward, the flotilla followed Drinkwater's example, their oars lifting horizontally, silver drops of water running along the looms, while the boats slowed, gliding in the admiral's wake.

Drinkwater watched as a perceptible ripple of excitement seemed to transmit itself from one bank to the other via the armed junks, at the sight of the single boat detaching itself from the others.

'What the devil's the admiral trying to do?' muttered Mount.

'Negotiate, Mr Mount,' said Drinkwater, 'and I'll trouble you not to open fire without my express authority.' Drinkwater repeated the order to the lieutenant in the adjacent boat, with instructions to pass it along the line. Drury had been explicit upon the point.

'Why the devil did he bring us then?'

'Something the celestials call "face" I believe, Mr Mount,' said Drinkwater, still watching Dawson's barge as he closed the hostile junks. 'A kind of ritual posturing to decide who shall have the upper hand in a matter. Ask Ballantyne to enlarge on the point . . .'

'Admiral's standing up, sir,' reported the bowman.

'Eyes in the boat,' snapped Frey as the idle and curious

oarsmen turned their heads to see what was happening.

'Bloody hell!'

A ground swell of voices like the stridulation of cicadas had accompanied their approach to the cordon. Against it they quite clearly heard Drury's voice and the shrill interpretation. The remarks had been cut short by a dense volley of stones that sent up tiny plumes of water all round Drury's boat.

'Advance!' signalled Drinkwater, and the assorted gigs and cutters, spreading out in a long line, pulled forward once more, closing the admiral whose oarsmen held water not twenty yards from a large, three-masted junk upon whose deck a knot of richly robed mandarins could be clearly seen.

Drury continued expostulating, moving his hands, though they could hear no more than the drone of his voice above the rising chatter of the vast crowd.

More stones plopped about him, some skimming across the placid river or falling alongside the supporting boats. Then suddenly it was not a volley. A sharp cry from the commanding junk and the jerk of a baton launched a hail of well-aimed missiles against the British. Ten yards away Drinkwater saw a marine drop his musket and clap his hands to his nose as blood gushed brightly through his fingers. Men moved dangerously in the boats as knocks and shouts told where others took blows and the boats received damage.

'Up marines, and present!'

Mount's order rang across the water and the marines in all the boats stood up and levelled their muskets. The sudden elevation of the soldiers further rocked the boats and Drinkwater realised they were blocking his view and that he had himself been standing for some moments.

'Hold your fire, damn you!' Drinkwater bellowed, suddenly seeing Dawson's face turn and blench at the proximity of the other boats. Drury turned too, took in the situation at a glance and bent to consult his interpreter.

He straightened up again and looked round. Astern of the admiral's barge the boats had drawn up in line abreast, their oarsmen dabbing at the river to maintain station against the current. Stones continued to fall about them. One concerted volley seemed flung with concentrated viciousness, hitting several men in *Russell*'s longboat. Stung by this furious assault her men suddenly dug in their oar-blades and, with a bending of looms, the marines in her were standing up again, cocking their muskets. Other men in other boats were being hit and cries followed one another with mounting rapidity. Men were shouting now; another boat moved forward and more marines, no longer hesitating like their officers, were flicking off their frizzens and snapping back the hammers of their flintlocks.

'Hold your fire!' roared Drinkwater. Drury had been adamant upon the point, this was to be a *show* of force only. To defy this mob with lead would call down a vengeful horde and the only result would be death for all of them, and a particularly senseless death at that.

'Hold your fire!' Drinkwater shouted again.

'Back-water and hold your fire, damn your eyes!' Drury, frustrated in his attempt to communicate with the Chinese admiral, was himself bull-roaring at his men. His pugnacious spirit was held in admirable check amid a crescendo of noise as cymbals and gongs now enhanced the cries of the Chinese and the curses and mutterings of the British. The marines lowered their muskets irresolutely, and sat down to lessen the target area they presented to the hundreds of Chinese who, leaning from the junks and sampans, seemed provided with an endless supply of pebbles and stones.

'They are driving us out as devils, sir,' volunteered Frey, 'that is why they are beating the gongs . . .'

'Your intelligence is ill-timed, sir,' snapped Drinkwater. 'Sit down, damn you!' he shouted at a midshipman who, in the *Dedaigneuse*'s cutter was standing in her stern sheets, waving his dirk and uttering a stream of obscene invective at the obdurate Chinese.

'Sit down at once and hold your tongue, sir!'

Even in such extreme circumstances the incongruity of the boy's torrent of filth annoyed Drinkwater. They were all

54

over-wrought and he was aware that his silencing of the midshipman was a vent for his own pent-up feelings.

Then suddenly it seemed as if a dark cloud had passed over them and their eyes were assailed by a sibilant vibration that rent the air above them. The volley of arrows splashed into the river astern of them, clearly aimed over their heads in intimidation. And then came a mighty roar, so sudden after the unnerving noise of the arrows that men's faces paled in fear, and so close that the wave of concussion and heat that seared them sizzled hair and added the sharp stink of its frizzing to the blast of powder. Their boats rocked dangerously. The huge bell-mouthed cannon, concealed until that moment by rush matting draping the sides of a war-junk, vomited a red and yellow tongue of fire.

No shot or langridge came from the dragon's mouth, but the message from its black muzzle was potent enough: the Chinese were not open to negotiations. Admiral Drury was waving the boats back. Dawson's barge was crabbing round, swinging her bow downstream. Willingly now the others followed suit and, helped by the current, dropped swiftly down towards the refuge of their ships.

Astern of them the clamour of the Chinese and their gongs rose to a victorious crescendo to which was now added the snap of fire-crackers. Banners waved and the huge dragon gun spat tongues of fire at their retreat. Aboard the greatest of the junks, the Viceroy of Canton received the congratulations of his court.

On either bank cavalry kept pace with them for a mile or so, then fell back, and their last sight of the citizens of the great city was a single draped palanquin that watched them from a low rise on the levee.

The red curtains fluttered a little as the brass ferrule of a telescope was withdrawn, and a few minutes later the bearers, obeying some command from within, swung it round and headed back towards Canton. Alongside it trotted a little Indian boy with an impish face and almost pointedly prominent ears.

CHAPTER 5

The Matter of Morale

'. . . A red flag from the foremasthead of the escort shall signify the convoy to form line ahead, to clear such armament as shall be borne by each ship and to maintain station until such time as the said red flag shall be struck.'

Drinkwater ceased dictating and stared over Derrick's shoulder as the Quaker clerk finished writing.

'I think that is all, Derrick. Now we must have fourteen copies, one each for our charges and two for ourselves, one of which is to be kept in the binnacle. You have my authority to impress the midshipmen on the duty of copy-clerks.'

'Aye, Captain.'

'And Derrick . . .'

The Quaker, gathering pens and ink-pot, looked up at Drinkwater.

'Ensure they make no mistakes . . .'

'Very well, Captain Drinkwater.'

A knock came at the door and Midshipman Belchambers's face peered round it. 'Beg pardon, sir, but Mr Quilhampton's compliments and there's a boy asking to see you.'

'A *boy*?' Drinkwater frowned.

'A native boy, sir . . .'

'A Chinese boy?'

'Looks more like an Indian boy to me, sir.'

Something about his assumption of mature judgement on

the part of the youthful Belchambers brought a smile to Drinkwater's face. There had been an atmosphere of something like farce attendant upon the affairs of the British ships at Whampoa following Admiral Drury's 'humane retreat' from Canton.

Drinkwater, in receipt of his orders, wanted only to be out of the river and on his way to Penang. Fortunately Drury had hauled down his flag from *Patrician*'s main-masthead and had returned to *Russell*, pondering his next move and reading the riot act to the dithering Selectmen.

'If neither peace nor commerce is to be had by an act of war, I never will sanction the slaughter of those defenceless multitudes,' Drury had said to them in Drinkwater's cabin before his departure. 'We have trampled under foot every moral law of man and nations, and the poor defenceless Chinese have been infuriated to a frenzy . . .'

Something of the fighting-cock had had to explode from this exemplary lecture and poor Drury, having been humiliated personally in his attempt to act to the satisfaction of all parties, suddenly reacted angrily, perhaps contemplating how fortunate the boat expedition had been in avoiding real casualties.

'However, gentlemen, if one of my seamen had been, or *is* killed, I will destroy Canton. Therefore recollect what *you* will have to answer for. I gave you quiet possession of Macao, but I tell you no hostile act shall be committed against the Chinese, unless a man is killed, which nothing but the most singular accident has prevented. The seamen under my control have borne to be fired at, but once let loose,' the admiral finished dramatically, 'no power on earth can stop 'em!' Out of tact or embarrassment no one mentioned Drury's failure to bring off a single piece of silver specie.

The Select Committee had been packed off to finish negotiations with the mandarins from the luxurious quarters of the *Stirling Castle*, East Indiaman, while Drinkwater gathered the few ships that were ready to proceed and prepared to depart with this small convoy.

And now a boy was asking for him.

'What does he want, Mr Belchambers, have you ascertained that?'

'Well, sir, beg pardon, sir, to see you.'

'You had better bring him down then.'

Belchambers seemed to hesitate.

'What is the matter now?'

'Well, sir, Mr Quilhampton voiced an opinion that the boy might be an, er, assassin, sir . . .'

Drinkwater laughed. 'That's most solicitous of Mr Q, Mr Belchambers. It does not occur to you that the lad is doubtless a servant from one of the Indiamen.'

'That's unlikely, sir . . .'

'Oh?' Drinkwater's temper was shortening. He had other matters to consider and a final letter of instruction to draft for the masters and commanders of the convoy.

'Yes, sir, he came down river in a sampan.'

'Bring him below,' Drinkwater snapped, meeting Derrick's eye as the clerk, penned in the cabin by this odd exchange, now slipped out to co-opt the midshipmen as copy-clerks.

Drinkwater bent over the chart that lay on his table. It was a survey by Huddart, and Ballantyne had laid off the best course for them to follow, south and then south-westward towards the tip of the long Malay peninsula. Such was his preoccupation that he had almost forgotten the announced visitor when the hobbling Belchambers showed the boy in.

He was shorter than the midshipman, and possibly two or three years younger. His features were neat and small, almost feminine, with huge brown eyes outlined with a hint of *kohl*. He bowed, displaying a jewelled turban, and drew from his loose sleeve a letter.

Drinkwater took the letter, an amused smile playing about his mouth, for in the shadows beyond the diminutive exotic, Mr Midshipman Belchambers stood anxiously, his hand on a half-drawn dirk.

Drinkwater slit the wafer, half turning to the window to read the message.

Canton
20th November 1808

To the Officer Commanding the Convoy Bound for India

> *Honoured Sir,*
> *Knowing your Imminent Preparations for Departure and the Frustrations your Party has Suffered in its Attempt to recover the Silver owed the British Merchants by the Rascally Hong, I have it in my Power to carry off most of the Specie at the time of your sailing if, in the First Part you Signify at what time this will occur and, in the Second Part you allow Myself and a Servant to Embark in your Frigate. The Matter to be Secret between ourselves.*
> *Please convey your Answer to the Bearer. He is dumb but understands English. I am, Honoured Sir,*
> *Your most humble and obedient Servant,*
>   *A Friend.*

Drinkwater read the letter through twice. It could be a ruse, of course. Information as to the convoy's sailing could be passed to the forts at the Bogue, or to the pirates of the Ladrones. But that information could as easily be signalled, for it would take several hours for the convoy to drop down river and they could scarcely do so unnoticed. In any case Drury had promised them the escort of the *Phaeton* until they were clear of land.

On the face of it this unknown 'friend' was obviously anxious to buy his way out of what might prove a dangerous place for a European, and had the decency to attempt to recover what the British merchants most desired. Yet why should the man insist on secrecy when he was proposing to achieve what the British merchants wanted?

To cheat them? Perhaps, and that was why he wanted passage in a frigate rather than a merchant ship. Drinkwater looked at the boy. He was dumb, yet the face was intelligent, and it watched Drinkwater with the passive observance of something feral. He thought for a moment of calling away his barge and

59

consulting Drury, but he knew this boy would take news of his indecision back to his unknown master.

Besides, Drury had employed Drinkwater on the task for his experience, and he had a mind to get to the bottom of what would doubtless turn out to be no mystery at all.

'Tell your master . . . no, wait, I'll write.'

He turned to his desk and picked up his steel pen, searching for the ink-pot that Derrick had moved.

The boy was suddenly beside him, the smell of scent wafting from his small body. Drinkwater felt a small brown hand on his arm and the dark, liquid eyes were staring up at his face. Behind them there was a shuffling movement, and the evening light glancing off the river gleamed on the naked blade of Belchambers's dirk.

But these were details on the periphery of Drinkwater's perception. Afterwards he considered the value of the stones in the boy's turban and the oddity of his prominent and pixie ears. In the moment of arrest, as the boy strove to prevent Drinkwater committing anything to paper, he was aware principally of the hollow of the boy's mouth, and the insistent grunts that filled its tongueless monstrosity.

He dreamed that night; a restless half-sleep full of terrors. He was flung down and drowning, drowning in waves of Elizabeth's hair that caught and clung to his struggling body, drowning in the laughter and shouts and smiles of thousands upon thousands of Chinese whose narrow eyes and loose, gaudy clothing seemed to have displaced his wife's tresses and moved with the overwhelming restlessness of the sea. Then he was fighting for air, surfacing in this very cabin, dark, lonely and cold. But there was a sweet and seductive laughter beyond the door and he struggled towards it in anticipation of all the delights of the flesh that he had for so long lived without.

But the woman beyond the door was ghastly; a horror of all the nameless, haunting horrors that mocked a man out of the darkness of his own desire. He drew back, pursued. The hag metamorphosed into the little Indian messenger who, mouth open, came to engulf him with his tongueless hole from which, Drinkwater fancied, the very sulphureous stink of hell itself seemed to emanate. And all about him laughter rang in his ears, laughter from Chinese and Indian and European faces . . .

He jerked awake, the sweat pouring from him, the thin laughter coming from beyond the cabin door. It was high-pitched and piping, and combined with the dream to bring him leaping from his cot, his heart thundering in his chest, his night-shirt sticking to his body and the lank locks of his loosely bound hair plastered to his scalp.

Pulling on breeches and tucking the tails of his night-shirt into them, he yanked his cloak from the hook by the door and stepped precipitately out on to the gun-deck. The dozing marine sentry sprang upright with a click of musket against buckles.

The giggling laughter came again, resolving itself into the now familiar sounds of pre-dawn coition from the berth-deck. His confusion clearing from his fogged mind, Drinkwater ran up the quarterdeck ladder, announcing his presence by a discreet cough.

Mr Meggs, the gunner, appeared from beyond the mizen mast. 'Sir?'

'What day is it?'

'Why, er, Sunday, sir.'

'And the time?'

'A little before three bells, sir,' and then added, as if sensing the captain's distraction, 'in the morning watch, sir.'

'Pipe all hands.'

'All hands, sir?'

'You heard me, damn it, and clear the ship. No showing of legs, Spithead style, I want the lower deck cleared fore and aft and the people mustered.'

'Ship's company to muster, sir, aye, aye.'

Somewhat bemused at this extraordinary behaviour, the elderly Meggs shuffled forward, hesitated, looked back at the captain, then called for the bosun's mate of the watch.

'Mr Meggs!'

The gunner turned at the captain's shout. He began to shuffle aft again.

'Mr Meggs,' said Drinkwater quietly, 'I am aware that only

the recent casualties force you to keep watch on deck, but be so kind as not to appear on the quarterdeck in your slippers.'

Meggs looked down at his erring feet. Habitual use of felt slippers in *Patrician*'s magazine, where the wearing of leather soles might rasp and ignite the coarse grains of spilt gunpowder, probably rendered it instinctive that the poor fellow put them on at the call of the watch. Perhaps, thought Drinkwater, catching a smell of the man, he slept in the festering things!

'I beg your pardon, sir.' Meggs looked crestfallen.

'Be a good fellow and have something more suitable on when you muster.'

'Very well, sir . . .' Meggs looked hard at his captain and Drinkwater suddenly looked down at his own appearance.

'Perhaps,' he said, recovering himself at last, 'that had better stand for both of us, eh? You may wait until four bells before turning up the ship.'

Fully awake and aware of the ludicrous appearance he would cut even in the pre-dawn gloom, Drinkwater hurried below. As he turned for his cabin above the companionway, he was aware of a face staring up at him. For a second he stopped, his heart beating as though this was some impish visitation from his dream, and then it was gone, the young Chinese girl vanishing into the stygian darkness.

'Pass word for my steward,' he growled at the marine, and the whisper went around the ship that Captain Drinkwater was awake and something was afoot.

Sluicing his face after the harsh ministrations of the razor Drinkwater called for a clean shirt. It occurred to him that the few days of relatively relaxed routine might prove fatal to the delicate matter of morale. He was aware that he had left the refitting of the ship to Fraser and though he could find little to fault with the first lieutenant's arrangements, only time would prove their thoroughness.

Drinkwater was unhappily conscious that any loosening of the bonds of discipline was a risky matter, and that mumblings of discontent had accompanied *Patrician* from the moment the crew of *Antigone* had been turned wholesale into her, topped up with the scum of a hot press and sent round Cape Horn to absent them all from European waters.

The long-service volunteers had had their willingness to serve eroded by lack of shore leave and the association of landsmen, lubbers, thieves and petty felons; men whose proper habitat was a gaol, but whom the Admiralty saw fit to pour into men-of-war to fill their impossible complements. It was for prime seamen to tolerate them, but to be reduced to their level was something that proud men, jealous of their expertise, could not submit to.

Drinkwater's greatest enemy was desertion. Jack had a simple understanding of the world and to him the foreign shore of China offered escape from the endless round of grinding labour expected of him aboard a King's ship. Drinkwater knew and understood all this, and before *Patrician* had sailed for the Pacific he had had to hang a man at the fore-yardarm for desertion, *pour encourager les autres*.

He shook the awful image from his mind's eye and summoned more cogent reasons for his attitude. He could not afford to lose a single man. Ballantyne had told him the Indiamen were often short of hands on a China voyage, of how they embarked Chinese to make up their complements, and how their commanders would be keen to secure the services of a dozen active topmen, even to the extent of hiding them until they were out of sight of land. To this must be added the potent inducement of the high and guaranteed wages paid on Company ships.

In short, Drinkwater mused as he tied his stock and reached behind him for the coat that Mullender held out, he would not be at all surprised if he *was* short of men. The question was, how many?

Beyond the cabin door the pipes squealed as four bells struck. Drinkwater stood before his mirror, head a-cock, listening to the sounds of reaction, judging by the inevitable sluggishness, the little shrieks of the whores and the suppressed oaths, the temper of his men.

Midshipman Count Vasili Chirkov felt his hammock shake.

'Come on, Vasili, get out . . . uniform . . . muster . . .'

Midshipman Dutfield was climbing into his breeches, rousing the indolent Russian between grunts of effort as he and his colleagues sought the neglected items of their uniform in the gloomy chaos of the gunroom.

'*Non* . . . no . . .'

The girl stirred in the crook of his arm and nestled comfortably up to him.

Dutfield shook the hammock violently and then Frey was standing close, holding up a glim so that it shone unequivocally over the exposed bodies.

'Come on, you lubber!' the acting lieutenant urged, 'Or the Captain will marry you to the gunner's daughter.'

'No . . .' Chirkov peered over the edge of the hammock. 'I have girl first . . .'

Dutfield and Frey exchanged glances. Frey winked and shrugged. He felt his new-found authority inadequate to the task. The midshipmen left the gunroom and joined the rush to the upper deck.

The ship was a babel of confusion. Everywhere along the berth-deck men were hurriedly drawing on clothes and unlashing and rolling hammocks. Small brown Tanka women, their usefulness now past and to whom the sudden shrill of the pipes and flurry of activity must have been beyond all comprehension, were being roughly shoved aside. In one place two men were busy thrusting their paramours through an open gun-port into a waiting sampan, in another one of these unfortunate creatures was crying like a child, her ankle badly sprained from too sudden a descent from a hammock.

'Clear lower deck! Out! Out! Out!' Bosun Comley was bawling, urging his mates to use their starters, and lashing about him with his cane.

'Get these whores over the side! This is a King's ship, not a kennel!'

'Bloody hypocrite!' remarked a Quota-man who had once entertained social expectations but had been found guilty of embezzlement.

'Clear lower deck!'

Lieutenant Mount appeared, buttoning his tunic and shouting.

'Ser'nt Blixoe! Pass word for Ser'nt Blixoe . . .'

'Here, sir!'

'Give the Bosun a hand to get these trollops into their boats . . . not too roughly, Ser'nt.'

Meanwhile, in the gunroom, Midshipman Count Vasili Chirkov was reaching the climax of his urgent love-making.

His sword hitched and his hat ready in his hand, Drinkwater half sat on the edge of his table, one leg swinging, awaiting the summons to the deck. When it came at last he affected not to notice the inordinate delay, not to enquire from Mr Belchambers, who had been sent limping down to inform him the muster was complete, why he had heard noises below decks that indicated a party of marines sent twice through the ship. He knew already what *that* signified.

It was growing light as he climbed to the quarterdeck. The men were massed amidships, over the booms and along the gangways, in the lower rigging and, still distracted by the departing women, craning over the rails. Beyond the hammock nettings he could see the trucks of masts as three or four score sampans rocked away from their sides.

'Eyes in the ship there!' Fraser touched his hat. 'Ship's company mustered, sir.'

'Very well, Mr Fraser.'

There was something wrong. He could see instantly the lack of symmetry in the ranks of marines who rigidly lined the sides of the quarterdeck. He caught Fraser's eye and raised an eyebrow.

'Four men missing, sir,' hissed the first lieutenant in a low, tense voice.

'How many marines?'

'None, sir. Corporal Grice is still searching the ship.'

'Any boats missing?'

'No, sir. Too many sampans . . .'

Drinkwater nodded a curt acceptance of what he had

65

already guessed. Affecting to ignore the report he stepped forward.

'Well, my lads,' he began, staring at the bleary faces that were taking shape in the growing light, 'the Chinese consider us barbarians, I'm told, and looking at the present state of the ship's company, I'm not entirely surprised . . .'

A collectively sheepish grin seemed to spread across the more tractable members of the crew.

'You have all enjoyed a little relaxation and the ship is almost ready to proceed . . .'

'Where are we bound, Cap'n?'

The voice was unidentifiable, but it might have asked for all except the Russian prisoners, for the light of interest kindled in their washed-out faces.

'We are escorting a convoy to Prince of Wales Island and then . . . then I think it time that we took ourselves home . . .'

He was aware that few of them knew where Prince of Wales Island was, and fewer cared, but they all wanted to hear their final destination. He was cut short by a spontaneous burst of cheering, cheering that only died away when Corporal Grice and his detail emerged from the after companionway half dragging, half shoving an able seaman named Ward, and escorting the protesting Chirkov and his half-naked flower-girl in to the ampitheatre of unoccupied deck before the captain.

Chirkov shrugged off the rough hands of the marines and turned as though to join his fellow prisoners, gathered about Prince Vladimir.

'Stand still, sir!' rapped Mount, pleased with his men.

'Make your report, Grice,' said Drinkwater quietly, nodding first at Ward.

'Caught him going out through a gun-port, sir. Into a sampan under number three gun, sir.'

Drinkwater nodded. 'Anything to say, Ward?'

The unhappy man shook his head. 'Put him in the bilboes, Corporal.' Drinkwater had no intention of marring the present moment with a flogging. On the other hand . . .

He turned to the sulking Russian. Not taking his eyes off the young nobleman, Drinkwater said, 'Captain Rakitin, this officer is under duty to you. He is responsible for a division of your men and has been publicly taken with this woman. Have you anything to say on his behalf?'

It gave Drinkwater a grim satisfaction to see the big Russian nonplussed, even if only for a moment.

'If it was one of *my* midshipmen he would be made to kiss the gunner's daughter!'

'No . . . no, that would be most irregular . . .'

'I shall punish him tomorrow, Captain,' Drinkwater said, 'when I deal with my own defaulters. Kindly be answerable for his behaviour until then.' He turned to Fraser. 'Pipe the men down, Mr Fraser, I want to be ready to weigh at first light tomorrow.'

'What about the deserters, sir? asked Fraser as the muster dispersed.

'No more sampans alongside, Mr Fraser, and a better guard boat tonight. Forget the deserters and let the men enjoy the anticipation of seeing Midshipman Chirkov's matrimony.'

Touching his hat, Drinkwater left the deck. Behind him Fraser and Mount exchanged glances.

'Forget the deserters,' muttered Fraser, 'that's no' wise . . .'

'I think,' mused Mount quietly to the worried first lieutenant, 'that we are more concerned with morale at the moment.'

The Concerns of a Convoy

'Well, gentlemen, that concludes matters . . .'

Drinkwater looked round at the faces of the dozen men gathered in his cabin. Most wore plain cloth coats, some sported brass buttons or a strip of gold leaf about their cuffs, but two wore the brass-bound uniform of the East India Company's livery.

'If there are no more questions I wish you all good-night and would be obliged if you would heave a-peak the instant you see my signal at daylight. We will make the best of our way beyond the Bogue and I will signal a boat from each of you before forming the order of sailing.' In this way Drinkwater could allow for any idiosyncrasies he noticed in the passage downstream.

There was a chorus of 'good-nights' and mutual exchanges between these masters of the convoy who all knew each other. An undercurrent of relief had permeated their gathering for Drinkwater's briefing: he knew that indecision had sent the Select Committee into a catalepsy and that these men, at least, were fortunate to have completed their cargoes and be home-ward bound.

Drinkwater nodded dismissal to Ballantyne who, attired in the more-or-less regulation dress of a warrant officer, had cleared away the copies of Huddart's charts that had been his passport to *Patrician*'s wardroom. Fraser, too, was about to leave the cabin, but Drinkwater stepped forward and restrained him with his hand.

'Captain Callan,' Drinkwater called, and one of the East India commanders turned in the doorway. 'Might I have a word, sir?'

'Of course, Captain . . .' Callan, a tall, slightly red-faced man with bushy eyebrows above deep-set eyes, was commander of the Indiaman *Guilford*, and senior of the two John Company men.

'I will be blunt with you, sir,' began Drinkwater, 'I am short of men.'

Callan nodded. 'I wondered when you would turn poacher.' He nodded at Fraser. 'We acceded to your first lieutenant's requests for spars from our stores in the bankshalls on Danes Island in the pious hope that we might assuage the Navy's rapacious appetite. It seems that, having plundered our stores, you now want our men.'

'It seems that you do not quite understand . . .' replied Drinkwater coolly.

'Oh, I *quite* understand, Captain Drinkwater. In fact I understand very well and that is why we, the masters in the convoy, have agreed a confederation united to oppose you if you send any men on board our ships with the intention of removing our people. Just attempt it, sir, just attempt it, by God!'

Drinkwater raised an eyebrow. 'You know my rights in the matter, Captain Callan . . .'

'Aye,' Callan retorted swiftly, 'such as they are this far from home and with the sworn affidavits of my colleagues to counter you. Besides, many of my men hold exemptions and it is a matter of record that we too are under-manned.'

'Captain, I do not submit to intimidation. Perhaps you need not threaten me if I assure you that I have no intention of pressing your men. I will give you my word of honour upon the point, if it pleases you.'

'Then, why . . . ?'

'But', Drinkwater pressed on, 'might I ask you how you feel about the boot being on the other foot?'

69

Callan's mouth was still open and it was clear that Drink-water's remark had caught him at a disadvantage.

'If I am not to poach from you, sir, you should not poach from me.'

'You heard?' frowned Callan.

'Three prime topmen. I guessed.'

A reluctantly appreciative smile hovered about the corners of Callan's mouth. Drinkwater wondered if Callan knew to what degree he had been bluffing. The commanders of Indiamen were no fools. A fortune of £20,000 was nothing to them, trading as they did on their own account. They were often part-owners of their ships, for the Honourable Company chartered rather than owned the great argosies, expecting them to make four or five voyages before they were worn out. The thought amused Drinkwater, making him smile in return. By Company standards *Patrician* was a hulk!

'I will return them in the morning, Captain Drinkwater.'

'No. Oblige me by holding them until I send for them. I do not want my own people disturbed by a flogging until we are out of soundings.'

'Very well.'

'A glass to warm the temperature of our meeting?'

'Obliged.'

'Pray sit down . . . Fraser, will you join us?'

'Thank you, sir.'

'My first lieutenant has done wonders to repair the damage wrought by the typhoon, Captain Callan, the least we can offer him is a drink . . .'

Fraser blushed and mumbled something as Drinkwater served from the decanter.

'I see you have taken on the younger Ballantyne, Captain Drinkwater,' remarked Callan conversationally.

'Yes. I lost my own master in action. You know him?'

Callan nodded. 'He's illegitimate, of course, Ballantyne has a wife in Lambeth. Rather a colourful fellow, the son . . .'

'He seems competent enough. I do not know that a little colour hurt a man of its own accord.'

'I meant in terms of manner, rather than blood, Captain, though there are those who would dispute the matter.'

'Well, I am not versed in these contentions. Let him serve until he proves himself one way or another.'

'Or a ball carries off his head.'

'You think that likely?'

Callan shrugged. 'You heard the opinion aired here tonight that the protection of the trade is inadequate. Pellew has a few frigates on station, but these are too well-known now and the Dutch and French have both got formidable ships in these seas.'

'You havena mentioned pirates, sir,' prompted Fraser, relaxing with his glass.

'Don't be a doubting Thomas, Lieutenant. The Ladrones will not touch us, but the Sea-Dyaks of Borneo are a different matter. They have taken four Country ships this last quarter, and all were richly laden, almost as if they knew . . . I tell you it's been a damned bad year for our trade, without this farce between the Selectmen, the Viceroy and our dear friend Admiral Drury.'

'You refer to the failure to extract the specie?' asked Drinkwater, refilling the glasses.

'Aye. The Chinese merchants of the Hong are a damnable tricky lot. The Viceroy wants the trade, the *Hoppo* of the Imperial Customs wants the trade and the European merchants want the trade, but if they can get it for nothing by hiding behind the Emperor's proscription they will, that's why we're so damned anxious to get our ships out of the river.'

'Captain Callan,' said Drinkwater, rising and walking round behind his writing-table to produce the mysterious letter he had received from Canton, 'what d'you make of this?'

He watched Callan frown over the thing, holding it to the candelabra to read it. He shook his head and looked up.

'I don't recognise the hand. Have you heard further from this *Friend*?'

'No . . . I made it clear that we would sail at dawn on the second, but we have heard nothing since his messenger departed.'

Drinkwater thought briefly of the boy and the dream, but dismissed the silly obsession.

'Did you mention it to your admiral?'

Drinkwater shook his head. 'No, he had already rejoined the *Russell* beyond the outer bar. Besides, if the thing had happened I could have sent word that we had got the specie via the *Phaeton*; she is due to drop down river with us tomorrow.'

Callan shrugged and appeared to dismiss the matter. 'I heard you took a Russian seventy-four, Captain,' he said, rising and holding out his hand.

Drinkwater nodded. 'We've a few of her people to prove it.'

'Here's my hand, Captain. I confess your escort is providential. Before your arrival the best we could hope for was Pellew's whipper-snapper Fleetwood. Perhaps we can dine during the passage, Captain, and with you, Lieutenant . . .'

Fraser saw Callan over the side and into his waiting boat. It was quite dark and Drinkwater stared out over the leaden surface of the great river. The mysterious letter seemed to signify nothing beyond some poor European thwarted in his efforts to get out of the beleaguered factories. Whatever its source it was beyond his power to do anything about it.

But thought of the letter worried Drinkwater now that he sat alone in his cabin. It resurrected the image of the tongueless child and the hideous dream. He knew the dream of old. With infinite variations the spectre and the sensation of drowning had accompanied him since the days when he had endured the tyranny of the sodomite bully of the frigate *Cyclops*. He had been an impressionable midshipman then, thirty years earlier, but the dream had come to mean more than the random nocturnal insecurities of his psyche; it had become an agent of premonition.

The thought stirred his imagination. He stopped staring out of the window, turned and picked up the candelabra. The halo of its light fell on the portrait of Elizabeth. Almost unconsciously his hand touched the carmine paint that formed the curve of her lips.

Had the premonition served warning of the deserters? Or

potential trouble with the Russian prisoners? Somehow neither seemed important enough to warrant the appearance of the spectre. Was the nightmare significant of anything corporeal?

He stood for several minutes willing his head to clear of these foolish megrims, cursing his loneliness and isolation, aware of the half-empty bottle on the table behind him.

That was too easy. He placed the candelabra beside it, paused, then resolutely took his cloak from its peg by the door and made for the blessed sweetness of fresh air.

Pacing up and down the deck he lost track of the time, though the watch, conscious of his presence among them, struck the half-hours punctiliously on the bell, while the sentries' assiduous calls were echoed by the guard boat rowing round the ship. It was not long before his mind was diverted, preoccupied by anxieties about the forthcoming convoy duty.

Below him the ship stirred slowly into life, prompted in part by the rhythms of her routine, in part by his own orders in preparation for departure. The first symptom of the coming day was the rousing of the 'idlers', those men whose duties lay outside the watch-bill. They included Drinkwater's personal staff, his steward, clerk and coxswain. This trio enjoyed the privilege of brewing what passed for coffee in the sanctum of the captain's pantry, a ritual that reduced itself to a formality of grunts and mutual acceptance as they went on to perform the tasks that bound them not to the ship, but to the person of Captain Drinkwater.

The Quaker Derrick had the lightest duties, clearing the captain's desk and ruling the ledgers and log-book. Tregembo, the old Cornish coxswain who had been with Drinkwater since the captain had been a midshipman aboard *Cyclops*, attended to Drinkwater's personal kit, to his razor, sword and pistols. It was to Mullender that fell the lot of the menial. The captain's steward was a self-effacing man who possessed no private life of his own, nor any personality to awaken him to the deprivation. He had been born to servitude and never questioned his lot, content with the tiny privileges that accrued to his rating.

The trio was dominated by Tregembo, for Tregembo was a

man of forthright stamp, whose wife Susan was cook to the Drinkwater ménage in distant Hampshire. Long service and Cornish cunning had ensured Tregembo exercised influence, even in the wardroom, and his protection of his master was legendary throughout the ship. It was Tregembo who first sensed danger.

'What means this 'ere?' he asked Derrick, holding out the letter from Canton that Drinkwater had left upon his desk.

'Thou should'st not read the captain's correspondence . . .'

'*Thou* knows I can't read, that's why I'm asking *thee*!' snapped Tregembo at the Quaker, ''tis what that boy brought . . .'

'Yes . . . 'tis only a request for a passage,' said Derrick dismissively, taking the sheet of paper and slipping it into the ship's letter book.

'I didn't like the cut o' that boy . . .' ruminated Tregembo, 'he put me in mind o' something . . .'

'Thou seest knots in a bullrush, Friend,' muttered Derrick, and Tregembo, staring through the stern windows at the emerging grey of the Pearl River, growled uncharitably.

'He put me in mind of a boy who used to be a whatsit to Captain Allen o' the *Rattler*.'

'And what does that signify?' asked Derrick.

'Nothing,' said Tregembo, 'but that Captain Allen was hanged for buggery.'

Lieutenant Quilhampton was called with the news that the captain was already on deck. James Quilhampton had suffered the agonies of sexual temptation while *Patrician* had swung to her anchor. He was near despair, for it was months earlier that he had received a letter already half a year old, that Catriona MacEwan would not repulse his advances if he pressed his suit. To the thin, one-handed young man, such a prospect offered a happiness that he had once despaired of, and the Captain's announcement that they were homeward bound only made their present tardiness the more reprehensible. He was suddenly, expectantly awake on this dawn of departure, eager to get the anchor atrip and loose off the gun that, with a shaking topsail, would signal the convoy to weigh. Waving aside the offered coffee he pulled on shirt and breeches, rasped his cheeks and wound a none-too-clean stock about his neck. Kicking his feet into pinchbeck-buckled shoes he strapped his wooden forearm in place, pulled on coat and hat, and hurried on deck.

His arrival coincided with the midships sentry's challenge.

'Boat 'hoy!'

In a frenzy of efficiency he hurried to the entry and peered over the side. 'It's only a junk, man,' he snapped at the marine, waving at the score or so of batwinged sails that moved slowly over the almost windless river.

'Aye, sir, but she's been standing towards us since she came through the Indymen . . .'

'She does appear to be approaching us, Mr Q,' remarked Drinkwater, coming up.

'Morning, sir.'

'Mornin',' replied Drinkwater, turning to the marine. 'Give her another hail.' Drinkwater raised his glass and levelled it at the junk. Quilhampton spotted activity about the mast, one of the three sails beginning to collapse, flattening the row of battens one on top of the other as the halliard was let go.

'Boat, 'hoy!' bellowed the marine.

'Ah, I thought so . . .' Drinkwater lowered his glass and Quilhampton could himself see the flash of colour in the grey dawn, like the blue of a jay's wing, where the gaily coloured figure of the little Indian boy stood at the junk's ungainly bow.

'I think we have a passenger or two, Mr Q, and a whip at the main yardarm might prove useful.'

'Aye, aye, sir.' Quilhampton turned away just as the bosun's pipes began squealing at the hatchways to turn up *Patrician*'s company. It did not seem to matter that they had thirteen or fourteen thousand miles of ocean to cross before a sight of the English coast would greet them: there was nothing so exciting as the final moment of homeward departure!

Behind him, watched by the marine and Captain

Drinkwater, the junk rounded to under the *Patrician*'s quarter and dropped alongside.

Tregembo watched the junk from the starboard quarter-gallery. Something in the appearance of that boy and the mention of sodomy had brought back unpleasant memories of the berth-deck of His Britannic Majesty's frigate *Cyclops* and the unpleasant coterie that had held sway under the leadership of a certain Midshipman Morris. Morris had been the evil genius who had presided over the cockpit and whose authority the young Drinkwater had challenged. Tregembo too had been mixed up in the dark and unacknowledged doings of the lower deck that had ended the tyranny by the quiet murder of one of Morris's confederates. Not that Tregembo possessed a conscience over the matter, rather that the disturbing influence had dominated an unhappy period of his hard life and the unbidden memory had made him introspective, in the manner of all elderly men. That is why for several moments he could not believe his eyes and thought himself victim of a trick of the light.

'It be impossible,' he muttered, for the figure was too gross, too robed in fantastical costume and too given to fat to be anything other than someone else. But just for a moment, as the mandarin hoisted himself up *Patrician*'s tumblehome by way of the man-ropes, Tregembo fell victim to the fanciful notion that he *was* the man Morris.

It was Quilhampton who first recognised the stranger stepping down on to *Patrician*'s deck. Quilhampton had known Morris when that officer had briefly commanded the brig *Hellebore* and Drinkwater had served as his first lieutenant. Unlike Tregembo he knew little of the man's history or his appearance as a younger man. Quilhampton recalled him already running to seed, though not as gross or disguised as he now appeared. Quilhampton had half forgotten the sick commander they had left in hospital at the Cape of Good Hope, forgotten the rumours that the ship's surgeon had been poisoning him, forgotten even the few facts from his own past that Captain Drinkwater had let slip. To Quilhampton recognition came most easily, though he too was surprised at the extravagant appearance of this quondam naval officer.

Drinkwater, his mind ranging from the forthcoming details of ordering his charges under weigh to the potential securing of the specie he anticipated off the junk's deck, saw only a large, obese man in the yellow silk robe of a mandarin. Recognition of the man as a European was incidental to the sudden flurry of activity about the deck. Fraser was alongside him, as was Ballantyne, and Acting Lieutenant Frey had his yeoman of signals bending flags on to halliards.

Reports flooded aft: the capstans were manned and the nippers in place, below in the cable tiers the Russians prepared to coil the huge, wet and heavy cable. Mr Comley had his fo'c's'le men at their stations and the topsail sheets and halliards were manned. On the quarterdeck a party of marines were tailing on to the main topsail halliards and a quarter-gunner, lanyard in hand, had a carronade charged and ready to fire as the signal for the convoy to weigh.

Gradually a calm settled over *Patrician*. Men stood expectantly at their stations; Fraser told off the acknowledged reports as they came in; Ballantyne stood by the wheel. Only Quilhampton seemed party to the drama at the embarkation point.

'Are you the gentleman from Canton?' asked Drinkwater, giving the newcomer his full attention now. 'D'you have that specie ready to heave aboard?'

The Indian boy stood beside his master, contrasting his bulk.

'I am he, Captain *Drinkwater*, and the specie wants only a tackle to secure it.'

It was the voice, the voice and the malignant and venomous inflection of hatred laid upon his own name that awoke Drinkwater to the stranger's identity. Suddenly the nightmare's premonition came to him.

And recognition slid beneath Drinkwater's rib-cage with the white-hot agony of a sword-thrust.

Morris

It was clear from the self-possession of Morris's smile that he was not surprised at the presence of Nathaniel Drinkwater in the Pearl River. The solicitations of the unknown 'friend' suddenly assumed a sinister aspect and the infallibility of the nightmare was proved once again, for here, at last, Drinkwater knew, was the cacodemon presaged by his dream. This realisation steadied him and he met again the eyes of his enemy.

Morris's gross figure was largely hidden under the yellow silk robe but his hooded eyes seemed to complete his strange oriental transformation.

'Captain Drinkwater, what a pleasure!' Morris bowed, the smile wider as he sensed Drinkwater's uncertainty. 'Please be so kind as to have my traps, and in particular the two bronze-bound chests, hoisted aboard.'

'Mr Q!' Quilhampton, casting a suspicious eye in Morris's direction, crossed the deck. 'Have the goodness to escort this gentleman and his . . . his servant to my cabin.' Drinkwater paused, then added, 'and look lively with those chests.'

'Mr Quilhampton, I do recall you too . . . still with Captain Drinkwater, eh?' Something offensive in Morris's tone lingered after he had left the deck and the boom of the signal gun made Drinkwater start, even though he had absently nodded his permission for its discharge, for he had been watching the heavy chests swing aboard. He disguised his exposure with a barked order: 'Lively with those halliards now!'

The topsail yards rose on freshly slushed masts. The braces were manned and trimmed so that, as the anchor tripped from the mud of the river-bed, *Patrician*'s head fell off downstream in a languid turn that carried her perilously close to the *Guilford*, before her long raking jib-boom pointed at the forts of the Bogue and the open sea beyond.

Drinkwater left the management of his ship to his officers and levelled his glass at the big Indiaman's quarterdeck. He could see Callan, arm outstretched as he got his own ship under weigh. A junk still lay alongside her and was being cast off as *Patrician* drew clear of *Guilford*'s quarter.

'Leggo and haul!'

The foretopsail swung on its parrel, flogged, then bellied out to the favourable air that, with the current, swept them southwards. Astern other ships were blossoming canvas, including Fleetwood Pellew's *Phaeton*, and beyond the convoy the remaining ships lay idle, awaiting the outcome of the negotiations with the Chinese. Among them Drinkwater could just make out the half-repaired masts of *Musquito*.

Beside the binnacle, his dark face working with anxiety, the younger Ballantyne ordered the helm eased a spoke or two, while Fraser, speaking-trumpet in hand, supervised the setting of more sail.

As *Guilford* fell astern, Callan raised his hat and bellowed something across the widening gap of water. Drinkwater was not sure of what he said, though his gesture indicated something of success.

'Pleased to be going, sir,' remarked Quilhampton, who had returned to the deck, nodding at the *Guilford*.

'So it would seem,' acknowledged Drinkwater, fixing Quilhampton with a stare. 'You have secured our guest, have you?'

'Aye, sir . . . he *is* Commander Morris, isn't he? I mean I didn't expect to see *him* here . . .'

'Neither did I, Mr Q, believe me, neither did I, and I doubt he still holds naval rank.' And then another thought struck him. 'Is Tregembo aware of his identity?'

'Yes, sir . . . leastways I think so, for he looked shocked when I entered the cabin . . .'

'Tregembo was in my cabin?'

'Aye, sir; with Derrick and your steward . . .'

'God's bones!'

Tregembo was a factor in the complex train of thought that assailed him with renewed force. It was clear that he could no longer avoid giving the matter of Morris his full attention. He looked about him. The convoy stretched astern of *Patrician*, each ship setting more canvas and with a red ensign at the peak, for Drinkwater had insisted they show a unity of national colours and that the East Indiamen forsake the grid-iron ensign the Company flew east of St Helena.

It seemed his orders were being followed to the letter and he grunted his satisfaction. Ballantyne and Fraser had the conduct of the ship well in hand and he anticipated no trouble when they passed the Bogue; he could absent himself from the quarterdeck for a while.

'Mr Fraser! Do you call me if you need me.'

Drinkwater went below. Enveloped by the gloom of the gun-deck he paused, rubbing his eyes as a worm of apprehension writhed in his gut. Should he send for Quilhampton as a witness, or keep this stinking matter to himself?

The rousing click of the marine sentry's musket against his webbing buckles stirred him. He must show none of the weakness he felt. Morris was the lowest kind of creature that crawled upon the face of the earth. God rot him.

Drinkwater nodded perfunctorily at the marine and passed into his cabin.

Morris was sitting at the table. The boy knelt beside him bare-headed and the pair were almost in silhouette, backed by the expanse of the stern windows. The bright picture of the following convoy, the teeming river and the green hills of China lent a mesmeric effect to the confrontation. There was no sign of Drinkwater's staff and the door to the pantry was closed. Morris's hand stroked the boy's head, his fingers playing with a pixie ear as though it belonged to a spaniel. The concupiscent gesture uninterrupted by Drinkwater's arrival appalled him. It was Morris, in perfect possession of his wits, who broke the silence.

'Necessity makes strange bedfellows, Nathaniel.'

The *double entendre*, the use of his Christian name, even the sound of Morris's voice seemed to strangle any reply from Drinkwater and, for a gasping moment, he felt the sensation of drowning revive from the memory of his dream.

'So . . . they gave you a frigate, eh? I always marked you for a coming man, did I not? In New York, I recall . . . and later . . . oh, I remember everything Nathaniel, everything . . . the humiliations I suffered at your hands, the termination of my career, my illness and abandonment at the Cape . . .'

There was no whining in this catalogue of grievance, but the sincere belief in a corrupt truth. Morris's tone brought Drinkwater to himself and swept aside the spectral remnants of his own fears.

'Hold your tongue, damn you! You cut no ice here, sir! I shall have you put aboard an Indiaman directly we . . .'

'No! No, you will not do that, Nathaniel, consider the matter of the specie . . .'

'D'you think I care a fiddler's damn for one per cent of anything that *you've* had a hand in?'

'Tch, tch, Nathaniel . . .'

'God damn you, sir, but desist from using my name!'

'We are excessively prejudiced, I fear, eh?' Morris was almost purring, his bloated face expanded laterally by a smile, his hand ever fondling the head and ears and nape of the boy. 'Come, come, then *Captain*, shed your tired old hypocrisy; make known what arrangements you have provided for my accommodation. You will not transfer me to an Indiaman, no, nor to one of those pestilential Country ships. For a start they will likely refuse me, for a second reason, if you need further persuasion, the specie, whether you wish to claim your percentage or not, will be at greater risk aboard another ship . .

the pirates are dangerously active in these seas, my dear fellow . . . Come, reconsider and do not be intemperate, you always were the very devil for duty, even as a tight-arsed little midshipman.'

'Morris, as God is my witness . . .'

'Oh, silence! And stop that prating cant before you start! What use would I have for *you* now, eh?' The sly, archly languid tone was shed in an instant. It had come upon Morris lately, like his fat. Remembered was the sharp trading of insult for insult, of venom flecking the very spittle round his mouth in the malignant outbursts that had first alerted Midshipman Drinkwater to the presence of an envious and inept rival. Later, the horrified young Drinkwater discovered the bully was a sodomite who dominated a faction among the weaker members of the lower deck of the frigate *Cyclops*.*

Morris's forbidden passion had awakened sympathetic lusts elsewhere on board, to become not a secret cabal which might have existed undetected by authority, but a hell's kitchen that dealt in intimidation and murder. It was whispered that sodomy was as old as the Bible; that some men deprived of any outlet for physical passion would inevitably be seduced by its specious attractions to relieve the misery of their lives aboard a man-of-war. Some such men might be forgiven the aberration if it impinged on no one unwillingly, whatever the raillings of the Articles of War. But Morris had made of his vice a weapon with which to terrorise, a means by which to indulge and fulfil a cruel megalomania. At the end of the affair, when he had been tactfully dismissed from the ship to avoid scandal, Morris had laid the blame on unrequited love. The thought still appalled Drinkwater.

'You sired siblings on your Elizabeth then.' Morris nodded at the portraits on the forward bulkhead. The indelicate remark presumed the familiarity of old friendship.

'You presume too much. Hold your tongue here!'

'Ah, I forgot. Captain Drinkwater *commands* here.' The sarcasm was as smooth as the yellow silk robe Morris wore. 'But *I* am beyond your orders, *muy Capitán*. I am no longer in your

* See *An Eye of the Fleet*.

navy. I resigned my commission from His Britannic Majesty's illustrious service. I am passed far beyond you and your lash.'

'Two boxes of specie do not purchase you immunity from authority,' Drinkwater cautioned, a horrible thought occurring to him of Morris and Rakitin in some unholy confederacy, combining with the disaffected elements of his tired and impatient crew. Morris smiled, unconcerned at Drinkwater's attitude.

'I have taken some insurance. More specie went aboard *Guilford*. Odious though it may seem to you, my arrival at Calcutta will be expected. You will have to attend to your duty most assiduously in respect of the *Guilford*, my dear fellow. As for me, I will not insist that you pander to my *every* whim; I doubt, candidly, that you would be able to . . .'

Drinkwater stood stock-still, half listening to Morris's baiting sarcasm. He could see, beyond the rim of the table, the lip of the half-opened drawer where, prior to his arrival, it was clear Morris had been inspecting the contents of his journal. He opened his mouth to inveigh further, but thought better of it. A knock sounded on the cabin door. Midshipman Dutfield announced Lieutenant Fraser's compliments and the intelligence that they were approaching the Bogue.

'Very well, Mr Dutfield, I will be up directly.'

'A handsome young man, Captain.' Morris's laughter followed Drinkwater in his retreat to the quarterdeck.

Lieutenant Quilhampton flung his hat on his cot and wrenched at the stock about his thin neck. He turned to find Tregembo at the door of his tiny cabin. 'May I speak with 'ee, zur?'

'What the devil is it, Tregembo?'

'Do 'ee know who's come aboard, zur?'

'You mean that fat mandarin is, or was, Commander Morris? Aye, I know, and I doubt the captain is much pleased about the matter . . . why?'

Quilhampton stared at the old Cornishman. He had never seen the weather-beaten face seamed with so much anxiety.

83

'Zur, forgive me for saying so, 'tis more than a fancy, but you only remember that bugger from the *Hellebore* . . .'

'I mind enough that he was an evil sod with one of the midshipmen there . . .'

'No,' interrupted Tregembo urgently and lowering his voice, 'I mean more'n that, zur; I mind him from way back on the old *Cyclops*, zur. 'E swore then as how he'd spavin the Cap'n, zur, and I know, zur, I *feels* it now as he's come to do just that.'

Quilhampton frowned. 'Spavin? You mean *ruin* Captain Drinkwater? How can he do that? You ain't suggesting this counterfeit mandarin fellow *knew* who commanded this ship? Come, come, Tregembo, I understand your dislike of matters as they stand, but he's clearly been engaged in trade and wants to leave Canton . . . anything else is sheer foolish conjecture.'

Tregembo opened his mouth, shut it and stared at the lieutenant.

'Beg pardon for troubling you, zur.' And he left Quilhampton staring at the closed door.

Morris had been put in command of the brig *Hellebore* at Mocha, at the end of 1799, or beginning of 1800, he could not quite recall. He had superseded Commander Griffiths, killed in action, and had relieved Lieutenant Drinkwater of his temporary command. Quilhampton remembered Morris getting the step in rank that properly belonged to Drinkwater. Surely that fact would atone for any earlier disagreement between the two men? Doubtless so partisan a champion of Drinkwater as Tregembo would see such a miscarriage of justice in an unfavourable light as far as Morris was concerned. But he remembered other things too; those rumours about Morris that concerned allusions of sodomy with one of the midshipmen, and the scuttlebutt that the surgeon and his woman, a convict they had rescued from an open boat, had been poisoning Morris.* He had dismissed it at the time; young Midshipman Quilhampton had not then learnt the extent of the perfidy of ordinary mortals.

Was there something in Tregembo's alarum? Or was the old man a victim of senility, of over-anxiety on behalf of his master?

* See *A Brig of War*.

Of course, that was it! He was known to be jealous of his assumed influence over the captain. So what if he remembered the petty squabbles between a pair of midshipmen in an ancient and long-rotten frigate? Lieutenant Quilhampton shrugged off the matter and bellowed at the wardroom messman to fetch him a basin of warm water from the galley. While he waited he fell to calculating how long it would be before he might present himself in the Edinburgh drawing-room of Mistress Catriona MacEwan and whether, after so long a commission, he had accrued sufficient funds to take a wife.

Drinkwater's thoughts were hardly on the convoy he was marshalling off the Bogue. *Patrician* lay with her sails clewed up, only her mizen topsail still sheeted home and backed against its mast. Above his head a flutter of bunting tested his signalling system and already, in conformity with his orders, boats from the various ships were converging on the frigate. First to arrive was *Phaeton*'s, to collect his final despatch to Admiral Drury. Her midshipman was of the same age as her commanding officer.

'Tell Captain Pellew that I'd be obliged if he would stand to the southward in company until sunset tomorrow.'

'Very well, sir.'

'And that I shall discharge him from his obligation at that time by a gun and the union at the foremasthead.'

'Union at the foremasthead . . . aye, aye, sir.'

Drinkwater turned to greet Callan. 'I did not expect you would come in person, Captain Callan,' he remarked, surprised.

'I do not think you understood my hail in the river, Captain Drinkwater, but I loaded several chests of specie from a junk, sent by order of the Hong without guard to avoid rousing the suspicions of the Imperial Customs. I counted the amount, ten thousand taels less a few score, some three and a half thousand sterling at seven shillings the *liang*. I think Drury and the Select-men should be informed.'

'I agree. I have sent the substance of your news by *Phaeton*'s boat.'

85

'You have?'

Drinkwater nodded. 'I also shipped specie, though I have not counted it, two chests.'

Callan's eyes lit up. 'By God, Captain, we've done it! The Hong must be under diabolical pressure . . .'

'Captain Callan,' Drinkwater broke in, 'I'm not certain you are correct. It is my understanding that the removal of the specie may not necessarily have been with the full approbation of the Hong. It was brought off by a European, a man in mandarin costume named, I believe, Mister Morris . . .'

Callan's expression darkened and his forehead furrowed. 'Morris? You say "brought off", is he here, on board?'

'In my cabin,' Drinkwater nodded.

'I must speak with him . . .'

'One moment,' Drinkwater restrained Callan. 'What d' you know of him?'

Callan reflected a moment. 'He is a man of irregular habits, Captain, not approved of by society in Calcutta, but not unknown in these parts. He was ostracised to Canton but was undeniably successful as a man of business, holding high influence over certain of the native houses in Calcutta, Rangoon and now, here, in China.'

'If by "irregular habits" you refer to the sin of Sodom, I take it you forgive him on the grounds that you and your colleagues find his acumen of use to you.'

The veiled sarcasm in Drinkwater's voice stung Callan, who flushed. 'This is the east, Captain, things are not ordered here the way they are in England.'

'Come, come, sir,' said Drinkwater acidly, relieving himself of some of the bile formed by the encounter with Morris, 'it is unfair to suggest that Mr Morris's pederasty is unique to the orient. You find him useful, that I understand . . .'

'Captain, you are under a misapprehension if you consider men of trade to be inferior to men of your warlike stamp . . .'

'I infer no such imputation, Captain Callan. I simply remark upon your tolerance. Mr Morris does not strike me as a man upon whom, sodomite or not, I would put the least reliance.'

Drinkwater paused, he did not want to give Callan the information that he and Morris were old acquaintances. 'Well, perhaps I am wrong. He brought off the silver and has redeemed the trade for this year, at least. Tell me, whence did he come? Is he Country born?'

'No . . . he came out in an Indiaman from the Cape, found employment in the Marine at Bombay, but shortly afterwards resigned. There was a whiff of scandal, I believe. I first knew him some six years ago when he arrived at Calcutta. He caused a flutter then for appearing in native costume. Shortly afterwards he moved to Rangoon on behalf of some Parsee interests, and then here, to Canton. But I must see him . . .'

Callan went below, escorted by Belchambers to admit him past the marine sentry. Drinkwater was fully occupied himself as officers, mates and a master or two came aboard from the merchant ships. Patiently he answered their questions and issued his last-minute orders. Chiefly he impressed upon them the necessity of keeping in company and of not passing the Rhio archipelago without escort, for which purpose he named Pulo Tioman the rendezvous. Few demurred, only an officer off the *Ligonier*, with *Guilford* the only other Indiaman, objecting on the grounds of delay, while the second mate of a Country brig, the *Hormuzeer*, claimed his ship was swift enough to outrun even the fastest cruiser the French could send against them.

'Well, sir,' Drinkwater replied testily, 'the responsibility for his vessel lies undisputedly with your master, but if I were he I would prefer the company of others to the risk of isolation.'

The man went off grumbling and Drinkwater turned away, only to be confronted with Callan. 'Have you answered the purpose of your visit?' he asked the India officer.

'Yes, thank you. I am not certain *I* trust him, Captain Drinkwater, but he has shown me accounts which indicate the money is indeed from the Hong in just and equitable payment of debts. I would *like* to believe him . . .'

'What possible advantage could he derive from the matter, his having admitted the sums to you?'

Callan shrugged. 'That is what makes me uneasy; on the face of it I cannot see any.'

'Then perhaps he will be content with a commission. Did you ask him from what he was running?'

'Why he abandoned his post at Canton?'

'Yes.'

'He volunteered that he was in danger of his life after the repulse of Admiral Drury and on account of the disfavour in which the native Chinese presently hold Europeans . . . but that will pass', Callan added, 'the minute their supply of opium is throttled.'

'Nevertheless, he himself may well be in fear of some retribution.' Drinkwater did not know why he sprung thus to Morris's defence. Perhaps, he thought, as Callan summoned his boat, because at the back of his mind was a suspicion forming that was too dark, too terrible and too preposterous to be anything other than the invented phobia of a disturbed mind.

Fair Winds and Foul Tempers

It was symptomatic of the confusion in Drinkwater's mind caused by the presence of Morris that he forgot the matter of the deserters during Callan's visit. Fraser reminded him later that day, asking also if he felt well.

'Quite well, thank you,' Drinkwater replied tartly, 'do I give you the impression otherwise?'

Fraser almost visibly quailed: 'I had it in mind that you were not yourself, sir . . .'

'Then who the devil should I be, eh?'

'I beg your pardon, sir . . .'

'Damn it, Fraser, I beg yours. Yes, I'm deuced distempered and out at all elbows with a festering passenger occupying my cabin. Needs must when the devil drives and the ship is so overcrowded, but tell Marsden I want the place screened . . . decently too, no parish-rigging, but a decent slat-and-canvas job.' Drinkwater paused, judging how far he could take Fraser into his confidence. 'That man is to be allowed as little liberty as possible. His boy-servant will attend his needs and he will be permitted the freedom of the quarterdeck only when I give my permission and at no time in the hours of darkness. He will dine at my table, damn it, and I shall be consulted in all matters concerning him. Mount is to advise his sentries of this. The invitation of the wardroom is not to be extended to him.'

'Aye, aye, sir . . . er, may I ask why you . . . ?'

'No, sir, you may not. You have your orders, now attend to them.'

'Very well, sir . . . and what about Chirkov?'

Drinkwater swore. 'We are down by the head with idlers, damn it! Send Mr Comley to the gunroom, Fraser, and in the presence of all its inhabitants have him administer a dozen stripes of his cane. Let's have done with that young gentleman once and for all!'

'And the deserters, sir? Word has it that the people know their whereabouts and . . .'

'And . . . ?'

'Begging your pardon, sir, but that you do too.'

Drinkwater stared at his first lieutenant. Fraser was a good, competent officer. Drinkwater had taken him as a favour to Lord Keith and though there was not the intimacy that existed between the captain and Quilhampton, there was a strong sense of mutual regard between them. He had never known Fraser attempt to meddle with his own method of command before, yet here was a direct, if obscure, inference.

'Go on, Mr Fraser, and do stop begging my pardon; you are, after all, the first lieutenant.'

Fraser's diffidence seemed to slip from him, and Drinkwater mentally reprobated himself for his cross-grainedness. He sometimes forgot the age difference between himself and his officers and the intimidating effect it could have on their confidences.

'Well, sir, I got wind o' scuttlebutt that the people had heard you knew the whereabouts o' the deserters . . .' (How? Drinkwater asked himself. Not Tregembo, certainly; perhaps Mullender or the Quaker Derrick, whose loyalty lay closer to his moral creed than any imposed regulations of the Admiralty.) '. . . and that you wouldn't reclaim them on account o' the fact that you didna' want trouble.'

'I see. But such an assumption of weakness might provoke trouble nevertheless.'

'Aye, sir, that's true,' said Fraser, relieved that the captain took his point.

Drinkwater recalled his remark to Callan about not wanting to disaffect the men when the ship was idle. Misinterpretation of such a speech was not surprising. He still had *Phaeton* in company, he could alter course for Macao and arraign the recaptured deserters before a court martial which would assuredly hang them. Or he could affect to ignore the matter a while longer, and deal with it when he judged proper.

'I shall recover the deserters tomorrow, Mr Fraser, if the sea permits it. In the meantime deal with Midshipman Chirkov and get Marsden to rig up those screens.'

In the gloom of the gunroom, lit by the grease-dips' guttering flames, the *Patrician*'s midshipmen stood alongside their Russian counterparts. In the main they had got on well together. Frey, partly by virtue of his personality, partly by his acting rank, was the acknowledged senior, and there was some evidence that Chirkov was not liked by the other Russians on account of his overwhelming idleness. There was, therefore, no particular objection to the first lieutenant's announcement of the punishment, nor any move to release Chirkov when he struggled, protesting the indignity of being held by two of Comley's mates. It was no fault of the other midshipmen, British or Russian, if Chirkov failed to understand that he was being let off lightly, given what amounted to a private punishment on a crowded man-of-war, rather than the spectacular public humbling of being beaten over the breech of a quarter-deck carronade.

Comley laid on over Chirkov's breeched backside to the count of twelve, and when he marched his mates out of the cockpit he respectfully touched his hat to them all. 'Gentlemen . . .' he said.

'There, sir,' Frey remarked reasonably to the straightening Chirkov who was choking back tears of rage, pain and humiliation, 'you have had the honour of a thrashing from one of His Britannic Majesty's bosuns, he is senior to you and therefore your submission is without prejudice to your character as an officer.'

Grins greeted this droll speech, but its humour was lost on Chirkov.

'A *Mister* Bosun is not superior to a Russian *Count*,' he hissed.

'Perhaps not, sir,' replied Frey quickly, 'but he *is* most assuredly superior to a midshipman.'

'Particularly a *Russian* midshipman,' added Belchambers boldly.

Enraged, Chirkov turned on the diminutive Belchambers, but the boy adroitly dodged him and the sudden movement sent agonies of pain through Chirkov's buttocks. As Belchambers slipped past his would-be assailant and made for the companionway to the deck, Frey, Dutfield and the rest barred his retreat. Chirkov was faced with an unsmiling wall of bodies.

'You deserved it, Count Chirkov,' said Frey, 'recall you are a prisoner of war. You would do best to forget the matter. I can assure you that Captain Drinkwater has dismissed it from his mind.'

'What do I worry about your Captain Drinkwater's mind? Captain Drinkwater can go to the devil! I am insulted. I cannot call for satisfactions from Mister Bosun but I can from you!' Chirkov rammed a finger into Frey's face. 'You are only *acting* lieutenant, you are challenged!'

A stillness fell on the gunroom. The midshipmen swayed amid the creaks and groans of the ship's fabric as it worked easily in the quartering sea. They watched Frey's reaction.

'Duelling is forbidden on board ship, sir, but I shall be pleased to meet you ashore upon our arrival at Prince of Wales Island.'

'Pistols,' snarled Chirkov, and stumbled unhappily from the circle of onlookers.

Captain Drinkwater looked about him. He knew he ought to be contented. The convoy was closed up in good order, spread over some five square miles of the China Sea, not in columns, but a loose formation centred on *Guilford* and *Ligonier*, the big

Indiamen, both of which had lanterns in their mizen tops that glowed weakly in the failing daylight. Clouds covered the sky, outriders of the northerly monsoon that drove them southwards with a fair wind for the Malacca Strait. In accordance with his Standing Orders the ships were taking in their topgallants for the night, snugging down to avoid the separation that might make one of them a vulnerable hen for any marauding French *reynard* cruising on the horizon. Drinkwater looked at the main crosstrees from which Midshipman Dutfield was just then descending. When the midshipman reached the deck he made his report.

'Two junks in the north-east quarter, sir, otherwise nothing in sight beyond the convoy.'

Acknowledging the intelligence, Drinkwater was peeved that the news brought him no satisfaction. He nodded and turned to Frey.

'You may fire the chaser, Mr Frey, and make *Phaeton*'s number . . .'

Drinkwater looked astern. Fleetwood Pellew's crack frigate dipped her ensign in farewell, hauled her yards and, on a taut bowline, stood to windward, returning to the coast of China. *Patrician* was in sole charge now and Drinkwater could go below.

But he lingered. There was no solace in the cabin, divided as it was and with Morris inert and inscrutable behind the canvas screen. So far Drinkwater had avoided all contact with his enemy, unwilling to stir any memory or allow Morris the slightest grounds for reawakening old enmities. Drinkwater did not know how Morris had got word of his presence in the Pearl River, though it was not hard to imagine in the circumscribed circle of gossip attached to the trading fraternity at Canton, but he was convinced Morris had some ulterior motive for selecting *Patrician* as his means of reaching India. And it went beyond the customary carriage of specie in His Majesty's ships, as witness the chests put aboard *Guilford*.

No, Morris had personal reasons for seeking passage with Nathaniel Drinkwater, and the quondam naval officer had once sworn he would professionally ruin the man who had displaced him on a quarterdeck.

Coxswain Tregembo lay in his hammock and stared at the dimly visible deck beam a few inches above his nose. During the night the sea had risen and *Patrician* was scending before the quartering waves. On either side of him the hammocks of other men pressed against his own in the fourteen inches allowed each man. Tregembo was part of a suspended island of humanity that moved almost independently of the ship, adding its own creaks and rasps and rub of rope and ring and canvas to the aching groans of the working timbers of the frigate.

To a less inured nose than Tregembo's, the stench would have been overpowering, for all Lieutenant Fraser's sedulous swabbing with vinegar, airing and burning of loose powder. Ineffectually washed bodies, the exhalations of men on an indifferent diet that whistled through badly maintained teeth and the night-loosening of wind combined with the effluvia of the bilge that rose from below. Rat droppings and the residual essences of the myriad stores concealed in the storerooms and hold added to the decomposing mud and weed drawn inboard on the cables so lately laid on the bed of the Pearl River. Flakes of green and noxious matter gave off gases as they broke down into dust, to be carried into the limbers of the ship by the trickling rivulets of leaks that found their inexorable way below.

Scarcely noticing this mephitic miasma that cast yellow haloes round the guarded lanterns by the companionways and dully illuminated the dozing sentries, Tregembo lay unsleeping. He too considered the presence of Morris in their midst.

Unlike his captain, Tregembo's intellect did not flirt with notions of providence or fate. Considerations of coincidence in Morris's resurrection aboard *Patrician* were quite absent from his thoughts. To Tregembo the world was not a vast, wondrous mystery in which his life held some fraction of universal implication; but a confined, tangible microcosm of discomfort, tolerable if one occupied the office of captain's coxswain under a man of Drinkwater's stamp. It was not that Tregembo lacked the intelligence to cast his mind beyond the compressing tumblehome of *Patrician*'s planking, nor that he was incapable of regarding the star-strewn sky with awe. It was just that his firmament was limited by the deck beam above him and that such considerations as Drinkwater could indulge in, for Tregembo bordered on the effete and were beyond the sensible limits of practical men. That Morris had turned up in China was, to Tregembo, not to be wondered at. He had been left half-way there, at the Cape of Good Hope some years ago, and it did not surprise the old Cornishman that he had made a new life for himself beyond the Indian Seas.

Listening to the noises of the night around him, to the soft, abrasive whisper of a hundred swinging hammocks and the labouring of the ship, the audible hiss of the sea beyond the double planking of the hull, the thrum of wind in the rigging far above him and the mumbles and grunts of dreaming men, Tregembo thought back to a gale-lashed night nearly thirty years earlier when he and another had sprung a man from a foot-rope when reefing a sail, flinging him into the sea, to disappear into the blackness astern of the hard-pressed frigate *Cyclops*.

It had been a judicial murder, secretly sanctioned by the tacit approval of most of the members of the lower deck, and it had put an end to the bullying and the tyranny of a certain Midshipman Morris and his sodomitically inclined cronies. Tregembo smiled to himself. He recalled the young Drinkwater seeking guidance when the same Morris turned upon his messmates for amusement. The eventual confrontation had matured the promising young midshipman, and had been the beginning of Tregembo's service to Drinkwater.

What worried Tregembo now, and kept him from sleeping, was the certainty that Morris would seek in some way to discredit the captain. When the young Drinkwater had sought out Tregembo for a confidant, the Cornishman had advised him that he had nothing to lose by opposing the cockpit bully.

Now things were different; Captain Drinkwater had everything to lose, and the thought made Tregembo uneasy.

Morris too was awake, listening to the breathing of Drinkwater beyond the canvas screen. The captain was asleep now, Morris knew, though it had been a long time before he had dropped off. Morris had heard also the revealing tinkle of glass and bottle after Drinkwater had come below.

Never, in his most extreme fantasies, had Morris imagined that Drinkwater would ever be delivered up to him so perfectly. In the days when, after his ousting from the *Cyclops*, he had smarted over his rival's luck, he had continued his pursuit of a naval career. He had been helped by petticoat influence, of course, but there was nothing unusual in that. Then had come the time when he had been appointed to the brig *Hellebore* and, delectably, had Drinkwater as his first lieutenant.

Only the onset of chronic illness had prevented him from fully exploiting that opportunity, and in his long convalescence at the Cape Drinkwater had slipped from his grasp. News had come to Morris there of the death of his sister by whose influence he had formerly gained employment, and a letter refusing to ratify his promotion to Master and Commander had left him high and dry at the tip of Africa. He could have gone home, but a welter of debts and creditors decided him against it. Besides, the frequent passage of Indiamen and the consequent society of one or two men of oriental taste induced him to try his luck in India.

Morris smiled to himself. He felt immensely benign, as good and calm as when the opium fumes took his soul and wafted it through paradise. Even in the gloom he could see the pale face of the sleeping boy. He had not paid much for the tongue-tied child, more for the services of the surgeon of the European infantry battalion in Madras whose fourchette had not simply sliced the frenum, but had excavated the child's mouth to make an apolaustic orifice for his master.

There was no abatement of the wind at dawn. Cloud obscured

the sky and a touch of mist hazed the horizon. The convoy remained in tolerably good order but Drinkwater, early on deck from an unsatisfactory night's rest, was frustrated in his plans to lower a boat and recover his deserters.

Tregembo had more success, entering the captain's cabin soon after Drinkwater had gone on deck and before either Mullender or Derrick was about. Slipping round the canvas screen he woke the corpulent mass of Morris by hauling his catamite off him. It was the first time Morris had knowingly laid eyes on the old Cornishman for ten years.

'What the . . . ?'

'Remember me, do ye?'

'You . . .' Morris's face creased with fear and the struggle to recall a name. The old man had been in Drinkwater's cabin when he had first entered it. Now he shook Morris with a horrid violence.

'Tregembo, Cap'n's cox'n. *I* remember *you*, an' I want words to tell 'ee that I'll see 'ee in hell before ye'll touch the Cap'n!'

Morris, still supine in the tossing cot, quailed under the venom of Tregembo's words. The boy had shrunk into a crouch, whimpering against the carriage of a gun.

'Tregembo . . .' muttered Morris, his eyes fixed on the glowering, over-zealous old man, recalling memories of Tregembo's past and how, like Drinkwater's, they lay like the strands of a rope, woven with his own. It was clear that Tregembo had come to threaten, not to murder. This realisation emboldened Morris. He eased his bulk on to an elbow.

'Ah, yes, Tregembo . . . yes, I recall you now. You are Captain Drinkwater's lickspittle, his tale-bearer. Yes, I recall you well, *and* your part in certain doings aboard *Cyclops* . . .'

'Aye. And you'd do well to keep your memories in your mind *Mister* Morris, for I'm not afeared of you and know what you'd do if ye had the chance. Just you recollect that old Tregembo will be watching you, and your dandy-prat there.' Tregembo gestured at the boy.

'Is that a threat, Tregembo?'

But the Cornishman had said his piece and retired beyond

the canvas screen. The boy whimpered fearfully and, as *Patrician* dipped suddenly into the trough of a wave, vomited over the deck. The sharp stink assailed Morris's nostrils and from pique he clouted the frightened and abject creature.

Tregembo felt satisfied with his mission of intimidation. He had hoped for an ally in Mr Quilhampton and had been disappointed. There was, however, one further thing to be done to complete the execution of the plan he had made during the night.

He found Drinkwater at the weather hance, wrapped in his boat-cloak.

'Beg pardon, zur . . .'

'What is it, Tregembo? . . .'

'That Morris, zur.' Tregembo's eyes met the Captain's.

'Well?'

''E knows me, zur . . . I spoke to him this morning.'

'You announced your presence, you mean . . . advised him to mind his manners, is that it?'

'Something o' the sort, zur.'

Drinkwater smiled. 'Be careful of him, Tregembo. Unfortunately we must bear with him . . .'

'*You* be careful o' him, zur,' Tregembo broke in, 'he's not forgotten nothing, zur . . . be assured o' that.'

'Thank you for your advice.'

Tregembo bridled at the faintly patronising air of Drinkwater's reply. 'He weren't never a gennelman, zur; he'm no longer quality.'

'No, you're right . . .'

'You shouldn't leave your pistols in your cabin, zur, I don't know that he's got any himself, but . . .'

'I've been thinking about that. I've decided to take over poor Hill's cabin and put Prince Vladimir in to share with Morris.'

Tregembo considered the proposition and a twinkle in his eyes caught an answering glimmer in Drinkwater's.

'I'll see to it, zur.'

'If you please.'

'Beg pardon, sir.' Lieutenant Quilhampton touched the fore-cock of his hat.

'Yes? What is it?'

'Weather's tending to thicken, sir.'

Drinkwater cast a look about the frigate, quickly counting his scattered charges. Two of the Country ships, small, round bilged brigs, were wallowing, dropping astern and fading into the encroaching mist that had dissolved the horizon, reducing the visible circle of sea on which the ships of the convoy drove southwards.

'Very well. Make the signal to shorten sail.'

Quilhampton acknowledged the order and the hitched bundles of coloured bunting soared aloft to break out at the main masthead. From forward an unshotted gun boomed to leeward, drawing attention to the signal. While the *Patrician*'s men leapt into the shrouds and lay aloft, Drinkwater watched the evolutions of the merchant ships. He knew the Indiamen were reluctant to crack on apace, believing in a leisurely progress as least wearing on cargo, company and passengers. If the convoy were being shadowed, now would prove an opportune occasion for an attack. But the convoy behaved itself. The Indiamen shortened down and the cluster of Country ships followed suit, the rearward sluggards sensibly holding on until they had come up with the majority.

'Bring the ship close to the starboard quarter of the rearmost brig, Mr Q.'

'On the wind'd quarter of the *Courier*, aye, aye, sir.'

If they were to be attacked, Drinkwater wanted *Patrician* to windward and able to crack on sail to support any part of his little fleet. He watched as the helm was put down and the men manned the braces, swinging the yards a point or two, easing the sheets and leading the weather tacks forward. The convoy drew out on *Patrician*'s larboard bow and then, yards swung again, she came back before the wind, reined in upon the quarter of the inappropriately named brig *Courier*, slowest vessel in the convoy.

Aware of someone beside him, Drinkwater turned, expecting

Quilhampton to report the adjustment to the frigate's station, but it was Rakitin.

'I have had a report, Captain Drinkwater, from one of my officers, that you have ordered him to be beaten. Count Chirkov is most . . .' Rakitin sought the right word for the humiliation of his subordinate with no success. 'Count Chirkov has . . . I protest most strongly.'

Drinkwater fixed the Russian with a glare and tried with difficulty to keep his temper. Morris, the Russians, such petty matters; relatively trivial when compared to the importance of the convoy and the dangers inherent in the latent disaffection of his crew. He knew that in the circumscribed limits of a ship such trifling irritations assumed an importance scarcely to be conceived by those on land, an importance that the rigid enforcement of naval discipline defused, but which grew and festered among those not held in such thrall with, moreover, the time and opportunity to dwell upon them. He rounded on the Russian.

'Captain Rakitin, if you did me the courtesy of maintaining order among your officers, a situation requiring punishment would not have arisen. As it was I ordered your officer punished according to the usage of the British service in which he is now a prisoner. He was not publicly humiliated in front of the ship's company and should not, therefore, complain. However,' Drinkwater continued, a mischievous idea occurring to him, 'I have made arrangements for you to transfer into my own cabin, vacating the one you presently occupy. I also deliver Midshipman Count Chirkov into your especial charge. He is to live and mess with you and not to contaminate my own young men any more. Good-day to you!'

Drinkwater strode purposefully across the deck, bent over the binnacle to check the course and took station with Lieutenant Quilhampton.

'For God's sake, James, talk some sense to me before I am constrained to do something I shall regret.'

Quilhampton turned, cast a glance beyond Drinkwater's shoulder and muttered, 'He's in pursuit, sir . . .'

'God's bones,' said Drinkwater through clenched teeth.

'Captain Drinkwater,' began Rakitin who had taken a moment to digest the import of Drinkwater's remarks, 'Captain Drinkwater, it is not . . .'

'Deck there!' came the lookout's shrill cry. 'Ship to loo'ard bearing up! Gunfire to the s'uth'ard!'

The dull boom of a gun rolled over the water and the sharp point of fire from a second discharge caught their eyes as the ships of the convoy began to swing to starboard across the bows of those behind them. Strict order seemed about to dissolve into chaos.

'Hands to the braces! Starboard your helm, Mister! Don't run aboard that damned brig! Call all hands!'

Drinkwater dodged Rakitin, hauled himself up into the mizen rigging and strove to make out what was happening ahead. He hesitated only a second as another stab of yellow gunfire flashed through the mist.

'Beat to quarters!'

Infirmities of Character

'Hold your course!'

Drinkwater moved beside the binnacle, steadying the helmsmen and countering a sudden and distressing nervousness on the part of Ballantyne, the new sailing master. *Guilford* loomed past a pistol-shot distant, her yards triced hard-up to avoid plunging into *Ligonier* under her lee. The latter, foul of the *Hormuzeer*, had broached and a brief glance showed men running out along her jib-boom, hacking at the mess of broken spars, torn canvas and tangled ropes where it had jammed in the Country ship's main rigging.

As *Patrician's* stern lifted, Drinkwater could see ahead. Only two more ships lay to leeward, and both were clearing from larboard, their heads laid on the starboard tack. Raising his glass he swept it across the misty horizon expecting to see the pale squares of enemy topsails taking substance above the low hull of a French frigate.

'Ship cleared for action, sir,' Fraser reported, and Drinkwater nodded. He had been so occupied with conning *Patrician* through the convoy that he had scarcely noticed the rattle of the marine drummer's snare, or the rushing preparations round the deck. Mount's marines lined the hammock nettings and the quarterdeck and fo'c's'le gunners knelt expectantly by their pieces. Midshipmen stood at their stations, little Belchambers, his ankle near normal, in the main-top. Drinkwater

102

thought of Morris, suddenly exposed to the vulgar gaze of the people as the cabin bulkheads were removed and the eighteen-pounder beneath his cot was manned by a dozen barefoot seamen. Drinkwater wondered if he was still fondling his pathic.

They were crossing the stern of the leeward-most ship now and Ballantyne was gesticulating.

'Please, sir! Something is not correct!'

'Eh? What's that?'

'They are waving, sir, on the ship to starboard . . .'

Drinkwater strode to the rail and peered over the hammock nettings. The square stern of the heavily laden *Carnatic* presented itself to his gaze. Two men were waving frantically from her rail and then a belch of smoke rolled from her waist as she discharged another gun.

'By God, it's an alarm!'

Drinkwater spun round. He had already detected the danger ahead by the sudden increase in the pitch of the deck.

'Braces, there! Lively now! Start 'em for your lives! Down helm! Down helm!'

There was no enemy frigate waiting to leeward of the convoy ready to snap up a prize; only an uncharted reef upon which the sea broke in sudden, serried ranks of rollers which exploded upwards, filling the air with an intense mist.

Mount saved them, slashing through the standing part of the main brace with his hanger, then cutting back into the strands of the topsail brace. As the yards flew round *Patrician* lay over assisting the helmsmen as they palmed the wheel-spokes rapidly through their hands. A member of the after-guard was already at the mizen braces while others started the main sheet at the chess-tree. The heavy frigate lurched to leeward, running her larboard gunports under water and taking gouts of streaming sea-water below as Lieutenant Quilhampton, in charge of the main batteries and suddenly aware of something amiss, ordered the ports secured.

'Jesus Christ . . .' someone blasphemed. The steady stern breeze seemed, now that they reached obliquely across it, to blow with the ferocity of a gale. The extra canvas, shaken out again as they had overtaken the convoy, now pressed them over. To windward the seas assumed a new and forbidding aspect, heaping sharply into breaking peaks as they felt the rising sea-bed beneath them.

Drinkwater turned to leeward. He was beyond the heart-thumping apprehension of anxiety, his mind perfectly cool with that detachment that feared the worst. At any moment, driven by his own impetuosity, he expected *Patrician*'s keel to strike the reef in a sudden, overwhelming shock that would carry her masts and yards over the side.

Beyond the narrow beam of the frigate's hull the seas down-wind bore a different look. Their precipitate energy was spent, they crashed and foamed and flung themselves in a thundering welter of white and green water upon the invisible obstacle of the reef.

'Hold her steady!' he ordered, his voice level as every man upon the upper deck who was aware of their danger held his breath.

For a minute . . . two . . . *Patrician* skimmed, heeling along the very rim of the reef, held from dashing herself to pieces only by the unseen, submarine run-off where the broken waves, spending themselves above, poured back whence they had come.

Ten minutes later they were in clear water and the white surge of foaming breakers with its cap of wafting spume lay fine on the weather quarter.

'I'm obliged to you, Mr Mount.'

'Your servant, sir,' replied Mount, still amazed at his own prescience.

'A damned close thing . . .' Drinkwater's heart was thump-ing vigorously now. Reaction had set in; he felt a wave of nausea and a weakling tremble in his leg muscles. 'Secure the guns and pipe the men down,' he said to Fraser between clenched teeth.

And then Morris was there, standing upon the quarterdeck watching Comley hustling a party along to reeve off a new main-brace, his loose, yellow silk robe flapping in the wind, the Indian, decorously turned out in coat, turban and aigrette, hanging by his side.

Men were nudging each other and staring at the bizarre sight. When Morris and Drinkwater confronted each other, the latter was still pale from his recent experience.

'You alarmed us, Captain,' Morris said smoothly, 'we thought you were going into action, but I see that, like Caligula, you had declared war on the ocean.'

The smug, urbane transition of remark into insult struck Drinkwater. He was reminded of how dangerous a man Morris was, that he was not without education, and came from a class that accepted privilege as a birthright. It had formed part of Morris's original enmity that the youthful Drinkwater was an example of an upstart family.

But Drinkwater's nausea was swiftly overcome by a rising and revengeful anger. He recalled something of the detached coolness that sustained him in moments of extreme stress.

'The bulkheads will shortly be re-erected. You will be able to return to your quarters very soon.' The words were polite, the tone sharp.

'But it is remarkably refreshing here on deck, Captain. You have a fine set of men . . . handsome fellows . . .'

The remark was loud enough to be overheard, on the face of it harmless enough, but tinged with notice of intent, judging by the amusement in Morris's deep-set, hooded eyes.

'Go below, sir,' Drinkwater snapped, facing his old enemy, and between them crackled the brittle electricity of dislike. Morris smiled and then turned to go. Drinkwater found himself confronted by Ballantyne. The master stood open-mouthed and Drinkwater thought of his earlier nervousness. He appeared to have a coward upon his quarterdeck.

'What the devil *is* it, Mr Ballantyne? Come, pull yourself together, the danger's past. Be kind enough to work out an estimate of our position so that we can amend the charts . . .'

'No, no, sir. It is that man.' Ballantyne's head shook from side to side. 'I know him . . .'

It occurred to Drinkwater that Ballantyne had not previously seen their passenger. For all Drinkwater knew, Morris had traded under a pseudonym.

'I knew him in Rangoon, sir,' Ballantyne persisted, 'he was up to mischief. He made much money.'

Mischief seemed a very mild word for what Drinkwater knew Morris was capable of.

'I should not believe all you hear, Captain Drinkwater, especially from a man of mixed blood.'

Overheard, Ballantyne paled, while Morris's head disappeared for the second time below the lip of the companionway coaming.

For two days nothing of note occurred. The wind eased, clearing the air so that the horizon became again the clear rim of visibility beloved by seamen. The convoy remained in good order and Drinkwater, immeasurably relieved by his move into the master's cabin, felt his spirits lighten. He dismissed his earlier fears of interference from Morris as foolish imaginings, recollections of the past when he had been a circumstantial victim of Morris's vicious and capricious nature. Now he had the upper hand; Morris was held aft under guard yet in the comparative freedom of the great cabin. His officers were loyal. The morale of his men was much improved by the news that their return home was now only a matter of time, and the convoy was well disciplined.

Privately, too, the move was beneficial. He had had Mullender take down the portraits, his journal was secure and his personal effects were removed from the defiling presence of Morris. What Morris did behind the canvas screen was his own affair, so long as it did not impinge upon the life, public or private, of Captain Drinkwater and his ship.

As Drinkwater's mood lifted, James Quilhampton's was damped by growing apprehension. The first excitements of departure from Whampoa had worn off, and the drudgery of watch-keeping imposed its own monotonous routines which combined with the demands of the ship and convoy to rouse dormant worries. It was Quilhampton who had, months ago, suppressed an incipient mutiny before its eruption. These were the same men, he thought as he paced the quarterdeck daily, observing them about their duties, the same unpaid labourers who were sorely tried by the hard usage of the King's Service. To Quilhampton, the spectre of mutiny assumed a new danger now that they were homeward bound; the danger that it might destroy any possibility of him marrying Mistress MacEwan. Part of his cavalier reception of Tregembo's warning was not so much because he did not believe in it, but because he did not want to contemplate any additional factor that might threaten or destroy his expectations.

Beyond the screen bisecting the captain's cabin Morris heard Captain Rakitin leave his indolent young companion while he took his exercise on deck. Morris, wrapped in his silk robe, touched the shoulder of his Ganymede and pointed at the screen. Impassively the boy rose and slipped past the end of the partition where, at the stern windows, communication between the divided cabin was possible. Morris waited, composing his face to its most benign expression, smoking a long, thin Burmese cheroot.

'Good morning,' he said as Chirkov, summoned by curiosity, followed the turbaned pixie. 'Please sit down. I hear you speak excellent English. Would you care for a glass . . . ?'

The boy produced a porcelain bottle and poured *samsu* into one of Drinkwater's glasses. Standing, Chirkov tossed back the glass, the raw rice spirit rasping his throat with a fire reminiscent of vodka. The glass was refilled. The Russian seemed reluctant to sit.

'We are both prisoners of Captain Drinkwater . . .' Morris began experimentally, pleased with the contemptuously dismissive gesture made by Chirkov.

'You do not like Captain Drinkwater?' Morris asked.

'No! He is doing me dishonour, great dishonour. I will fight and shoot one of his officers soon.'

'A duel, eh? Well, well.' Morris motioned the boy to

produce more *samsu*. 'And what is this great dishonour the ignoble Captain has done you?' Morris's voice had a soothing, honeyed tone.

'He ordered me to be beaten!' Chirkov spluttered indignantly.

'Beaten?' Morris's tongue flickered pinkly over his lips in a quicksilver reaction of heightened interest. He flickered a commanding glance at the Indian boy and more *samsu* tinkled into Chirkov's glass to be tossed back by the impetuous Russian. 'How barbaric,' Morris muttered sympathetically. 'And it is still painful, eh?'

Chirkov nodded, watching the boy pour yet more *samsu*. '*Oui* . . . yes.'

'I have a salve . . . a medicine, specific against such a wound. If it is not treated it may fester.' Morris smiled, reassuringly. 'You do not want gangrene, do you?' Abstractedly Morris touched the glowing end of his cheroot to a bundle of sticks by his elbow.

'Gangrene?' Chirkov frowned.

'Mortification . . .'

Chirkov understood and the dull gleam of alarm deliberately kindled by Morris appeared in his fuddled eyes.

'Would you like me to . . . ? Morris's hands made a gesturing of massage and he addressed a few words of Hindi to the Indian boy.

Samsu and sympathy and the strange scent that wafted now about the cabin from joss-sticks burning in a brass pot beside Morris dissolved the young man's suspicions. The turbanned boy returned to his master's side with a pot of unguent. Morris made a sign for Chirkov to expose himself. Morris smiled a complicit smile and Chirkov, drunk and of sensuous disposition, did as he was bid. Morris dipped his hands in the salve and began to apply it as Chirkov, holding on to the edge of the table, stood before him.

For a few seconds a heavy silence filled the cabin. Morris felt the fierce triumph of discovery as Chirkov's compliance revealed his own hedonistic nature and then the Russian too was aware of the most pleasurable and undreamed of sensations flooding through him as the tongueless boy obeyed his master's instructions.

'A glass, Mr Ballantyne?'

'Er, thank you, Mr Quilhampton.' Ballantyne struggled with the awkward surname. In the post-daylight gloom of the wardroom Quilhampton pushed the glass across the table, taking two fingers off its base as Ballantyne seized it. Then, holding the neck of the decanter in one hand, his own glass in the other, he tipped his chair back against the heel of the ship and with the unthinking ease of long practice, threw both feet on to the edge of the table. Ballantyne watched with fascination, for the hand in which Quilhampton held his glass, his left, was of wood.

'A rum thing, ain't it?' remarked the unabashed lieutenant.

'I beg your pardon, Mr Q . . .' Ballantyne's overwhelming predilection for formality was one of his characteristic features. 'You lost it in action, I believe?'

'Yes. Damned careless of me, wasn't it? Have a biscuit. No? Then pass the barrel, there's a good fellow.'

'Have you had much experience of action?' There was an eagerness in Ballantyne's question that, together with other remarks he had made, had provoked a character analysis from Mount that suggested the new sailing master nurtured a desire to distinguish himself. 'To prove himself,' Mount had explained, with a knowing look that attributed Ballantyne's desire for glory to his coloured skin.

'Action?' remarked Quilhampton. 'Yes, I've seen enough. And you, have you had much experience with women, Mr Ballantyne, for I'm woefully ignorant upon the subject.'

'Women?' A faint light of astonishment filled Ballantyne's eyes. 'But you talk often of your woman, Mr Q . . .'

'Because I am a besotted fool,' Quilhampton said in an attempt at flippancy, 'but I want to know of *women*, of the gender as a whole, not one in particular.'

'What is it you want to know?'

'Have you known many women?'

'Of course. Many, *many* women.' Ballantyne rolled his head in his quaint, exotic manner.

'Can a woman love a man with a wooden hand?'

'Now you are asking about one woman, Mr Q, and I am not comprehending you.'

'But to answer honestly you need to have known many women,' Quilhampton replied, a faint edge of desperation entering his voice.

'That is true. But I cannot answer for the particular . . .'

'No.' Quilhampton's face fell. In the silence the messman entered with a lantern.

'But . . .' said Ballantyne as the man retired, 'but I think it would be easier for a woman to love a man with a wooden hand than for a man to love a woman with a wooden leg.'

Quilhampton paused in the act of refilling his glass and stared at Ballantyne. The master was deadly serious and suddenly Quilhampton burst into laughter, giggling uncontrollably so that he only got all four chair legs and both his feet back on the deck with difficulty.

'What the devil is this rumpus?' asked Mount, emerging from his cabin, unfamiliarly attired in shirt-sleeves.

'Ballantyne,' gasped Quilhampton, 'Ballantyne is making up riddles . . .'

Mount leaned against the door frame of his cabin and looked upon the young lieutenant indulgently as Quilhampton recounted the conversation. Switching his glance to the master Mount was aware that Quilhampton's unbridled mirth had irritated Ballantyne. He was bristling with affront, unable to see anything beyond Quilhampton's ridicule of his remark. Mount was quick to retrieve the situation.

'Perhaps, Mr Ballantyne, you would favour me with an answer to a more serious question than a young jackanapes like James is capable of framing.'

'What is it, Mr Mount?' Ballantyne asked, suspicious now that the two Englishmen were going to bat him back and forth like a shuttlecock.

'I heard you remark to the Captain that you knew something of our somewhat unusual passenger. Who, or what exactly is he?'

Quilhampton was still giggling, but Mount's question almost silenced him for he could make his own contribution to its answer. Almost, for his amusement was sustained by the sudden overwhelmingly serious cast that Ballantyne's swarthy features assumed. It seemed to Quilhampton that this gravity of its own accord drew Mount to a vacant chair, and his amusement only subsided slowly, for his sensibilities still lingered on Catriona MacEwan, the point from which his question arose.

'He is a bad man, Mr Mount. It is said that he was formerly a naval officer, but he was in Calcutta for some years and then moved to Rangoon where he traded with a Parsee. My father had some business with their house and they cheated him. My father has never divulged the particulars of their transactions, for I believe the loss was too shameful for him. Some time after this the Parsee was found dead, and although nothing could be proved against this man he moved on to Canton where he had considerable influence with the Hong in the interest of the opium trade. It is said that he had connections with the Viceroy and these enabled him to travel outside the normal limits imposed by the authorities on the foreign devils . . .'

'Foreign devils?' queried Mount, frowning.

'The Europeans in the factories . . .'

'Ah . . . please go on . . .'

'I cannot tell you much more, except that I know of his dishonest connections with my father and that when, on one or two occasions I saw him in Canton, my father warned me against him.'

'But you are not going into trade, are you, Mr Ballantyne? You have volunteered for King George's service, at least for the time being.'

'I should like to serve His Majesty,' said Ballantyne. 'Is it true that by being master I cannot obtain a commission?'

'It is unusual, certainly, unless you distinguish yourself in action against the enemy. I suppose if you earned Captain

Drinkwater's approbation and were mentioned in the *Gazette*, a commission might be forthcoming.'

There was a dry edge to Mount's voice that only Quilhampton recognised as faintly mocking. Now all suspicion was gone from Ballantyne's mind.

'And do you think we shall see action on a convoy escort?' Ballantyne asked.

Mount shrugged. 'One can never tell . . .'

The noise of the fo'c's'le bell rang through the ship and the frigate stirred to the call of the watch. 'On the other hand the call of duty is remorseless,' he added. 'Your watch, Mr Ballantyne . . .'

'You should not bait him, James,' remarked Mount, stretching himself and yawning.

'I didn't . . .'

'Then keep your love-sickness to yourself.'

'It ain't contagious.'

'No, but misery is and a long commission's fertile ground for that.' Mount rose. 'Good-night, James, and sweet dreams.'

Quilhampton sat alone for a few moments. Soon Fraser would come below demanding a glass and the remains of the biscuit barrel. Quilhampton threw off his thoughts of Catriona, for the image of Morris had intruded. He wondered why he had not added his own contribution to the pooling of knowledge about Morris. Was it because he could not admit that such a man had once held a commission as a naval officer?

He would confide in Mount. He would trust Mount with his life, but Ballantyne . . . ? Ballantyne was not quite one of them; a merchant officer, a man of colour, a man for whom the grey seas of Ushant and the Channel were a closed book. Was Drinkwater truly going to confirm his appointment as master?

Quilhampton shrugged, drained his glass and made for his cabin. He did not want to socialise with Fraser, only to thrust his mind back to the pleasurable agony of dreaming of Catriona MacEwan.

On deck Mr Ballantyne paced up and down and dreamed of

glory. He had set down upon Captain Drinkwater's chart the estimated position of the reef upon which the *Patrician* and her convoy had so nearly met disaster and earned a word of approval. He had modestly demurred from appending his own name to the shoal and now he fantasised about earning a more durable reward from the taciturn Captain Drinkwater. A commission as a lieutenant in the Royal Navy could lead him to social heights denied him on the Indian coast, for his mother had not been the Begum of Drinkwater's fancy, but a nautch-girl stolen from a temple by his lusty father, a beauty, true, but a woman of no consequence in Indian society. His father cared little for the conventions of the coast and had set his heart on an estate in the English shires if fortune smiled on him. But Ballantyne the son had a sharper perception of values, forced upon him by bastard birth, a tainted skin and opportunities that had raised him from the gutter in which an Indian Brahmin had once suggested he belonged. Something of a subconscious resentment of his father for the predicament in which he had been placed prevented him from accepting a life in merchant ships, and the turn of events which took him from the labouring hull of the dismasted *Musquito* and placed him aboard the puissant mass of *Patrician* had awakened a sentiment of predestination in him.

It was this happy mood, combined with a lack of appreciation of the exact status of Midshipman Chirkov that led him to indulge the Russian prisoner when he requested to take the air on deck.

Mr Ballantyne, Master of His Britannic Majesty's frigate *Patrician*, felt a certain lofty condescension to Count Anatole Vasili Chirkov, and indulged the young and apparently interested Russian officer in a dissertation on their navigational position in the South China Sea.

CHAPTER 10

A Small Victory

In the stuffy hutch that had formerly been inhabited by *Patrician*'s sailing master Drinkwater sat writing his journal. For a few moments he reflected before dipping his pen. Then he carefully scribed the date, forming the numerals of the new year with care.

> *We are now south of the twelfth parallel in less misty weather and lighter winds. My apprehensions of attack by Spanish cruisers from the Philippines seem unfounded and I assume their recent loss added to the knowledge of Drury's squadron in the area has made them more concerned for their own register ships than the plunder of our India trade.*
>
> *The convoy continues to behave well. The discipline of the Indiamen is excellent and the Country ships seek to emulate them to the extent of making the throwing out of recriminatory signals unnecessary. This good behaviour is not consistent with the conduct of all convoys . . .*

Drinkwater paused. While he allowed himself a certain latitude in personal asides, he was conscious of a desire to scribble all his random thoughts on to paper. He knew it was a consequence of his loneliness and the thought usually stopped him short of such confessions. Besides, they were too revealing when read later. But the urge to place something on record about Morris was strong, though the nature of the words he would employ eluded him. All he had written to date was a brief entry that Morris, *formerly Master and Commander in His*

Majesty's Service, now a merchant at Canton, has come aboard for the passage with a quantity of specie.

It was a masterpiece of understatement, making no allusion to their previous acquaintance. Drinkwater knew the omission begged the question of for whom he wrote his journals. He had been ordered to destroy them, but had refused, considering them personal and not public property. In accordance with John Barrow's instructions his ship's logs had been dumped, so that no record of her activities in the Baltic existed; but even a man in the public employ was not to be utterly divested of personal life at the whim of another so employed.

He knew that, in truth, he wrote his journals for himself, an indulgence taken like wine or tobacco. It was unnecessary for him to have written anything about Morris beyond the fact that, like a phoenix, the man had risen from the ashes of the past. Out of the uncertainties and passions of adolescence when their antipathy had first found form, to the hatred of maturity aboard the brig *Hellebore* where Morris had indeed been 'Master and Commander', they had come now to a snarling and wary truce.

'Like two senescent dogs,' Drinkwater muttered, half lifting his pen as if to write down the words. But he laid the pen aside and closed his journal.

'We are too old now, too interested in feathering nests for our old age to disturb our lives with the revival of former passions.'

He spoke the words to himself, a low mumble that at least satisfied him in their formation, even though they failed to find their way on to the written page.

The improvement in the weather, the convoy's discipline in maintaining station and the apparently resigned behaviour of Morris persuaded Drinkwater that, subject to a degree of vigilance, his *bête noire* might be permitted the occasional freedom of the quarterdeck. The incongruous sight of Morris, corpulent under the shimmering silk of his robe, pacing beside Rakitin, became familiar to the other occupants of the quarterdeck during the first dog watch. As the hour of tropical sunset approached, Drinkwater also kept the deck, maintaining his own watch upon the two men. Little appeared to pass between them beyond the odd word, and the Russian seemed to have shrunk beside the obscene bulk of Morris. No longer filling his elegant uniform, Rakitin paced with hunched shoulders next to his enforced companion. The relentless nature of the ship's routine soon removed the novelty of this odd, morose promenade.

Midshipman Chirkov was also more in evidence, showing active signs of growing interest in professional matters and receiving instruction from Mr Ballantyne in a most gratifying manner. Drinkwater hoped the young man was taking advantage of the opportunity to increase his knowledge and that, reconciled to his fate, circumstances had wrought a sea-change in him.

The lighter winds slowed their southward progress and allowed fraternising between the ships so that, late one afternoon, Drinkwater found himself aboard the *Guilford*, dining at Callan's ample table.

Throughout the meal Drinkwater felt a sense of detachment. It was partly due to the fact that he was an outsider and not one of the small band of intimates who had grown wealthy in the service of the Honourable East India Company. Among the diners, four of Callan's own officers and an equal number from the *Ligonier*, including her commander, had been joined by several of the masters of the Country ships, men who considered themselves, equal to, if after, the lordly Company captains. Drinkwater found the overt and artificial social posturing rather amusing, though their knowledge of the trade and navigation of the eastern seas, expressed in an argot with which he was unfamiliar, increased his sense of being an outsider.

The assumed superiority on the part of the East India commanders, whose wealth and power conferred on them a cachet that found its greatest expression in these remote oriental waters, seemed to Drinkwater a bubble ripe for pricking. He had accepted Callan's invitation, he privately admitted to himself, for motives other than the anticipation of a good meal. Looking down the table, however, he could see James Quilhampton entertained no such ulterior considerations for the meal was sumptuous, served on crisp, white linen, eaten off splendid porcelain with fine silver cutlery and accompanied by wines drunk from glittering crystal glasses.

Drinkwater enjoyed the luxury of the meal. He played up to Callan's efforts to engage him in conversation, but both men knew that unfinished business lay between them and only the convention of good manners prevented its open and indelicate discussion before the other guests. Quilhampton and a handful of his own subordinates were being entertained by the Indiamen's. Drinkwater's attention was engaged by the senior men about him, portly men, for the most part, fleshy and rubicund from the climate and its alcoholic antidotes. They were men of strong opinion, products of almost unbridled licence and power, and although this fell short of the life-and-death power of a post-captain in the Royal Navy, it was clear that the opportunities their commands gave them for making money had given them confidence of another kind.

It occurred to Drinkwater that Callan might have assembled these men as allies to shame him into passing over the matter of the deserters. He smiled inwardly. He was quite capable of enjoying the fruits of Callan's table with as much insouciance as was Callan in accepting the protection of his frigate's cannon.

''Twas a trifle of a near-run thing t'other day, Captain Drinkwater,' remarked one of the masters of a Country ship. 'We were firing alarm guns and you took 'em for shots at an enemy, eh?'

A silence had fallen and faces turned towards him. A conspiracy to embarrass him seemed in the air, or was it a remark provoked by over-much liquor? At the lower end of the table, too, there was a stir of interest and Drinkwater was gratified at the sudden irritation in Quilhampton's loyal eyes. Deliberately Drinkwater drained his glass.

'I took 'em, sir, for what you say they were, alarm guns. I would have been failing in my duty had I ignored them. Had you perused your instructions you would have observed a signal to indicate the convoy was standing into danger . . .'

Drinkwater watched the face of his interlocutor flush. The company shifted awkwardly in its chairs and he was persuaded that there *was* at best some practical joke afoot to throw him in a foolish light, for another spoke as though trying to regain the initiative.

'I don't think there was time for the hoisting of flags, Captain Drinkwater . . .'

The diners sniffed agreement, as though implying such niceties were all very well for a well-manned frigate, but a tightly run merchant ship could not afford the luxuries of signal staff.

'You were damned lucky to get away with it,' remarked the commander of the *Ligonier*.

'Now there I *would* agree with you, sir,' Drinkwater said smoothly, 'but a miss is as good as a mile, they say . . .'

'And we were fortunate not to lose your services,' said Callan soothingly.

'Yes,' agreed Drinkwater drily. 'What bothers me, gentlemen, is how such experts in the navigation of these seas as yourselves came to be so misled in your navigation.' He paused, gratified by a suggestion of embarrassment among them.

'I take it,' he went on, 'that we nearly ran ashore upon a hitherto uncharted spur of the Paracels? I trust you have all amended your charts accordingly . . .'

Drinkwater looked the length of the table. It had been a foolish attempt to mock him, of that he was now certain, and unwittingly they had given him a means to get his own back.

'A delightful meal, Captain Callan, and one in which the humour of the company induces me to ask you for the return of my men.'

There was only the briefest of pauses and then Callan urbanely agreed.

'Of course, Captain Drinkwater, of course . . .'

Was there the merest twinkle in Callan's eye? Drinkwater

could not be certain, but he hoped so, for they had measured blade for blade and Drinkwater was fencer enough to know he had the advantage.

Contrary to expectations aboard *Patrician*, Drinkwater did not punish the deserters immediately. He had, he admitted to himself as he sat, wooden-faced, in the stern of his barge, fully intended to, but the sullen faces of his barge crew as, eyes averted, they rocked back and forward, half-heartedly pulling at the knocking oar-looms, dissuaded him. Not that he was afraid of the consequences of the flogging as he had earlier been. Indeed his mood was almost one of light-heartedness, so clumsy had been the efforts of the merchant masters to disconcert him, but Drinkwater possessed a strong, almost puritanical sense of propriety born of long service, and he would have despised himself if, after a magnificent dinner, he had viciously flogged the deserters.

It was impossible that he could excuse or exculpate them, for he had hanged a man for the same crime before leaving for the Pacific and such unheard-of leniency would, by its inconsistency, lead others into the same path. But their downcast misery as they sat in the stern sheets of the barge, in such close proximity to their captain, filled Drinkwater with an odd, angering compassion that, by the time he reached the ship, had dispelled his good humour.

'Put those men in the bilboes,' he curtly ordered Fraser as the first lieutenant stood with the rigid side-party, 'and prevent anyone approaching them,' he said to Mount, before hurrying below, only just catching himself in time to turn aside for the master's cabin and not walk, seething, into the main cabin. Suddenly the confines of his self-imposed prison oppressed him, and he as quickly returned to the deck, to pace up and down, up and down along the line of quarterdeck guns until he had mastered himself.

'He doesn't want to hang 'em,' said Quilhampton to the lounging officers in the wardroom.

'He'll have to. A court martial at Prince of Wales Island will condemn them without a thought . . .' remarked Fraser.

'Not if he punishes 'em now, quickly . . .'

'You mean flogs them?' asked Fraser.

'Yes,' replied Quilhampton, ''twill serve as an example to the rest.'

'Good God, man, we were hanging people before! D'you think their blessed Lordships 'd approve of a mere flogging? They want stiffs for desertion, not red meat. He'll no' flog them, but keep them in irons until he can have them court-martialled by a full board at Penang.'

'But he doesn't *want* to hang 'em,' persisted Quilhampton.

'Och, you presume on your knowledge o' the man, Jamie. I sympathise but not even Captain Drinkwater can get awa' from the fact that desertion's a hanging offence.'

'Tomorrow will tell who's right. If he hasn't flogged 'em by seven bells in the forenoon watch I'm not James Quilhampton.' Quilhampton rose, yawning. 'I've the middle tonight, and I'm weary . . .'

'What do you think, Mister Lallo?' Fraser asked of the surgeon who had sat silently through this exchange.

Lallo shrugged. 'I've no idea. Mr Q's solution seems the most humane, yours the most in conformity with the regulations . . .'

'And the easiest for you,' added Fraser drily.

'Ah yes.' Lallo's tone was unenthusiastic. 'Mr Fraser,' he said, suddenly shifting in his chair and reaching for the decanter on the wardroom table, 'there are other problems that confront us, you know.'

'Oh . . . ?' Something in Lallo's voice caught Fraser's attention. 'What?'

'I thought I had three cases of lues as a legacy of California, now I have five, maybe six.'

'And is that so unusual? I saw the venereal list myself only this morning.'

'Two of the cases I'm certain are syphilitic, but the others . . .'

'You are not sure?'

'No, I mean, yes, I'm sure.' Lallo rubbed his hand across his forehead in a gesture of extreme exhaustion. 'But it isn't the pox.'

'Well what is it?' snapped Fraser, a sudden fearful cramp contracting the muscles of his belly.

'Button-scurvy . . .'

'Scurvy?'

'No! *Button*-scurvy, Mr Fraser, framboesia, the yaws . . .'

'The yaws!'

'Aye, and it's contagious.'

Midshipman Chirkov's quarterdeck appearances had begun to assume a semblance of normality, so much so that the flattered Ballantyne remarked upon his regular interest to Quilhampton when handing over the deck to him at midnight. Together with the details of the course steered and the bearings of the merchantmen, the information made no impression upon the still sleep-dulled Quilhampton until he had been on watch for some time and had dismissed the more immediate preoccupations of his duty. It occurred to him then that Midshipman Chirkov's sudden enthusiasm was singularly uncharacteristic and that, for reasons of his own, he was currying favour with the vulnerable and somewhat pathetic Ballantyne. Had Quilhampton also known the state of hostility that existed between Chirkov and Frey, he might have associated Chirkov's sudden interest in navigation with something more sinister. But that was a matter of honour, a matter of honour forbidden on board ship, and so a closely guarded secret of the gunroom. As it was, his conversation with Ballantyne led him to make other assumptions, blinding him to what was going on almost under his very nose.

Morris had made no attempt to convert the indolent and sensual Russian to his own particular vice. Indeed, age, jaded appetite and excessive corpulence had rendered him less active himself in its pursuit. Besides, his seduction of the Russian

121

youth had aims other than the fulfilment of his own overt desires; what Morris meditated was something infinitely more pleasurable than the mere gratification of lust, something that still appealed to a man far gone in lechery, holding out the budding promise of the most exquisite pleasure.

The boy he had had fashioned for his unique and effortless delight could be employed with equal facility to enrapture the libidinous Chirkov without too much arousing the young man's disgust at himself. Morris was delighted for the gift of so compliant an accomplice as Chirkov.

Nor did the lounging Chirkov, half drunk, half drugged by *samsu* and Malwa opium during the nights in which Rakitin slept and he and Morris held their unholy court, realise the extent to which he was being used. Morris had explained the dislike Drinkwater felt for them both as an unmannerly prejudice, offering Chirkov a spiteful little revenge upon the British captain by finding out the location of the frigate from the log and traverse board so that he, Morris, might be kept abreast of events that Drinkwater, out of malice, denied him. In return, the extravagant pleasures of Morris's half of the cabin amused the young man as an acceptable alternative to the gypsies who had first introduced him to the gratification of the flesh.

And unbeknown to anyone, even his helpless catamite, Morris plotted the southward progress of the convoy on a chart of his own.

Blood and Rain

'One!'

Spread-eagled against the triced-up grating the man's body jerked in reflexive response to the first stroke of the cat. The flesh of the back was surprisingly pale, turning bronze at the nape of the neck. As he watched, his face a grim mask, Drinkwater saw the red weals begin to streak the skin . . .

'Two!'

As the second weals emerged beneath the unruptured skin, the first were rising in sharp relief. Drinkwater watched the man's face, the mouth distorted by the leather pad upon which he bit. The deserter had his eyes screwed tight-shut and Drinkwater knew he was bracing himself for the dreadful assault upon his body . . .

'Three!'

The stretched skin, pressed upwards from below by the bleeding tissues beneath, began to break. At first the stretched pores exuded suppurations of blood and plasma, giving the impression of a rosy sweat that spread in bands across the man's back . . .

'Four!'

Was this better than hanging? Was this man's life confined in the wooden bulwarks of His Britannic Majesty's frigate *Patrician*, in which even the ship's very name emphasised the subordination of her company, better than a swift and final agony at the end of a yard-rope? Was there, Drinkwater wondered as the bosun's mate laid on the tailed whip again, not one sublime second of freedom before the awful darkness of oblivion? One infinitesimal fragment of time and space where the spirit was free of obligation, of duty, of subservience?

'Six!'

His own freedom to think such thoughts suddenly overcame him. He wanted to ask whether, in that conjectural moment, a man would be free too of the awful obligation to have another man whipped; as if, in some way, the recipient of those lacerations should feel grateful to him for the moderation of the punishment his crime had merited. Drinkwater's eyes flickered to the mass of the ship's company gathered in the waist. Were they, could they fail to be aware of the condign nature of this thrashing? Did they not see in it a spirit of leniency, of sympathy, almost? Or did they see in it a weakness in himself, a weakness, perhaps, to be exploited?

They watched without expression. They had watched such punishments before and those that were intelligent enough to realise knew he *had* been lenient. Three dozen lashes was more than he normally administered, but it was downright *soft* on four bloody fools who had run in a place like China and had then been discovered in the very convoy the bloody ship was escorting!

'Twelve!'

Mr Comley intoned the strokes like those of a bell. The bosun's mate stopped and handed over the cat to another that the thrasher might not ease the violence of his stripes through fatigue. Their Lordships thought of everything . . .

'Thirteen!'

Old Tregembo watched, sensing the mood of his fellows as vaguely contemptuous of the four men for having been caught so easily. Quilhampton watched full of the knowledge that Drinkwater had agonised over the decision and confident that he had come to the right, the only decision open to a reasonable man. Fraser, the cares of first lieutenant weighing upon him, felt a stirring of disapproval. He would have preferred the matter handed over to the admiral at Madras, or Calcutta or wherever he was, removing the stigma of it from the ship. Sometimes he envied Drinkwater's impeccable, irreproachable acceptance of his responsibilities, sometimes he disapproved of it. Like every second-in-command in history, Fraser knew what *he* would have done in the circumstances, and that it would have been diametrically opposite to what was now happening . . .

'Twenty!'

It never occurred to Fraser that he would have handed the matter over through weakness, for there were half a dozen good reasons why, in his heart, he felt his own decision would have been the right one. Nor did it occur to him that Drinkwater had given more than the most superficial consideration to the matter.

'Twenty-four!'

The bosun's mates changed again for the last dozen. The man's back was laid open now. The cat bit into one vast bruise that had burst into a flayed mass of dark, bloody flesh. Lallo, the surgeon, stared at it, only half seeing more toil for him and his mates, his eyes fixed with a greater calculation on the men amidships, computing, or attempting to compute, how many had already taken the infection of the yaws . . .

'Thirty!'

He had heard someone mutter the words 'humane punishment' as they had assembled on the quarterdeck in response to the cry for all hands to muster. It seemed a sophisticated conceit to run words like that together in justification of so barbaric a ritual. Not that Lallo condemned the flogging from any lofty principle; he was too old to think the world would ever set itself to rights, but to talk of 'humane punishment' was almost as stupid a thing to do as to run away from a man-o'-war; almost deserving of the same treatment too, he thought morosely . . .

'Thirty-one!'

Derrick made himself watch, though revulsion rose in his throat on hardly suppressed upwellings of bile. He had seen this evil so often now, perpetrated on the whim of a man he both liked and respected. Intellectually he understood all Drinkwater's motives, both official and unofficial. But the inherent brutalising of them all he condemned as utterly evil. It reaffirmed his pacifism, revived his faith, for without war there would not be this grim, so-called necessity . . .

'Thirty-two!'

The deserter was hanging by his wrist lashings now, unconscious like some early martyr. Blood ran down to the deck and trickled from his mouth where the leather pad had become dislodged. Senseless he hung there in the sunshine upon the golden, scrubbed timber of the grating so that Midshipman Chirkov was reminded of an icon, the glittering uniforms of the marines an encrustation of rubies, the naval officers a semi-circle of sapphires. Fumes of opium still whirled in his brain, enhancing his hearing so that he heard the involuntary exhalations of the man's lungs as the sodden cat thrashed its final strokes upon the rib-cage. Chirkov felt nothing for the victim. All sensations were inwards. The flogging did not even remind him of his own humiliation. He saw only the strange beauty of the agonised body.

'Thirty-five!'

Midshipman Belchambers waited to faint. To his eternal shame he had fainted several times when witnessing punishment and, although he had since that humiliating period seen action and distinguished himself, he still feared that irresistible loss of control . . .

'Thirty-six! Water! Cut him down!'

The man's body twitched as the green-white water slopped not ungently over his bloodied back, but he was unconscious as the bosun's mates sliced the lashings at his wrists and dragged him to one side where his messmates took him. Midshipman Belchambers took a deep breath. He was rather pleased with himself . . .

'Next!'

Like Chirkov, Morris's hearing was acute. A pipe of opium

126

made it so and the sounds from the quarterdeck revived old, old memories in Morris's mind, memories that the drug uncoiled in lascivious scrolls drawn in graphically slow motion across the mind's eye.

He fondled the boy's ear, realising that these were days of sublime happiness. Not only was he basking in the anticipation of personal success, but that was heightened by the unexpected bonus of encompassing the ruin of a man he had once attempted to love. To the expectation of revenge he now found added the knowledge that that youthful paragon had been brought low in the world, low enough to have his delicate nature sullied by the grim necessity of ordering floggings.

'Ah, my fine friend, how has the bloom withered upon the stalk, eh?' He chuckled, pleased, seeing in his mind's eye that it was Drinkwater's back that received the thrashing of the cat.

His grip suddenly tightened on the boy's ear, turning the puckish face towards his own bloated and puffy flesh.

'Tonight! Tonight we will do it. It will have to be tonight. And then, my little imp, we shall see, oh, yes, we shall see . . .'

The boy grunted, the spittle in his throat, his mouth opening.

But Morris had averted his own hooded eyes, for above his head he heard more noises of punishment . . .

'One! Two!'

And he smiled.

Despite his conviction of the rightness of Drinkwater's decision to mete out swift and humane justice to the deserters, Lieutenant Quilhampton did not share the captain's analysis of the people's collective attitude. For one thing he was less accustomed than Drinkwater to thinking of the ship's company as one amorphous mass. Rather, to him they were a sum of many separate parts, some of whom, those who fulfilled their duties in his division, were well known to him. But part of this disagreement was attributable to his own involvement in the stilling of their mutinous spirit in the Baltic. He knew that for a while he had sat on a powder keg and alone had snuffed out an already sputtering fuse. He was, therefore, upon his guard in the hours following the floggings. Loyalty, this apprehension about the explosive mood of the hands and his eager longing to return home, stopped him from sleeping, and men nudged each other from mess-table to mess-table and hammock to hammock, as Quilhampton prowled about the ship on one pretext or another.

But the mood of the ship was not threatening, for with that swift change that occurs at sea like the lifting of cloud shadows or a shift in the wind, the reported sight of blue islands to the south of them set their minds on a new tack, dispelling the gloom of the morning and setting their imaginations on anticipation of arrival at Prince of Wales Island, Pulo Penang, first stage on their homeward track.

'Where away?' asked Drinkwater with boyish eagerness, glad of some image to feast on after the shambolic succession of raw backs that had imprinted itself on his consciousness.

'Three points to larboard, sir. The Natunas,' replied Ballantyne confidently. The Dutch name alerted Drinkwater to the possibility of the presence of Dutch cruisers. He swung round and examined the convoy: still in good order, only one ship a trifle too far to leeward.

'Make to *Hindoostan*, "Keep better station".'

'The *Carnatic*'s run a little ahead of her station, sir,' offered Ballantyne helpfully.

'No matter. She's in the grain of the convoy and another pair of eyes up ahead saves us a little trouble.'

'We may encounter a Dutchman or two, sir.'

'Yes,' Drinkwater said shortly, still peering through his glass, once more levelled at the serried blue summits of the Natuna Islands. He would almost welcome an action with the enemy, welcome it as being his proper business, as purging to his blood and cathartic to his ship. And if he died during it he could hug the satisfaction of duty well done to his crushed bosom as he enjoyed that vital, sparking moment of ineffable knowledge of freedom . . .

Bloody stupid thought!

He snapped the Dollond glass shut. 'Very well, Mr Ballantyne. Send the men to quarters, we'll exercise the great guns!'

Drinkwater stayed on deck long after they had resecured their brutish artillery and the men, delighted with their exertions and the pulverising they had given the three beflagged casks, raced aloft and made sail to catch up with the convoy from which they had become separated in their manoeuvring. They had resumed their station long before the red sun reached down and touched the green horizon on its strange, tropical setting. It seemed quenched by the lambent rim of the visible world, cutting the sun in two so that a lenticular fragment of it lingered, gradually changing from fire to ice and then facing and etiolating the sky in the suddenness of the tropic night.

There was a magic in the moment and Drinkwater lingered to savour it, so unlike the attenuated twilight of the grey northern seas with which he was more familiar. One by one the heavily brilliant stars began to appear, those near the horizon coruscating with sudden apparent changes of fiery colour so that he fell into the simple game of identification, cudgelling his wits to remember their names and sad that command removed him from the daily necessity of knowing what he had once been adept at.

Beside him Ballantyne performed the mysteries of navigation, grunting figures to Midshipman Dutfield who read the corresponding times on the chronometer and noted the altitudes on a tablet. Drinkwater indulged his game and noted the disappearance of Canopus, half-alarmed that a squall would reach treacherously down and strike them.

'Wind's falling away, sir,' Acting Lieutenant Frey remarked as he took over the deck for the first watch.

'Yes.'

Having regained their station they were snugged down under easy sail, watching over the convoy as they had since leaving the Pearl River. One was tempted to call it an uneventful passage, setting aside the intrusion of Morris; but even that seemed contained since his judicious move to the master's cabin.

'I shall be below if you require me, Mr Frey.'

'Aye, aye, sir.'

He read for a little, but the cabin was stuffily hot despite the wind-sails rigged amidships. He turned to his journal but the threat of megrims brought on by over-long introspection on the morning's floggings led him to conclude the task in as concise a form as decency allowed. In the end he amused himself with a letter to Elizabeth. If they were not sent home from Prince of Wales Island then he could forward the letter and, in any case, it was better written now, while his mood was light, than when he learned, pledges to his men notwithstanding, that *Patrician* formed a welcome addition to the East Indies squadron.

He must have dozed, for he found himself shaken awake with no idea of the time and the candle burnt low. He blew it out and, in his shirt-sleeves, went on deck.

The watch were busy, attentive to the shouts of Frey and his subordinate petty officers as they braced round the slatting sails. It was not a strong squall, but it had struck them from out of nowhere and the topsails and their blocks were flogging wildly.

'Lively there, damn it!' Frey cannoned into him. 'Get out of my . . . Oh! Beg pardon, sir!' Frey drew back, hand to hat barely perceptible in the sudden impenetrable blackness. 'Taken aback, sir, damned squall hit us without warning.'

'It's uncommon dark,' replied Drinkwater. 'Have a mind for the convoy, Mr Frey.'

'Aye, sir.'

Frey turned and bawled for Mr Belchambers, sending him forward with the night-glass to keep a sharp lookout.

Drinkwater scrambled up the heaving deck to the starboard hance, went to fish in his pocket for his glass and then realised he was coatless. Not only was the night dark, it was damnably warm too.

'Only to be expected in four degrees north, I suppose . . .'

'Beg pardon, sir?' It was Frey again, looming up and staring forward at men working at the midships pinrail. Drinkwater was not conscious of having spoken and the revelation of talking to himself startled him.

'Black as the Earl of Hell's riding boots.'

'Yes, sir.' Drinkwater heard the grin in Frey's voice. 'There're the lights of the convoy, sir, fine to starboard . . . see?'

Drinkwater stared. Yes, he could see the faint glimmer of stern lanterns to the southward. And *Patrician* was steadying on course now, her yards braced round as the wind picked up, suddenly cold. Seconds later they were leaning to the pressure of it and rushing through the water at a rate of knots. Then with an equally bewildering suddenness the night was riven by lightning, a flash of intense brilliance that showed the dark spots of the convoy ahead and to starboard of them, leaving an almost indelible image on the retina so that it seemed nature had obliged them with a brief spectral revelation to ease their anxieties.

The next minute they were soaking from the deluge of rain that poured upon them, blotting out all but a narrow silver-slashed circle of sea around them, their heads split with the thunderous assault of the exploding cloud above them.

In the confusion of steadying on their course Drinkwater bumped into another body. It recoiled, half apologetically, and in a further, less brilliant flash of lightning which seemed to strike the sea with a sizzling alongside them, he recognised the startled face of Midshipman Chirkov.

'What happens if lightning strikes the ship, sir?' asked Frey anxiously, the cocks of his hat spewing water like gutter-pipes, his face a pale gash in the darkness.

'I should think it'd consume our masts . . . possibly set us on fire . . .'

Drinkwater tried to think. He had heard of such a thing, surely? But there was nothing they could do to avert it. 'Steady on south by west, Mr Frey,' he said coolly. It was the only thing to do in this shivering cold. The rain fell so heavily that he felt the weight of its volume upon his head and shoulders.

'Binnacle light's out, sir . . .' he heard one of the helmsmen report.

'Well get below and fetch a light,' Frey snapped.

'Keep her full and bye, Mr Frey. Steer by the luff of the main tops'l.'

'Aye, aye, sir.'

A note of weary tolerance had crept into Frey's voice. Drinkwater peered upwards, water pouring into his eyes. The main topsail was a pale, almost imperceptible ghost seen as through a rain-beaten window.

'Do your *best*, Mr Frey,' he said with asperity.

In the hiatus that followed, as they waited for the rekindled light for the binnacle that, to judge by the curses muttered from the companionway, was extinguished as soon as it reached the deck, Drinkwater remembered Chirkov.

'Was that Mr Chirkov on deck?' he asked Frey in a more intimate, conversational tone.

'Chirkov? Oh, yes, sir, I expect so. He's taken to coming on deck. Ballantyne says he's interested in the navigation of the ship.'

'Well keep the lubber below after dark. You know my orders.'

'Aye, aye, sir,' replied Frey, thoroughly peeved, and ready to shoot Chirkov any moment the Russian gave him opportunity.

Going below, Drinkwater found the ship in a state of disruption. The two Chinese pigs kept in the manger forward of the breakwater were terrified by the over-charged atmosphere and had begun squealing. Men below in the berth-deck were grumbling and Corporal Grice had turned out some of his men, so that a foot patrol in cross-belts and drawers had emerged from the orlop deck and were just then going below again to the hoots and jeers of those able to see the fools they had made of themselves. There was something chaotic about the ridiculous scene as it met Drinkwater's eyes, reminding him of one of the seditious drawings he had seen by Mr Gillray. For, at the foot of the ladder, a little pool of light was formed by half a dozen purser's glims from which an obscenely swearing quartermaster was trying to relight the binnacle lamp. It was this bizarre source of illumination that drew attention to Corporal Grice's folly. Drinkwater stepped over the hunched and cursing backs, leaving them to their task without his presence being known. Rain was streaming over the coaming of the companionway and he was chilled to shuddering by it.

He found Tregembo waiting for him with a towel.

'Thank you, Tregembo'

'Zur . . .'

The remains of the candle he had extinguished earlier guttered on its holder. As he dried himself he felt the heel of the deck ease and a few moments later little Belchambers came below to report normality established on deck.

'Is the convoy in sight?'

'No, sir, the rain is still obscuring it, though it's much lighter now than it was, but Mr Frey says he had a good look at the convoy's bearing in the lightning, sir, and he's quite happy.'

'Very well, Mr Belchambers. Thank you.'

'Good-night, sir.'

'Good-night.'

'Thank you, Tregembo. You may get your own head down now.'

'Aye, zur . . . G'night, zur.'

Outside the cabin Tregembo bumped into the surgeon.

'Cap'n's just turning in,' he said defensively, standing in Lallo's way.

'Very well,' said Lallo. The surgeon had been meditating all day when to tell Drinkwater about the epidemic of yaws that he might anticipate and had turned in irresolute. Woken by the general agitation of the ship and the clap of thunder he had resolved to act immediately. Now he felt a little foolish, and not a little relieved. A night would make no difference.

'I'll see him first thing in the morning,' he said, turning away.

But Mr Lallo was not the first officer to report to Drinkwater next morning; he was beaten by Mr Ballantyne who, head shaking and excited, burst in to Drinkwater's cabin with such violence that he fetched up against the rim of the bunk. Drink-water started from sleep as if murder was in the wind.

'Sir! Oh, sir, calamity, sir!'

'What the devil is it? Why have you left the deck, Mr Ballan-tyne?' Drinkwater spluttered.

'The convoy, sir, it is not in sight!'

PART TWO

Nemesis

'The only thing necessary for the triumph of
evil is for good men to do nothing.'

Edmund Burke

A Council of War

A sickeningly empty horizon greeted Drinkwater's eyes as he cast about the ship. In a despairing movement he looked aloft to where, astride the main royal yard, Midshipman Dutfield scanned the sea. Looking down, Dutfield shook his head.

'God's bones!' Drinkwater swore, then strode to the binnacle and stared at the compass. The lubber's line pointed unerringly at south by west. Drinkwater looked aloft again, the sails were drawing, all seemed well. He stood, puzzling. Some instinct was rasping his intelligence, telling him something was wrong, very wrong, though he was totally at a loss to understand what. Full daylight was upon them, the rising sun, above the horizon for fully half an hour, remained below a bank of wet and coiling cumulus to the east. For a long moment he stared at that cloud bank, as though seeking an answer there, cudgelling his brain to think, *think*.

Both he and Frey had seen the convoy last night. The cluster of ships had been quite distinct, to leeward of them, perhaps a little too far off the starboard bow for absolutely perfect station-keeping, but . . .

Had that squall, local and intense, affected only *Patrician*? It was possible, but it had not lasted long enough to carry the frigate beyond the visible horizon of the group of ships.

A slanting shaft of sunlight speared downwards from a rent in the clouds. A moment later it was joined by another, and another. Three patches of glittering sea flared where the sunbeams struck, scintillating intensely.

'Bloody hell!'

Drinkwater's eye ran up the beams, seeking their theoretical intersection where, still hidden, the sun lurked behind the bank of cloud. In a stride he was beside the binnacle, sensing something was definitely wrong, electrified by suspicion.

He could not be sure. It was difficult to take an azimuth in such a way . . .

He fumed, impatient for a sight of the sun. Not one of the three patches seemed to move nearer to them, then one disappeared.

'Is there something . . . ?' Ballantyne's voice was nervously hesitant.

'Get an azimuth the moment the sun shows, get my sextant and chronometer up here upon the instant!'

It had to be the lightning, a corposant perhaps, that had run unobserved in all that black deluge the previous night. There was no other explanation . . .

'Look, sir, the sun!'

Neither sextant nor chronometer had arrived but Drinkwater did not need to work out the calculation. It was too blindingly obvious. Though they crawled across the face of the globe and altered the bearing of the sun at any given time of the day, and although the sun was almost imperceptibly moving towards them as it orbited further and further north towards the equinoctial and the vernal equinox of the northern spring, he could see that an error existed in their compass; an error of perhaps thirty of forty degrees, sufficient to have misled them into sailing on a diverging course from the convoy. It was with something like relief that he offered the worried faces on the quarterdeck an explanation.

'Our compass is thirty or forty degrees in error, gentlemen. We have been sailing more nearly south-east than south all night. It must have been disturbed by the lightning.'

A murmur of surprise, mixed with wonder and relieved suspense, crossed several faces. Drinkwater looked at the dog-vane and made a hurried calculation, a rough estimate in triangulation that he would work out more carefully in a moment when he had the leisure to do so. For the time being a swift alteration of course and speed were needed.

'Lay me a course of south-west, Mr Ballantyne, and have the watch set all plain sail!'

'Sou' west and all plain sail, sir, aye, aye, sir!'

Drinkwater looked about him again. The wind was a light but steady breeze. God alone knew what the convoy commanders would think when they realised *Patrician* was absent, but he could imagine well enough! A creeping anxiety began to replace the feeling of relief at having discovered the cause of the navigational mystery.

The Natunas were astern; suppose they had concealed a Dutch cruiser, or even a French one? He rubbed his chin, feeling the scrubby bristles rough against the palm of his hand.

Canvas flogged above him and the cries of 'Let fall! Clew down!' and 'Sheet home!' accompanied the sudden bellying of the fore and main courses. Above the topsails the topgallants and royals were spreading *Patrician*'s pale wings in the morning sunlight. His eye was caught by a sudden movement lower down. Midshipman Chirkov was on deck. Drinkwater recollected the presence of the young Russian the night before. He suddenly vented all his bile on the good-for-nothing young man.

'Mr Chirkov! Damn you, sir, but my orders are explicit! You are forbidden to be on deck at this hour!'

There seemed something vaguely dreamy about the young man, something weird that Drinkwater had neither the time nor the patience to investigate. Doubtless the young devil had got his hands on liquor, probably Rakitin gave him access to it . . .

'Go below, sir, at once!'

'All plain sail, sir,' reported Ballantyne, recalling Drinkwater to normality.

'Very well, Mr Ballantyne, thank you.'

'Sir?'

'Well, what is it? Hurry man, for I want to set the stuns'ls.'

'Would not the lightning have affected other ships? We were, by all accounts, no distance from the convoy.'

'What?' Drinkwater looked sharply at the master. Did Ballantyne have a valid point, or did that single, fateful glimpse of the convoy argue that it had been immune from the lightning? He recalled the bolt hitting the sea quite close. Surely *that* was what had disturbed the magnetism in the needles suspended on their silken threads below the compass card. It had all been something of a nightmare, Drinkwater thought, recalling vignettes of evidence, lit by flashes of lightning or the unholy gathering of men round the binnacle light on the gun-deck.

'No. I think not,' he said with assumed certainty. 'There was a thunderbolt struck the sea quite close to us, Mr Ballantyne, I think it was that that mazed our compass . . .'

And so he came to believe for the time being.

'Trouble never comes in small bottles, does it, Mr Lallo?'

'No, sir.'

'What should we do? Quarantine 'em?'

'We may be too late for that, sir,' Lallo cautioned.

'Is it as contagious as the Gaol Fever?' Gaol fever they called it aboard ship, and ship fever they called it ashore, ascribing its spread to the least desirable elements of each of the societies in which, amid the endemic squalor, it spread like wildfire.

'It's hard to say, sir. I'm not over-familiar with the yaws, but typhus . . .'

'We've contained outbreaks of *that* before . . .' Drinkwater said hopefully. It was true. Clean clothes and salt-water douches seemed, if not to cure typhus, at least to inhibit its spread. Perhaps the same treatment might stay this present unpleasant disease. He suggested it. Lallo nodded gloomily.

'We must *try*,' said Drinkwater encouragingly, bracing himself as *Patrician* leaned to a stronger gust under the press of canvas she was now carrying. Suddenly Drinkwater longed for the luxury of his own cabin; to be watching the white-green

140

wake streaming astern from below the open sashes of the wide stern window, and the sea-birds dipping in it.

Lallo coughed, aware of Drinkwater's sudden abstraction. He stared at the surgeon's lined face. Was he going out of his mind to be thinking such inane thoughts? How could he stare, delighting in the swirling wake, when Lallo was here, bent under the weight of his message of death?

'Quarantine 'em,' he said, suddenly resolute, 'station 'em at the after guns; to be issued with new slops at the ship's expense (we've widows' men to cover the matter), ditch their clothing. They're to be hosed down twice daily and dance until they're dry. Keep their bodies from touching anything . . .'

Lallo nodded and rose. 'I'll tell Fraser to re-quarter them. You said after guns, sir?'

Drinkwater nodded. Yes, he thought, after guns, close to Morris . . .

'Sail ho!'

Drinkwater stirred from his doze, fighting off the fog of an afternoon sleep.

'Two sails! No three-ee! Point to starboard! 'Tis the convoy!'

He was on deck before the hail was finished, up on the rail and motioning for the deck glass. Someone put it into his hand and he watched the sails of a brig climb up over the rim of the world, saw them foreshorten as she altered course towards them and then he jumped down on deck and felt like grabbing both Fraser's hands and dancing ring-a-roses with him for the sheer joy of finding the lost ships. Instead he said:

'Put your helm down a touch, Mr Fraser, let's close with 'em as fast as possible and offer our apologies . . .'

The two vessels came up hand over fist. On the horizon to the south-west they could see the rest of the convoy close together.

'Odd, sir, they seem to be hove-to.'

'Shows they've been waiting for us. They've been buzz-nacking.'

Drinkwater's cheerful tone was redolent of the relief he was feeling at overtaking the convoy before dark. It was *Hormuzeer* that approached them, a trim little brig that had once been a privateer and now ran opium to China under the command of an elderly but energetic Scotsman named Macgillivray. Through their glasses they could see her come into the wind with a large red flag flying at her foremasthead.

'That's a damned odd signal for her to be flying,' someone said among the curious little knot of officers who had gathered on deck.

'Into action?'

'They're hoisting out a boat . . .'

'Get the stuns'ls off her, Mr Fraser, if you please,' snapped Drinkwater, his face suddenly grim. 'If that's the convoy over there, we've two ships missing.'

'Aye, sir, we sorely missed you. Your absence, sir, was ill-timed. Dolorous, sir damned dolorous.' Macgillivray's face was thin, hollow-cheeked and pitted by smallpox. A hooked nose that belonged to a larger man jutted from between two deep-set and rheumy eyes that fixed Drinkwater with a piercing glitter. Across the nose and cheeks, red and broken veins spread like the tributaries of a mapped river, contrasting with dead-white skin that seemed to have been permanently shaded by a broad-brimmed hat. As if to augment the ferocity of his expression, grey whiskers, sharply shaved below the cheekbone, grew upon his face below his eyes.

'I have explained, Captain Macgillivray, why I failed to keep station last night. The matter is done, sir, and the time for recriminations is past . . .'

'No, sir! Damn no, sir! We shall have time for recriminations at Penang, you mark my words. We demand the navy protects us, sir, and you are missing. We lost two ships, sir . . .'

'Captain Macgillivray, you have told me three times that two ships are missing and I have told you twice why we lost contact with you.' Drinkwater was almost shouting down the furious Scotsman, bludgeoning him into silence with his own anger. 'Now, sir, will you do me the courtesy of telling me *which* two ships and how they were lost?'

Macgillivray subsided, then he opened his thin mouth as though diving for more air. 'Pirates, sir, pirates. Sea-Dyaks from Borneo forty *praus* strong, sir, forty! Pirates with gongs and shrieks and stink-pots and blow-pipes in red jackets. Straight for the *Guilford* they came, took *Hindoostan* as well, swarmed aboard and carried her off before you knew it.'

'When?'

'At dawn.'

'Did you attempt to drive them off?'

'Aye, we opened fire, but the wind was light . . .'

'And you were spread out?'

'Aye, maybe a little . . .'

'Ah . . .'

'Not for reasons of slackness, Captain, oh, no, not for that, I assure you. We had spread out to seek yourself. Some of us saw you struck by lightning, like you said, but we were mistaken, for you are here, now.'

That 'now' seemed like an accusation of a crime.

'And they carried the *Guilford* off, from under your noses? You didn't pursue . . . ?'

'It's *your* job to pursue, Captain, not ours to lose our cargoes. We did what we could. I followed a little myself. They went sou' b' west, for the Borneo coast . . .'

The two men fell silent. After a while Drinkwater looked up. 'I will make the signal for all commanders in an hour, Captain Macgillivray. Then I shall decide what to do.'

'There's damn all you can do – now.'

Drinkwater looked up into the undisguised contempt in the Scotsman's eyes.

He had wanted the hour to work *Patrician* into the main body of the convoy. That was the reason he gave out on the quarter-deck. In reality he wanted the time to re-establish himself, albeit temporarily, in the more impressive surroundings of his cabin, to remove the screen and evict Morris and Rakitin. In the event it was noon before the last indignant master was pulled alongside and the ships rocked gently upon the now motionless sea. The wind had died and the calm was glassy, as though the ocean lacked the energy to move under the full heat of the brazen sun. Drinkwater had fended off the verbal assaults of each and every one of the merchant captains, reiterating the circumstances of *Patrician*'s separation until he was only half-convinced of its accuracy. It was too extravagant a tale to be wholly believable, particularly by men with little faith and large axes to grind.

The cabin, as he called the meeting to order, seemed to heave with indignation and Drinkwater himself was very close to losing his temper. Only the thought that an outburst of anger would carry to Morris on the quarterdeck held him in check.

'Gentlemen! Gentlemen!' He managed at last to quieten them. 'What has happened is a matter of regret to us all. Both you and I are incredulous at aspects of events, you that my frigate was absent, I because your pursuit seems to have been non-existent . . .'

'There were forty *praus*, damn you, and poisoned darts all over the place and cannon . . .'

'And bugger-all wind . . .'

'There was sufficient of a wind to return me to station . . . but let that all pass . . .'

They subsided again. Drinkwater pressed doggedly on. 'What we must now decide is how to proceed.'

'Proceed?' queried one voice. 'Why to Penang, of course.'

'Aye!' A chorus of voices rose in assent.

Drinkwater frowned. Did they intend to abandon Callan? Was the motivation of these men solely and wholly governed by profit? So different from his own thinking was this conclusion that he stood for a moment nonplussed.

'Captain Drinkwater, I think you misunderstand us.' Drinkwater looked at the speaker, glad at last that one reasonable voice spoke from the hostile group before him. It was that of Captain Cunningham, commander of the *Ligonier*.

'I rather hope I do,' replied Drinkwater curtly.

'It is not that we wish to abandon Captain Callan; in all likelihood he will be repatriated by the Dutch, for this kind of thing has happened before. The Sea-Dyaks are interested only in booty. They will strip *Guilford* of all that they require or can trade with the Dutch; powder, small arms, shot, plus cargo. Since hostilities with the Batavians began, the wily squareheads have sought out the princes of the Sarawak tribes and offered them bribes for the capture and surrender of any of our Indiamen. I doubt Callan or his officers will come to any *personal* harm . . .' Cunningham paused and a stillness filled the hitherto noisy cabin. Drinkwater sensed the compliance of the other masters: Cunningham was poised for the *coup de grâce*. 'Your own predicament, Captain, is perhaps even less certain of its outcome than Captain Callan's.'

A further pause, pregnant wth opprobrium, let the implied threat sink in. Macgillivray, a man of little subtlety, could not let the matter rest on so insubstantial a foundation; besides, he had concocted a phrase of such obscurity that he flung it now like an accusation of untruth.

'The fulmineous intervention of nature you *say* you experienced, Captain Drinkwater, offers poorly against the loss of two ships.'

'One of which carried specie,' put in another.

They were the kicks of a cowardly mob, delivered after a man was in the gutter.

Drinkwater stood before his accusers. Inwardly he felt crushed. Fate had dealt him a cruel blow! To be singled out by Macgillivray's 'fulmineous intervention of nature' seemed so cruelly unjust as to anger some primitive inner part of him so that, although silent, he raked their faces with a baleful glare. He mastered the inner seething with the realisation that he wanted a drink. He would have one in a minute, immediately he had disposed of these men, bent to their wishes.

'Very well, gentlemen. I shall accede to your request and escort you to Penang.'

'Well let us hope you *do*, Captain,' said Macgillivray, as the downcast company turned for the cabin door. Drinkwater stood stock-still as they filed out. Then, almost out of habit, he turned towards the pantry and bawled for his steward. The cathartic bellow did him good and Mullender, by some small miracle of intuition, appeared with a bottle and glasses.

Drinkwater took a glass. As he stood impatiently waiting for Mullender to fill it with blackstrap, unannounced Morris re-entered the cabin. His expression bore witness to the fact that he had gleaned knowledge of Drinkwater's discomfiture.

'Where is Captain Rakitin?' Drinkwater asked, delaying his need to swallow the cheap port.

'On the quarterdeck, zur.'

It was Tregembo who answered, stooping at the pantry door, ancient, worn, like a futtock of the ship itself. It seemed oddly appropriate that Tregembo, like Mullender, should have mustered in the pantry, for all that his occupation of the cabin was to be short-lived.

'Thank you.'

Drinkwater fixed both steward and coxswain with the stare of dismissal. Mullender put down the bottle and the pantry door closed behind them, though their listening presence beyond the mahogany louvres was almost visible.

'Your health, Nathaniel.' Morris helped himself to a glass, an ironical smile about his hooded eyes. 'And, of course, your damnation.'

Drinkwater merely glared, then seized gratefully on the excuse to gulp his drink, making to leave the cabin.

'Don't go,' said Morris, divining his purpose, 'we have been so little together. Intolerably little for such old shipmates . . .'

'Morris, we never made the least pretence at friendship. We fought, if I recollect, some kind of duel, and you made numerous threats against my person. You behaved abominably to members of the *Cyclops*'s company and, if there was such a thing as natural justice in the world, you should have been hanged.'

He tailed off. Morris was laughing at him. 'Oh, Nathaniel, Nathaniel, you are still an innocent I see. Still dreaming of "natural justice" and other such silly philosophies . . . How much have you missed, eh? You and I are old men now and here you are beset by worries, buggered upon the altar of your duty . . . You left me at the Cape a sick man . . . I hungered for the destiny you had before you and hated you for seeming to command fate. That was ten years ago, before Bonaparte burst upon us all . . .'

'Bonaparte?' Drinkwater frowned, bemused by this drivel of Morris's.

'Yes, Bonaparte, blazing like a comet across the imaginations of men. "Do as you will," he screamed at the world. "Do as you will . . ."'

There was something about Morris that was not quite drunkenness, but nevertheless reminded Drinkwater of intoxication. There was also, now he came to think of it, a faint, unfamiliarly sweet aroma in the cabin, gradually reasserting itself after the sweaty stink of the convoy masters. Of course! A man of Morris's disposition, influenced by every sensuous inclination of the human body, would be an opium eater. Drinkwater poured himself another drink.

'So I forsook my duty,' went on Morris, 'she was a raddled whore that had nothing to offer me but the pox of responsibility that now consumes you. I counted myself lucky to have found my destiny half-way to India, and took ship to find what I knew to exist if prudish knaves like you did not stand in my way . . .'

'You charm me by your tale, sir,' said Drinkwater unmoved. 'No doubt your little Indian Ganymede approves wholly of tearing out his tongue for your unnatural pleasure! I doubt even the monstrous genius of Bonaparte would approve of that!'

Drinkwater half turned away but his arm was caught by Morris. Both the speed and the force of the grip surprised Drinkwater and he felt himself pulled back to face his enemy.

'D'you dream, Nathaniel? Eh? Of course you do – unholy dreams here, on your cot, eh? Coiled by the legs of . . . of whom, eh? Your Elizabeth, or other, secret women? Well, I dreamed my own dreams . . .'

With a violent gesture Drinkwater shook himself free. The compulsion to run, to escape the cabin and Morris's contaminating company was strong in him, but some dreadful fascination kept him rooted to the spot. As abruptly as he had advanced, Morris fell back. The intense, almost complicit tone vanished and he spoke again in his arch, mocking manner.

'Do you know,' Morris said, 'they say in Peking that the Son of Heaven finds the most exquisite pleasure in impaling a goose who, at the appropriate moment, is strangled . . . ?'

'Damn you . . .'

Sickened, Drinkwater turned away. As he made for the door he caught sight of the boy. He was asleep, had slept, it seemed, all through the noisy council and its revolting aftermath, half-naked, a brown curl in the corner of Drinkwater's quondam cabin.

There was nothing he could bring himself to do in the remaining hours of that disastrous day but pace up and down the quarterdeck, biliously angry as the convoy stood for the entrance of the Malacca Strait. Great clouds reared on the horizon, huge anvil-shaped thunderheads that rose over the steaming tropical rain forests of the distant land. As night fell these huge, billowing clouds were illuminated from within, possessed by flickering demons as lightning, too far away to crackle with thunder, sparked and flashed tremendously within their charged and coiling vapours. The sight tormented Drinkwater as he continued his lonely, self-imposed vigil, recalling over and over again Macgillivray's facetious phrase: 'fulmineous intervention of nature'.

In deference to his savage mood, men moved quietly about the upper decks and the officers, alternating as the ship's routine ground its remorseless way into time, gave their orders in low voices. It seemed, as he gradually emerged from the depths of introspection, that they were humouring him, like a child. The thought made him unreasonably angry and he cast about for some weapon of chastisement. Was that Frey on watch? No, Quilhampton.

'Mr Quilhampton.'

'Sir?'

'Have we established, sir,' spat Drinkwater, with unbending formality, 'why the binnacle lamp was extinguished last night?'

'Er . . . I . . . I've no idea, sir . . . was it not the rain, sir?'

Drinkwater's temper fed deliciously on such foolishness. 'The lamp has a chimney, sir, is set in a binnacle for the purpose of protecting it from the weather. Its wick may have become soaked when it was removed from such protection, but that was not the reason for its extinguishing. May I suggest a lack of oil as a plausible explanation, eh? I recognise it as one out of favour with the officers as bespeaking a slackness on their part, but . . .', he faltered. He was going to say something about a lack of oil providing a natural explanation, but it smacked so of Macgillivray's phrase that it cut his tirade dead.

'Oh, for God's sake check the damned thing now!'

He cast Quilhampton aside and stalked off into the night, ashamed of himself. God! How he hated this commission! Ever since that poor devil had been swung to the yard-arm at the Nore there had been ill-luck aboard. Now they even had to compensate for a compass deviating thirty-eight degrees, at least until the effects of the thunderbolt wore off . . .

'Sir!'

Something urgent in Quilhampton's tone brought him up. Any peevishness Quilhampton might have felt at his commander's unspeakable behaviour was absent from the imperative note in the lieutenant's voice. Drinkwater turned. Quilhampton was advancing towards him. The binnacle lamp had been extinguished to check the reservoir, but in the gloom Drinkwater could just make out the faint sheen of the glass door of the locker and something in Quilhampton's hand.

'What is it?'

'This, sir.' Drinkwater was aware that Quilhampton was holding out his hand.

'I can't see a damned thing.' Then he was vaguely aware of a dark shape, like an irregular musket ball darkening Quilhampton's palm.

'Bit of metal, sir,' said Quilhampton in a low voice, 'half filling the oil reservoir. Could have put the lamp out prematurely . . .'

'God's bones!'

An act of sabotage? The thought was in both their minds, for it would not be the first that had occurred. A similar event had happened on the coast of California when the ship was found to have developed a persistent and elusive leak.

'Say nothing more,' Drinkwater whispered urgently, then raised his voice to a normal level. 'Very well, Mr Q, relight the lamp.'

Drinkwater walked across the gently leaning deck and stopped beside the wheel. In such light winds only two men stood beside it, staring aloft at the main topsail, steering by the wind until the light was re-established in the binnacle. It was all clear to him now. It was no mere reduction of the volume of the reservoir that had been sought, it was something far more sinister. In a few moments the lamp would come back on deck and prove him correct, but the metallic lump he held in his hand was no melted leaden musket ball poured molten into the base of the lamp. It resisted the imprint of his thumb-nail with an almost crystalline stubbornness.

'Here, sir . . .'

Drinkwater stood aside. The lamp was placed back between the two copper grooves that held it in place, throwing a gentle radiance across the neatly inscribed compass card.

'What course, sir?' asked the puzzled helmsman, sure that he had held the ship's head steady relative to the wind during the last quarter of an hour.

'You may steer sou' west a-half west.'

'Sou' west a-half west, aye, aye, sir.' There was a brief pause, then the helmsman said, 'She's that now, sir.'

'Yes,' replied Drinkwater quietly, 'I know she is.'

'Sir?' In the dim glow the rumple of a frown creased Quilhampton's forehead.

Drinkwater held up the small nugget. 'It's a piece of magnetic lodestone, Mr Q, perfect for deliberately inducing a deviation in the compass.'

CHAPTER 13

A Round Robin

'What d'you intend to do, sir?'

Fraser's voice was tight with anxiety. Ever since the flogging of the deserters he had been half expecting some such outbreak among the people.

'What the devil can I do, Mr Fraser, except abjure you and all the officers to be on their guard?'

'Could be the quarantined men, sir,' suggested Fraser.

'What? Some kind of collective revenge for their misfortune?'

Fraser shrugged. 'Ye canna let it pass, sir.'

'No. But they all know we discovered the thing, 'tis common gossip throughout the ship. Such scuttlebutt spreads like wildfire . . .'

'Could you not . . .' Fraser looked conspiratorially about the deck, to make sure that no one was within earshot of the pair of them, '. . . ask Tregembo to . . . ?'

'Spy, you mean? Carry lower-deck tittle-tattle?'

'Aye, sir.' Fraser seemed rather relieved that Drinkwater grasped his meaning.

'If it was known, I'm damned certain Tregembo would have told me. The trouble is Tregembo don't know.'

Fraser subsided into unhappy silence. Drinkwater was aware that Midshipman Dutfield was trying to catch his eye.

'Beg pardon, sir, but Mr Ballantyne's compliments and the entrance to the strait is in sight.'

'Very well, Mr Dutfield, thank you.'

They had, for the past two days, been aware of the presence of land. At first they had seen the electric storms above the distant, jungle-covered mountains, then the clusters of islands forming the Anambas archipelago lifted over the horizon. Odd tangles of floating vegetation, bound by the roots and stumpy remnants of mangroves, drifted past. 'Floating islands' Ballantyne called them, recounting how sometimes they reached astonishing size and had once concealed a host of Dyak canoes from which he and his father had only escaped with difficulty and the prompt arrival of a breeze.

Of Dyaks they had seen nothing, gliding over a smooth, empty sea, and now picking up their landfall with gratifying precision. Rank upon rank of hills were emerging blue and low from the clouds hovering over them, a seemingly impenetrable barrier whose nearer bastions were turning slowly green as they approached. Stretching away into the northern distance the long finger of the Malay peninsula crept round almost a third of the horizon, its distal point Pulo Tumasek. To larboard rose a wild jumble of islands, the Rhio archipelago, which, from this distance, retained the impression of a continuous, if indented coastline. Beyond, indicated as yet by clouds, lay the vast island of Sumatra, parallel to the Malay coast and containing, between the two, the Malacca Strait, highway to Prince of Wales Island, as Penang was then more familiarly known. Beyond all lay the Indian Seas.

Drinkwater strained his glass further to larboard. Somewhere to the southwards, beyond the Rhio islands, lay the Gaspar and Sunda Straits, shortest route to the Cape of Good Hope, and barred to the China fleet by Dutch and French cruisers. But today he could see nothing, nothing but an empty blue sea, glittering beneath a brazen sky. And, curiously, it brought him no pleasure. Somehow he would rather have seen an enemy, been faced with a task; somehow the very emptiness of the ocean seemed ominous.

'Beg pardon, sir.'

Belchambers's face, poked round the door of the tiny cabin, was more readily seen in his shaving mirror, thought Drinkwater, as he rasped the razor upwards over the stretched skin of his throat.

'What is it?'

He forced the query through the clenched teeth of a jutting jaw.

'This, sir.'

Drinkwater swivelled his eyes a little. The image of Belchambers's hand could be seen in the cracked mirror. The fingers unfolded to reveal a crushed scrap of paper.

Drinkwater had seen one before and the shock made him nick himself. It was a round robin, a message from the ship's company, and it cast his mind uneasily back to the days of ninety-seven, the year of the great mutinies. They had been a common thing then, demands, protests, both reasonable and unreasonable, sent aft to the officers in this anonymous, yet neatly demotic way.

'What does it say?'

Affecting a *sang-froid* he did not feel, Drinkwater dabbed at his bleeding throat and completed his shave. 'Read it,' he commanded, a little more forcefully.

Belchambers cleared his throat. The self-conscious gesture relaxed Drinkwater. 'Are they going to cut my throat, or should I complete the matter myself, Mr Belchambers? Eh? Give the thing here, thank you.'

He took the crumpled and grubby paper and the boy fled gratefully. Captain Drinkwater's mood had been dangerously unpredictable of late.

Drinkwater smoothed the sheet and stared at it. In all justice to the midshipman, it was not easy to read, almost obscured by the creases into which it had been balled, the easier to be thrown on to the quarterdeck. It would have been tossed at Quilhampton's feet, no doubt, with not a man on deck anywhere near it as the lieutenant bent to pick it up. Or, of course, it would have been dropped during the night. No matter now; here it was, in the hands for which it was intended, and the

153

writing was well formed, legalistic and educated – a bad sign. Drinkwater frowned; he was seeing ominous signs in everything these days. He read:

To Captain Drinkwater, Esquire
　　　　Y'r Honour,

　　We, the Ship's Company, with our Humble Duty beg to Acquaint Your Honour of our Reprobation of the Events of this Day. Knowing Your Honour's Mind to be of Lofty Principles, we, the Ship's Company, Entreat you not to be Misled by former Occurrences. We Solemnly Swear that no Malice Aforethought attaches to the Heinous and Hideous Interference with the Binnacle Lantern that Must be Contemptible to the Minds of British Seamen.

　　We, the Ship's Company, Desire to Inform Your Honour of our Loyalty to Our Duty and Our Country.
　　　　　　Signed,
　　　　　　　　By Us All,
　　　　　　　　　　One and Indivisible.

It was a concoction worthy of the most appalling Patriotic Club, but its outrage rang with sincerity. Its very vehemence suggested a wiping out of the shameful acts off California. These were men, quite capable of outrageously mutinous behaviour, angrily repudiating any suggestion of its initiation in *this* case.

'They want to go home,' muttered Drinkwater, smiling at himself in the battered glass, and crushing the round robin in his hand.

But it offered little peace of mind, merely diverting his suspicion elsewhere. Morris he knew to be too motivated by self-interest to have attempted such a stupid thing. Morris had nothing to gain by diverting *Patrician* and could not possibly have known of the Dyak presence. Drinkwater was tempted to seek its motivation in mischief rather than malice. He recalled Midshipman Chirkov's sudden interest in navigational matters, and the suspicion, once it crossed his mind, seemed a reasonable one, redolent of idle folly and petulant resentment over earlier humiliation.

Dangerously stupid and consequentially disastrous as the

matter had been, he realised his suspicions were circumstantial and unprovable. He knew only that his own vigilance must increase, and that the burden of his responsibilities weighed even heavier upon him. When later that day, as the sun dipped crimson towards the thunderheads above the blue mountains of Sumatra, the masthead reported two sails, Captain Drinkwater could not have cared whether or not they were enemies.

They made contact with the two ships just before daylight finally vanished from the tropic sky, two sloops from Penang sent questing down the Malacca Strait after reports of enemy cruisers off the Rhio archipelago. They were not naval ships, but belonged to the East India Company's Bombay Marine, the *Arrow* and the *Dart*, nattily smart twenty-two-gun ship-rigged sloops aswarm with lascars and a commander not much older, or so it seemed to Drinkwater's jaundiced eye, than Fleetwood Pellew.

Convoy, escort and new arrivals lay to in a calm through the night. The continuing windlessness of the following morning, with the sea like blue steel, pricked here and there by the lifting spearheads of flying fish, allowed much boat-trafficking between the ships. Drinkwater, watching the masters rowed about the wallowing fleet, knew that tittle-tattle was being plied about, mostly pejorative to his reputation, a fact confirmed by the boats' avoidance of the *Patrician*.

After an hour or so of this feeling of having been sent to Coventry, Drinkwater ordered the signal hoisted for 'all captains'. In the event only two boats pulled towards the frigate, one from the *Ligonier*, bearing an embarrassed Cunningham, the other from the *Arrow*. Cunningham made the introductions and Drinkwater was aware that, in the Company's service, the commander of an Indiaman outweighed an officer of the Marine. For this he was profoundly grateful, for the young prig seemed ready to read Drinkwater a lecture.

'. . . And so, sir,' concluded Cunningham with a decent preamble about Drinkwater's able, though unfortunate, escort, 'Captain Hennessey here . . .', Hennessey footed the meagrest of bows by way of identification, 'is of the opinion that he should take over the escort.'

'And what is *your* opinion, Captain Cunningham, might I ask?'

'Why, sir, that you continue to accompany us to Penang; only a fool would opine that your guns are not valuable.'

There was the slightest emphasis on the word 'fool'. Clearly Hennessey was attempting to arrogate command of the escort against Cunningham's inclination. The young commander flared his nostrils in a spiritedly equine fashion, registering well-controlled indignation.

'Well, sir, since I am *ordered* by Admiral Drury to command and escort this convoy, I shall continue to do so until I see it safe at anchor at Penang. Captain Hennessey and his colleagues are welcome to join us, subordinate to my command, of course.'

It did not gratify Drinkwater to argue about such matters. The thing was plain as the nose on one's face if one took the trouble to look at it.

'Might I ask what Captain Hennessey's orders are?'

The young man spoke for the first time, a nasally superior voice, just as Drinkwater had expected, wondering, in an errant moment, if the salons or withdrawing rooms, or whatever they called them in Calcutta, made a point of turning out such stuffed shirts.

'I am ordered upon a cruise, sah, reports having reached Fort Cornwallis that Dutch and French cruisers were active in the Rhio Strait. Captain Cunningham informs me that you saw nothing and passed safely through. Therefore I shall consider it my duty, there being, according to Captain Cunningham, no further trade coming down from Canton, to see these ships back to Prince of Wales Island.'

'Are you apprehensive of attack between here and Penang, sir?' asked Drinkwater.

'I have no reason to be, but one never knows, and the Company cannot stand the loss of a second of its own ships . . .'

'*Ligonier* will be the only Company ship to get through from Canton, Captain Drinkwater,' broke in Cunningham, as though to add a reasonable weight to Hennessey's plan.

'It occurs to me, gentlemen, that Captain Hennessey, with his local knowledge of these waters, might double that score and recover *Guilford*.'

Cunningham and Hennessey exchanged glances; it was clear they had already discussed the matter and Cunningham's anxiety had prevailed.

'I would go myself, but for a lack of charts,' Drinkwater added quickly. Hennessey shot him a swift glance. Was the young dandy subtle enough to spot the gauge flung at his feet? 'Is Admiral Pellew at Penang?'

'He is expected, sah,' drawled Hennessey, speculatively, adding, 'I have charts, Captain Drinkwater, Dutch charts . . .'

'Perhaps you will allow me the use of them. Now I shall escort the convoy to Prince of Wales Island and then we shall see . . .'

He ushered the two men to the rail. Hennessey left first, Cunningham hanging back a little.

'I am sorry for the outcome of all this, Captain Drinkwater. I am aware that you have done your utmost.'

'You imply repercussions, sir. I am conscious of having done my duty. There may be a little more I can do. At any event I shall make my report to Admiral Pellew in due course.'

'Pellew will stand by you. He is himself under attack by the merchant houses of Calcutta as well as the Company.'

Drinkwater was close to grinning. With Dungarth dead and John Barrow hostile at the Admiralty, he expected little further employment. What did it matter if providence had made his name smell in the noses of the Court of Directors in Leadenhall Street? The baying of the Calcutta merchants could touch him very little. He longed to be home with Elizabeth and the children. 'Let us hope poor Callan survives,' he added, as Cunningham shook out the man-ropes that lay down the curve of *Patrician*'s tumblehome.

'Indeed,' said Cunningham, 'but I fear 'tis not Callan that will upset the Directors, but his thirty thousand sterling . . .'

'I beg your pardon?' Drinkwater's sharp interrogative held Cunningham one-footed at the rail.

'The specie, aboard *Guilford* . . .'

'*How much*, though, sir? *How much* did you say?'

'Thirty thousand sterling.'

'God's bones, the man told me three!'

Cunningham frowned. 'Three? Three thousand? Good heavens, no. Mind you Callan was a thoughtful fellow, perhaps he did not wish to worry you.'

Drinkwater stared after the boat as it pulled Cunningham back to the massive bulk of the Indiaman. What a bootless concern, Drinkwater thought ironically, as if anything could stop him from worrying.

It took some eight days to work their way northwards in the capricious winds of the land-locked strait, eight days of bracing yards and tacking, of easing sheets and hauling tacks, of setting studding-sails and dousing them when they began to outrun their charges. And for Drinkwater eight days of brooding introspection. He had decided to return and make a sweep along the Borneo coast; perhaps his luck might come back and he would catch a sleeping Dutchman in a river mouth – he hardly dared hope for the recapture of *Guilford*. At any rate Pellew would approve, he had no need to report to the Admiral in person, merely to send in his written account via Cunningham and then turn south off Pulo Penang.

The green and lush island hove into view at last, and the cluster of ships, steadied finally before a westerly breeze, stood north along its west coast to avoid the shoals to the south of the island.

They bore away round Muka Head and Drinkwater stood in until he could see the low, embrasured ramparts of Fort Cornwallis commanding the anchorage on the eastern flank of the heights, between Prince of Wales Island and the mainland. Here he anchored, hoisted out all boats and divested himself of his Russian prisoners. Pellew was not at the anchorage, but a frigate was, commanded by an officer far junior to himself, who grudgingly obeyed the order by the hand of Acting Lieutenant Frey to hold the prisoners against his return. Three of the *moujiks*, Lithuanians from the old Duchy of Kurland, swore their oaths to King George and remained aboard *Patrician*.

Drinkwater bade a civil farewell to Rakitin. The man was far gone in lethargy, a catalepsy tending, according to Lallo, to suicide and common among the Slavic peoples. Rakitin had eaten Morris's opium, but it was not the white poppy that killed him, nor remorse over his defeat. He died within a week of leaving *Patrician* of a cancer undiagnosed by Lallo.

Midshipman Count Vasili Chirkov left under protest, swearing that when *Patrician* returned, he and Frey must settle their affair of honour. It was perhaps fortunate that Frey was employed upon his errand in another boat at the time, for Drinkwater was impatient to be gone. Frey had secured the promised charts, poor enough things by the look of them, and had filled them a few stummed casks of fresh water.

All day Drinkwater was active on deck, aware that below Mullender and Tregembo were clearing his cabin, dislodging Morris from it and burning gunpowder within, to stum it like the water-casks of any impurities.

'Mr Fraser, do you see the launch? Damn it, but I want to be under weigh within the hour, before sunset at the latest . . .'

Both men strained their eyes to locate the launch amid the anchored ships and bum-boats, *praus* and *tonkangs* that teemed in the sheltered waters.

'Beg pardon, zur.'

Distracted, Drinkwater turned. Tregembo stood before him.

'Well? What the devil is it now?'

'It's Morris, zur . . . he won't leave your cabin.'

The Winds of Fortune

'I can help you, Drinkwater.'

This was a different Morris. Gone was the overt hedonist, the flaunting amoral character that sought to discomfit his old enemy. This was the wily man who had succeeded in trade, swindled or earned his enviable position at Canton and wherever else the winds of fortune had blown his perverted and unlovely carcase. Drinkwater saw, to his surprise, flashes of the old Morris he had first known, the tyrannical bully, but also the seaman and officer, the man of gentle birth whose sexual excesses, had they been discreet, might not have disturbed the outward life of a gentleman of substance and quality.

Drinkwater thrust aside Morris's blandishments. 'I do not want you on my ship a moment longer than necessary,' Drinkwater stated bluntly.

'But you want that Indiaman back, don't you?' Morris stood his ground. 'You are returning to search for her and have, I'll warrant, not the slightest idea where to look . . .'

'What interest can you have in the matter? You and your silver are safely here in Penang; you can leave for Calcutta with the trade, my orders were only that I should see it safely this far . . .'

'Do you think I have no interest in the specie aboard *Guilford* . . . ?'

'You showed precious little interest in the m. er at the time . . .'

'My dear Nathaniel, how you misunderstand and misjudge me. Of course I relished your embarrassment. I do not hold your values, I seek my amusements where I may find them. I do not offer my help out of friendship, you know me too well for that . . . no, no . . . But I *do* have an interest in the fate of that silver . . .'

'Well, of what help can you be? broke in Drinkwater impatiently. 'Do you know where *Guilford* is now? How can you? Do you know anything of this coast? And what motivates this sudden about-face, this, this impetuous urge to assist?'

'Nathaniel, Nathaniel, your questions are too fast. Listen, I have told you, I have some interest in the silver; I alone brought it out of Canton in defiance of the Viceroy, its loss alone may be held against me, my business interests will suffer from its loss; my "face", my standing, my good name will be diminished. As to the coast, let me tell you I know both the estuaries of the Sekrang and the Sarebas Rivers, for I travelled on two Dutch ships and know them for haunts of the Sea-Dyaks.'

'But why . . . ?' Doubts assailed Drinkwater, but Morris pressed on.

'When the *Guilford* was taken I was more amused by your discomfiture than the loss. Recollect how long I have waited for your humiliation. But now you are determined to return. That is a different matter. For a while we have something in common . . .'

'You are offering me . . .'

'Terms . . . an alliance.'

'God's bones . . .'

'Furthermore,' Morris persisted, 'I have charts, better charts than those there . . .' Morris pointed to the half-unwound rolls of Hennessey's charts flung upon the cabin table until, later, Drinkwater could study them.

'See . . .'

Morris turned, drawing the top off a leather tube that he

took from a fold of his robe. He drew a tightly rolled paper and held it out. Drinkwater took it and opened it. It was remarkably detailed, annotated with neatly pencilled notes. He moved across to hold it in the light from the stern windows but Morris took it from him, rolling it up again with his pudgy, beringed fingers.

'A sprat, Nathaniel, to catch the mackerel of your good favour . . .'

Drinkwater looked at Morris. The odium of him! He was almost wheedling in that mincing mode the seamen called nancying.

'You will let me have access to those charts?' Drinkwater asked.

'I will pilot you, using them. You need them only for the estuaries, your boats may search the edges of the swamps and mangroves.' Morris paused and Drinkwater hesitated.

'You need me, Nathaniel,' Morris said softly, almost seductively, 'you need me to rescue your reputation . . .'

It was true. Despite the doubts and uncertainties, it was true.

'Do you think we have the slightest chance?' Drinkwater asked.

Morris noted the plural pronoun. He had hooked his prey. He forced his features into a grave, counselling expression.

'A good one . . . with a little luck . . .'

Drinkwater prevaricated a moment longer, though both men knew his mind was made up. 'How much specie was aboard *Guilford*?' he asked guilelessly.

Morris shrugged. 'Oh, ten, twenty thousand perhaps, certainly ten.'

Was the imprecision of Morris's reply sinister? And why had Callan himself lied about the amount of specie aboard his ship? For a moment or two Drinkwater stood indecisively, gauging the intentions of the man before him. He was already determined to turn back in quest of the lost ships, but he knew that he was without resources and that, intolerable though it was, Morris might be able to help. If, as he claimed, the good

162

name of Morris himself would be impugned, then for a while they might hold something in common. Repugnant though the consideration might be to Drinkwater, honour and duty compelled him to submit to this personal humiliation in the hope of recovering the captured ships.

Drinkwater sighed. 'Very well, I'll give the order to weigh.'

By the light of the candles Drinkwater studied Hennessey's charts. They were not comparable with Morris's, but adequate for strategic planning . . .

Strategic planning!

The whole business was a mockery, a wild goose chase of the utmost folly, an attempt to save his . . . what was it Morris called it? His 'face'. That barometer of a man's standing in the world. 'You need me to rescue your reputation,' Morris had said, and Drinkwater ground his teeth at being so beholden. There was a knock at the cabin door. 'Enter!'

'You sent for me, zur?'

'Aye, Tregembo . . . what is the temper of the men? This is a testing time. Today they saw Penang and know it for an English post, now we sail south-east and only a fool knows that ain't for home.'

'Like you said, zur, I've given out that you've to clear the Dutchies out o' the strait, zur; said you'd orders for a month's cruise and that after that the Admiral's promised to hoist his flag aboard us for passage to the Cape.'

'Damn it, Tregembo, I didn't ask you to embroider my intention. Now you've made me a liar!'

'I've bought ye a month, zur.'

'Damn me!' Drinkwater's eyes met those of the old Cornishman. 'Yes, you have, and I thank you for it.' Drinkwater smiled. 'A month to keep us out of the Comptor, eh?'

'It'll not come to that, zur.'

'No.' No, it would not come to that. He no longer feared poverty, but there were other things. 'Thank you, Tregembo.' He bent over the chart, but the old Cornishman did not budge.

'Zur . . .'

'Well, what is it?'

'Morris, zur, don't trust him.'

'I don't . . . only I must, just a little.'

'Zur, I knows how you judged it were that young devil that played hokey with the compass.'

'Chirkov? Yes . . . though I can prove nothing.'

'No, zur. Mullender'll tell 'ee, though it took me long enough to get it out of him, he's the wits of a malkin, but he's certain sure it were the Russian. Mullender was in an' out, tendin' to 'em all in here.' Tregembo waved a hand about the cabin, disturbing the candle flames and making shadows leap like the spectres he invoked. 'You know 'ow 'e comes and goes silent like. He says how he saw 'em all smoking and drinking together, right little hell's kitchen they made o' this place, zur, beggin' your pardon . . .'

'Go on.'

'The boy too, zur, that little Turk. You know what he's for?'

'I can guess, Tregembo. Morris hasn't changed his habits.'

''Tis worse than a Portsmouth knocking shop . . . Mullender didn't say much. Learnt to keep his mouth shut, I s'pose, or didn't want to start Derrick a-Quakering at him . . .'

'If all he saw was Morris and Chirkov . . .'

'Not buggering, zur, though I daresay they did that too, but in *conversation*, zur . . .'

'Conversation?'

'And Morris gave Chirkov a lump o' something . . .'

'A lump of opium, perhaps?'

'Only if opium's hard enough to rattle on the deck when it's dropped, zur.'

'The lump of lodestone?'

'Aye . . .'

Both men looked at each other, recalling the web of intimidation and cruelty that Morris had once cast over the helpless seamen aboard *Cyclops* thirty years earlier.

'So, the leopard hasn't changed his spots, has he?'

'No, zur.'

But why had Morris engineered such an act? The question tormented him after Tregembo had gone, and he sat slumped at the cabin table, toying with an empty glass and staring at Hennessey's charts. There was no reasonable explanation. Even though personal revenge was a powerful motive, particularly to a man as amoral as Morris, Drinkwater was convinced that Morris's pecuniary interests would have outweighed any other considerations during their passage from Canton.

As Drinkwater wrestled with the problem he felt a rising tide of panic welling in his gut. His loneliness seemed to crush him and in his weakness he reached out for the bottle. From forward, beyond the barrier of the cabin door, came the tinny, quadruple double strikes of eight bells and he heard the ship stir as the watch changed. He withdrew his hand from the bottle and swore. He commanded a fine ship, he had sufficient fire-power at his finger-tips to bolster his courage better than any damned bottle! And he had Morris close by, damned near mewed up under lock and key.

Drinkwater rose and, leaning forward on his hands, stared unseeing down at Hennessey's charts. He was a fool and Tregembo an alarmist. Certainly Morris had put Chirkov up to the stupid act of tampering with the compass, but they had been drunk, or drugged, befuddled to an act of gross irresponsibility. Their jape had misfired and gone disastrously wrong. It was not Drinkwater who needed Morris, but Morris who needed Drinkwater! Surely *that* was the explanation, for not even the malevolent Morris could have foreseen that the convoy would be attacked by piratical Sea-Dyaks the following dawn and that the treasure aboard *Guilford* would be spirited away.

Thirty thousand sterling!

No wonder Morris had been imprecise about the amount, for its enormity was a measure of his consummate folly. Morris had wished to make trouble, to discredit Drinkwater and, like a good puppet-master, pull strings to rob his enemy of influence in London. Recovering his spirits, Drinkwater thought there was an ironical satisfaction in this line of reasoning, a grimly humorous if somewhat chilly comfort. Providence, it seemed, had failed them both.

'Devil take it,' he murmured reaching for his hat, 'but it argues powerfully for the bugger's co-operation.'

And with that conclusion, Captain Drinkwater went more cheerfully on deck.

'Red cutter's in sight, sir.'

Drinkwater looked up from Hennessey's chart pinned to a board a-top the binnacle and covered the three yards to Quilhampton's side in an instant. The lieutenant had his eye screwed to the long-glass, bracing its weight against a mizen backstay as *Patrician*, her main topsail backed to the mast, lay hove to off the Borneo coast. It was the second week of their search and January was already over. Another hot and almost windless day had dawned. There was barely enough movement in the air to press the heavy canvas against the main-top and the sea was flat, metallic and seemingly motionless, reflecting the refulgence of the sun.

Drinkwater stared in the direction of Quilhampton's telescope. He could just make out the wavering quadrilateral of the red cutter's lugsail as she cleared the Sarebas River. The estuary was invisible from this distance.

'Damn coast looks all the same,' Drinkwater muttered. 'Is she signalling?'

'Not at the moment . . . I think they're trimming the sheets, sir.'

Even from the mastheads the entrance of the creeks and obscure rivers that wound their way into the interior were impossible to make out. There seemed no appreciable difference in the endless miles of coastline they had patiently worked along. Endless vistas of ragged-edged blue-green swamp formed an indeterminate littoral. Distant hills rose blue-green, climbing into rolling cloud, evidence of firm footing beyond the sub-aqueous morass of the swamp which lay steaming under the sun.

'Cutter's signalling, sir . . .'

A tiny bubble of expectation formed in the pit of Drink-water's stomach: perhaps this time . . . ?

Drinkwater knew their chances of finding *Guilford* and *Hindoostan* had diminished to the point of impossibility. They would have been burnt, or disposed of by now.

'Nothing to report.' Quilhampton lowered and closed the glass with a snap. The tiny, half-formed bubble in Drink-water's gut burst. He felt the sun hot upon his shoulders. With every day that passed it had climbed further up the sky as it approached the equinox. Its relentless heat paralysed his will.

'Make the signal for recall.'

'Aye, aye, sir.'

The bark of the carronade drawing attention to the numeral flag jerking aloft drew Morris on deck. With him came his helot, small and brown, near-naked, but for a loin-cloth and the jewelled turban.

'No luck?' Morris asked.

'No,' Drinkwater answered flatly.

Morris met Drinkwater's eyes. The sight of Drinkwater's wilting resolve brought a thrill of both pleasure and sudden alarm to Morris. He had intended torture, but he must not lose the initiative. Drinkwater must not be driven to give up the search. Besides, he was as eager to reach the location of that mighty haul of specie as was Drinkwater! He bent over the chart, his fat, fleshy and glittering finger indicating a head-land where the coast swung sharply east.

'Tanjong Sirik, Captain,' he said, drawing Drinkwater's attention to the point. 'Our last hope is here, Sumpitan Creek, Blow-pipe Creek we called it, naming it for the ferocity of its inhabitants and their use of poisoned darts.'

Drinkwater stared at the pointing finger. It was beautifully manicured and reminded Drinkwater of a fat Duchess's digit. More significantly, it pointed to a white blank on Hennessey's chart. Where the coast swung round Tanjong Sirik, a gap appeared, an area of unsurveyed coastline unknown to the Dutch hydrographers.

'Into uncharted waters,' Drinkwater said ruminatively: a

last chance. Morris had played his fish with infinite cunning. Drinkwater had will enough for one last throw.

'Not quite, Captain,' Morris said in a low voice, 'perhaps uncharted, but not quite unknown.'

Beyond Tanjong Sirik there was no mystery. The endless jungle of mangroves dipped south and seemed to disappear in an inlet beyond which it curved north and then eastward as far as the keenest eye at the masthead could discern. They passed small native *praus* and men fishing, and the smoking fires and *atap*-roofed huts on stilts which emerged like excrescences of the jungle itself. Small strips of sand with beached dugouts gave indications of firmer ground and the reason for these remote habitations, but of the mighty war-*praus*, the sea-going assault craft of the Sea-Dyaks called *bankongs*, there was no sign.

Drinkwater had originally nursed some vague plan of coasting this wasteland in the hope of attracting attack, of appearing sufficiently like an Indiaman to mislead whatever lookout the putative pirates employed. But they were either non-existent or knew full well that *Patrician* was no Indiaman, but a man-of-war. Not even the subterfuge of hoisting Dutch colours, resorted to two days ago, had made the slightest difference. Apart from the fisherfolk, the coast had remained obdurately uninhabited.

As *Patrician* stood inshore, coasting slowly to the east of Tanjong Sirik, Drinkwater allowed Morris on the quarter-deck. The sun was westering and the blessed cool of evening was upon them. Morris scanned the line of the shore through his glass, his silk robe fluttering about his obese form.

'Blow-pipe Creek lies to the southward,' Morris remarked.

Drinkwater raised his glass and stared at the impenetrable barrier of the mangroves. He would give the game one last throw of the dice; one last opportunity to see if providence would change his luck. He had nothing to lose by sending the boats away for a final search before he admitted himself beaten. His only satisfaction was the knowledge that Morris, too, had failed.

'You may bring the ship to an anchor here. It is good holding ground, if I recall correctly.'

Drinkwater grunted assent and gave the requisite orders.

Before the last of the daylight was leached out of the sky the launch and both cutters lay alongside, stores aboard and crews told off. The sentinels stood vigilant, their muskets loaded, primed and with fresh flints new-fitted, and the officers had been ordered to maintain a keen-eyed watch. Drinkwater was too old an officer, and too good a fencer, to sleep well with his guard down.

He was very tired, tired beyond what the exertions of the day justified. Perhaps it was age, or the strain of rubbing shoulders with Morris in this quotidian way. Morris had proved an expert pilot for the place and, Drinkwater was reluctantly compelled to admit, appeared to have justified all his claims made at Penang. If only this were the place . . .

Drinkwater closed his eyes. The last thing he heard before sleep claimed him was the gentle knock of oars on thole pins as a guard boat rowed watch about the ship.

He slept as he rarely slept, deeply. The near-silence of the anchored ship released his nerves so that nature overcame his seaman's instincts. He did not hear the sudden roar of torrential rain that abruptly opened like the sluice gates of heaven. It drowned the watch, the heavy drops bouncing off the wooden decks so that a ghostly mist seemed to rise a foot from the planking. It pummelled the toiling oarsmen in the guard boat that laboured the small hours through under Midshipman Dutfield's command, beating them into inactivity and forcing them to crouch, dull-witted in the drifting boat.

It stopped almost as suddenly as it had begun. Those on duty gasped with the relief, blew the droplets off their noses and scraped back the hair from their foreheads, shivering in the chill. It was some time after the air cleared before anyone discovered what had happened under the cover of the downpour.

It took Frey a further five full minutes to coax Drinkwater into wakefulness.

'What is it?' Drinkwater was dazed by the depth of his sleep.
'Sir, the boats, the launch and cutters . . .'
'What about them?'
'They are missing!'

The Bronze-bound Chests

'*What*?'

Drinkwater was awake now, scrambling out of his cot and reaching for his breeches. 'Where's the guard boat? How the devil did the boats break adrift?'

'They didn't, sir,' said Frey unhappily, 'they were cut adrift.'

'*Cut*?' He paused, thinking furiously. There was little doubt but what *that* meant. 'Turn up the hands, muster the ship's company at once, and pass word for my coxswain!'

Drinkwater finished dressing as *Patrician* came alive to the shouts and pipings of the duty bosun's mate. Two hours before dawn her people were hustled unceremoniously out of their hammocks.

'Pass word for my coxswain!' Drinkwater roared the command at the bulkhead and heard it taken up by the sentry beyond. He cast angrily about for a lost shoe. Mullender answered the summons.

'I sent for Tregembo, man, not you!'

Mullender's face seemed to tremble in the lantern light. The cares of endless servitude had removed all traces of individuality from its customary mien so that Drinkwater took his distress for a trick of the guttering flame he held up.

'S . . . sir . . .' Mullender was stuttering, a blob of saliva gleaming wetly on his stubbled chin.

'What the hell is it?' Drinkwater spotted the lost shoe and bent to pull it on.

'Tregembo, sir . . .'

Drinkwater stood. The ship was growing quiet again, evidence that her company were standing shivering on deck.

'Well?'

In a moment Frey or Dutfield would come down and report the lower deck cleared.

'He's missing, sir.'

'What d'you mean he's missing? How the devil d'you know?'

Cut boat-painters, deserters, Tregembo missing . . . what the deuce did it mean? They were taking a damned long time to count heads. How many had run?

Suddenly he had no more patience to wait the conventional summons. Shoving poor Mullender aside he made for the ladder.

He met Fraser in the act of turning from the last divisional report.

'Ship's company all accounted for, sir, except Mullender and Tregembo.'

'Mullender's in my cabin . . .'

The dark pits of Fraser's eyes stared from the pale oval of his face. Was Fraser implying Tregembo had absconded? Slashed the painters of the boats and disappeared? What was it the orientalists called it? Running *amok* . . . had Tregembo run *amok*?

'Are you certain you have accounted for every man? In this darkness one could answer for another.'

'Certain, sir. I've had the divisional officers check each man individually.'

That accounted for the delay. But Drinkwater was too dumbfounded to accept Tregembo was responsible. He opened his mouth to inveigh against the inefficiency of the guard boat when Fraser pre-empted him.

'He must have gone in the rain, sir. Frey said you couldn't see the hand in front o' your face, and the noise and wind were terrific.'

Drinkwater noticed the sodden decks and dripping ropes for the first time. But not Tregembo . . .

And then a thought struck him.

'Morris! Has Morris been called?'

'Er . . .'

No one had called the passenger, but he could not have failed to have heard the noise, nor have resisted the impulse to see what had provoked it. And even if he had not turned out himself, he would certainly have sent his catamite to spy.

'Mr Frey!'

'Sir?'

'Check the master's cabin. See if Mr Morris is there!'

'Yes, sir.'

Drinkwater paced across the quarterdeck. The entire ship's company waited, the men forward, heaped in a great wide-eyed pile across the booms, indistinguishable as individuals, but potent in their mass. Beside and behind him stood the rigid lines of marines and more casual grouping of the officers. Only Drinkwater moved, measuring his paces with the awful feeling that he was on the brink of something, without quite knowing what it was . . .

Frey's returning footsteps pounded on the ladder and Drinkwater already knew he was right in his suspicions.

'Gone, sir . . . taken his effects and gone . . .'

'What about those chests?'

'Didn't see them, sir, but,' Frey gasped from his exertion, 'I didn't search his cabin properly . . .'

'No matter. Mr Mount!'

'Sir?' The marine lieutenant stepped forward. He was in his night-shirt but wore baldric and hanger.

'Which of your men was on duty at Morris's door?'

'I . . .' Mount drew a step forward and lowered his voice. 'I withdrew the sentry there, sir . . . I had not thought him to be necessary after the cordiality you showed Mr Morris and he was removed from the presence of Captain Rakitin. I beg your pardon . . .'

'God damn it, Mount, *cordiality?* God's bones, you had no

authority! No orders to . . . to do such a thing!' Drinkwater met Mount's confidential tone with his own muted fury. 'You have let me down, sir . . .'

'Sir, I beg your pardon . . .' The agony of Mount's sincerity twisted the stock phrase. 'I merely thought . . .'

Recriminations were of no avail now and in his heart Drinkwater perceived the logic of Mount's misplaced initiative. It was not really the marine officer's fault. How could he have communicated his worst fears when he had not admitted them to himself? In any case the time for dithering was past. He raised his voice: 'Get your men to turn the ship inside out. I want every store and locker thoroughly searched. I want to know if any clue exists as to where the three missing men have gone . . .'

He called for the purser and surgeon to get their keys and assist. What he did not say was that he sought the body of his coxswain.

'Mr Frey, get a fresh crew told off for the barge. The minute you can see what you are doing I want you to carry out a search for those boats. Mr Fraser, you will remain here with the people until Mount's search is completed. Then you may pipe 'em below.' He paused, considering addressing the patient multitude that still waited, then thought better of it. Instead he caught sight of Ballantyne's figure in the gloom.

'Mr Ballantyne, you attend me. Do you get a lantern upon the instant.'

'Aye, aye, sir.'

He waited for Ballantyne to return, remarking to Fraser, 'Tregembo's a victim, Mr Fraser, not a causative factor in this mystery. Morris is a man of consummate evil. Tregembo and I knew him thirty years ago. We may find Tregembo on board, in which case he will be dead. But we may yet find him alive, for Morris could not have got far in a cutter with only a boy to help him . . .'

'I don't understand, sir, are you suggesting . . . ?'

But Fraser was denied a word of explanation, for Drinkwater, seeing Ballantyne with a lantern, disappeared below. He led the master to the cabin Ballantyne himself should

174

rightfully have occupied, had the accommodation aboard *Patrician* not been so disrupted.

'Hold the lantern up.'

Drinkwater examined the louvred door, then pushed it open. There were no signs of struggle. Morris's cot was rumpled, a single sheet thrown aside. The boy's bedroll almost bore the curled, foetal shape of the creature. A robe, a heavy brocaded mantle of crimson silk lay in a crumpled heap, the only sign of hurried departure, but the heavy leather portmanteau with which Morris had come aboard was empty, its lid flung back and its interior void. The smell of opium, which was for Drinkwater the very scent of Morris's corruption, filled the stale air in the tiny cabin.

'Lower,' Drinkwater commanded, bending and wrenching open the lockers built below the cot. The lantern light fell on the dull gleam of brass locks and bronze banding.

'Ahhh . . .' Ballantyne could hold his tongue no longer.

'D'you have a pistol, Mr Ballantyne?'

'In my cabin, sir . . .'

'Get it,' Drinkwater snapped, adding 'loaded . . . here, give me the lantern.'

He set the lantern on the deck as Ballantyne scrambled off excitedly in search of his pistol. Reaching into the locker Drinkwater's hand found the corner of a chest and dragged it out of the locker beside the lantern. It was heavy, very heavy. He struggled with the second and was panting slightly as Ballantyne returned. He had Mount with him.

'I've found nothing, sir,' said the marine officer.

'It's loaded and primed, sir. Shall I?'

'Yes.'

Drinkwater drew back into the doorway and felt Mount's breath on his neck. Ballantyne squeezed himself into a corner of the cabin and held the pistol with both hands, arms extended. It was a heavy, double-barrelled weapon. Ballantyne's thumbs cocked the hammers. He braced himself. Drinkwater saw for the first time that the bronze bands on the chests were low reliefs of fantastically writhing dragons. Each lock was shaped in the head of a Chinese lion, their hasps of steel.

Ballantyne squeezed the trigger of the first barrel. The hammer struck the frizzen and the brief flash became a sharp bang that momentarily deafened them in the confined space. The small discharge of smoke cleared to reveal the first lock shattered. Shifting his aim Ballantyne blew the second apart.

'Reload,' commanded Drinkwater. 'Your hanger, Mount.'

Drinkwater took the marine officer's sword and inserted its point under the bent hasp of the lock and twisted it. Mount drew his breath in at the outrageous use of his prized weapon.

Damn Mount! Half of this was his fault!

The lock fell to the deck and Drinkwater attacked the second; it too gave way.

'Ready, sir.' Ballantyne raised the pistol to repeat the process on the second chest.

'Wait!'

Drinkwater gave a final jerk with Mount's sword and passed it backwards without turning. He felt a mean satisfaction at the damage he had inflicted to the perfection of its *pointe*. Then, with both hands, he lifted the curved lid of the chest. He had expected the glitter of silver or even the soft gleam of gold.

'What the hell . . . ?'

Drinkwater ignored the comments of the impatiently watching officers and put out a hand. The dull metallic sheen resolved itself into irregular lumps of mineral. As he lifted one and half turned to show it to Mount and Ballantyne he felt his hand move under a curious impulse.

It was irresistibly drawn towards the blued steel barrels of Ballantyne's pistol.

'Lodestone, gentlemen,' he said, standing and tossing the lump of magnetic ore back where it came from.

Blow-pipe Creek

'It's pointless going any further, Belchambers, put your helm down.' Frey turned aft from his position in the bow of the barge. 'This is a cul-de-sac.' He slapped the insect stabbing his cheek and swore as the mosquito buzzed away unharmed. The dry leaves of the mangroves plucked at him, like the claws of hideous succubi in a nightmare.

'Backwater larboard, pull starboard.' Belchambers was having difficulty turning the barge in the root-choked gullet, a green and slimy inlet that wound out of the bay and into the jungle. It was one of the innumerable such creeks that they had attempted to penetrate since dawn.

Already the sun was lifting above the shelter of the over-hanging branches, and the coils of mist that had clung like samite to the water were evaporating. Occasional birds, bright flashes of brilliant hue, whirred across the thin finger of water, shrieking or rasping alarm with a noise that had, at first, frightened them with its raucous suddenness. When they rested upon their oars they could hear the strange burp of trumpet fish coming to them through the planking of the boat and the distant chatter of monkeys was once interrupted by the sullen roar of a tiger cheated of its prey.

'It's no use . . . there's nothing here . . .'

The heat was filling the air with a weight of its own. The men were sodden with their own sweat and Frey's shirt clung to him like the dress of a Parisian courtesan. The effects of the early breakfast and the Spanish *aguardiente* with which the boat's crew had broken their fast were wearing off.

'Give way . . .'

'Look, sir!'

Belchambers's order, partially obeyed but ignored by two men who had seen the same thing, caused a moment's confusion.

'What is it?' Frey asked sharply, starting round.

'There, sir. Under that branch . . .'

Frey and Belchambers stared in the indicated direction. It was almost submerged. Just the upper curve of it, with the notch cut for a sculling oar, showed vermilion above the murky water. It might have been a dead bough but it was the scarlet transom of the red cutter, its stern painted for easy identification at a distance. It was no more than ten yards from them, sunk beneath the overhanging branches of a mangrove bush.

'We'll need kegs to refloat it . . . this bottom's so damned soft . . .' said Frey, probing with a boat-hook.

'Might work a spar underneath, sir, and jack 'er up on this 'ere root, like . . .'

'Damned good idea, Carey,' remarked Belchambers eagerly, 'let's try with the boat-mast, Frey . . .'

'*Mister* Frey, if you don't mind,' said Frey archly. 'Very well . . .'

'Hey, sir . . . look!'

They could see the tip of a pair of thole pins just breaking the surface a few yards further into the swamp.

'It's the launch!' Frey and Belchambers chorused simultaneously.

'But *why*, sir?'

Fraser waved his hands, pacing about the cabin, unable to keep the seat Drinkwater had provided for him. Quilhampton and Mount sat watching, while Drinkwater stood silhouetted against the stern windows, staring moodily at the green

178

curtain of jungle that stretched across their field of view. Ballantyne was supervising the rigging of a spring upon the anchor cable, sounds of which came from beyond the bulkhead.

Drinkwater appeared to ignore Fraser's question. Mount, still smarting from his own idiocy, sat silent. Quilhampton knew better than to speak. He guessed something of what Drinkwater was thinking; he had been aboard *Hellebore*.

'I don't understand why this man Morris . . .' Fraser began again, jerking his hands like a hatter with the shakes. But it was not mercurial poisoning that motivated the first lieutenant, it was the incomprehension of an unimaginative man. This time Drinkwater responded. Turning from the windows, he cut Fraser short.

'*I* don't understand precisely *why* this man Morris chooses to act the way he does, Mr Fraser.' He lowered his voice which was strained with a tension that Quilhampton knew to be fear for the life of old Tregembo. 'Sit down, sit down . . . you see, gentlemen, I have cause now to believe that this man Morris quite deliberately engineered the separation of *Patrician* from her station on the night of the storm of thunder and lightning. In short I have been fooled – mightily fooled.' Drinkwater paused, inwardly seething.

'Oh yes,' he went on, looking round at their astonished faces, 'believe me, he is quite capable of such an act, for I knew him many years ago. We were midshipmen together. There is no need for details, except to tell you that we formed a mutual dislike; he affected a grievance against me for some imagined advantage I possessed over him. I was, it is true, briefly preferred before him . . .'

Drinkwater broke off. It was impossible to tell these men who stared at him with wrapt attention that Morris had, in his twisted and perverse way, declared a desire for the young Drinkwater. The thought was repulsive to him even now.

But he had to tell them something of the man's character, if only to prepare them for what they were up against.

'He was, is, also a sodomite, a sodomite of a particularly

179

cruel disposition. Mr Q may recall his conduct aboard *Hellebore*, for we had the misfortune to meet again in ninety-nine. Morris corrupted a midshipman who was later drowned.'

The sceptical Fraser turned to look at Quilhampton who gave a corroborative nod.

'Prior, however, to this, while still aboard *Cyclops*, Morris was involved in a cabal of similarly inclined men. One of them was later tossed overboard. Tregembo was involved in this rough justice. I don't know whether Morris knew that, I suspect not, but Tregembo knew enough about Morris and was loyal enough to me to have risked his life . . .'

Drinkwater paused and drew a hand across his perspiring brow. 'Perhaps Morris simply took him to man a pair of oars . . . I don't know . . .'

'You say Morris took *him*, sir,' said Fraser, 'suppose Tregembo took Morris.'

'That is possible, sir,' added Quilhampton hurriedly, 'Tregembo might well have done that. He came to me once, sir, weeks ago . . .' he faltered.

'Go on,' snapped Drinkwater, 'you interest me.'

'Well, sir, he came to me,' Quilhampton frowned, trying to recall the circumstances, 'asking if I had recognised Morris when he came aboard at Whampoa. I said yes, and Tregembo reminded me of the character he had assumed aboard the *Hellebore*. Then he told me something about your earlier association . . .'

'Aboard *Cyclops*?'

'Exactly. He seemed to want to enlist me in some way.'

'Enlist you?'

'Yes. He said he knew Morris would – what was the word? Spavin you.' Quilhampton paused and looked down. 'I'm afraid I told him the whole thing was nonsense. Rather let him down, sir.'

'Was there anything else?' Drinkwater quizzed.

'No, sir, only that I believe words to have passed between Tregembo and Morris. Perhaps Tregembo chose last night to act, to protect you.'

'It makes a kind of sense,' said Mount, speaking for the first time, an edge of sarcasm in his voice, 'but it begs a lot of questions.'

'What questions?' Quilhampton asked defensively.

'Why Tregembo should choose last night; why, if he contemplated some violent act, he had to make off in a boat which he could hardly have handled alone; and why he should cut all the others adrift. It makes no sense for Tregembo to run off into the jungle denying us our boats.'

'But it is exactly what Tregembo *would* do, Mount, don't you see?' argued Quilhampton. 'Precisely to prevent us from following . . .'

'That's too fantastical,' Mount said dismissively, the pragmatic soldier routing the quixotic young lieutenant. They fell silent.

'Is it too fantastical, gentlemen,' said Drinkwater slowly, 'to suggest that Morris separated *Patrician* from the convoy out of more than mere malice aforethought towards me? Is it too fantastical to suggest that . . .'

Drinkwater paused at the knock on the door. 'Enter! Ah, Mr Ballantyne, I trust the spring is now clapped on the cable?'

'Yes, sir.'

'Very well. Please take a seat. I am theorising, please bear with me.' Drinkwater continued. 'As I say, is it not possible that Morris knew of our progress? He was a seaman, remember, and could, knowing our position, detach us from the convoy when he wished.'

'You mean he knew the convoy was to be attacked?' asked an incredulous Fraser.

'I mean he caused it to be attacked.'

'Well done, lads.'

Frey grinned appreciatively at the gasping men. Two hours of furious activity had refloated the red cutter. By dint of hard levering they had got her stem on a mangrove root and, by placing the barge's bottom boards underfoot, managed with much awkwardness, to find a footing themselves sufficient to work the boat so that its entire gunwhale was lapping the surface of the viscid water.

By jamming a thole pin into the empty bung-hole, they had been able to bale and now she floated, not quite empty and low in the water, astern of the barge. Sodden and mud-besplattered, the men tumbled back into the barge and got out their oars.

'Give way, Mr Belchambers, back to the ship for reinforcements, some kegs and lashings, and we'll have that launch up in a trice.'

With renewed hope the seamen bent to their oars.

'I'll see you get a tot for your trouble, lads,' said Frey magnanimously, raising grins of anticipation.

'I never thought I'd say it, sir,' said Carey, the man who had spotted the scuttled boat, 'but I'd rather have a tumbler o' water . . .'

A silence greeted Drinkwater's hypothesis. Fraser crossed then recrossed his legs in an unconscious gesture of disbelief. Eventually Mount spoke.

'That's rather unlikely, sir.'

'Is it?' Drinkwater looked at Ballantyne. 'Mr Ballantyne, how familiar were you with Midshipman Chirkov?'

Ballantyne, a little mystified at the direction of the discussion, rose like a fish to a fly. 'Count Chirkov did me the honour of requesting instruction upon navigation, sir.'

'And you discussed such matters as the navigation of the ship?'

'Yes.' Ballantyne's head shook slightly, a note of uncertainty in his voice.

'To the extent of disclosing our position?'

'Well, to the extent of illustrating my talks about the day's work, the traverse and so forth, yes . . .' He stared about him. The faces of the other officers were turned towards him, their eyes hardening as he spoke. 'Have I committed some indiscretion?'

'Unwittingly, I think you have. Chirkov, by your own admission, was able to keep Morris informed of our position.

We follow a predictable route, it was only necessary for Morris to detach us near the Natunas for his allies to attack. You see Morris had a most detailed chart of this area. I caught only a glimpse of it, and accepted his assurance that Hennessey's was adequate enough for our navigation.'

'And Chirkov interfered with the compass too?' asked the embarrassed Ballantyne.

Drinkwater nodded. 'I believe so, he too was capable of such a thing. Then Morris, knowing of my intention to return and search for the *Guilford*, persuaded me to accept his own offer of assistance . . .'

'And led us here?' said Mount, only half-questioningly. 'But why?'

'Because somewhere out there in that wilderness is, if not *Guilford*, then the fruit of a long matured plan . . .'

'I don't understand,' puzzled Fraser.

'*Guilford* was carrying thirty thousand sterling.'

Whistles of wonder came from his listeners. '*Thirty thousand . . . !*'

'A prodigious sum, you'll allow, and Morris had planned to seize it at a time when the naval command on the East Indies station was changing, when the Selectmen were making such a racket in Macao and Canton that Admiral Drury was distracted and had no spare frigates to escort the small and vulnerable convoy that Morris *knew* would get out of the Pearl River before the negotiations reached stalemate. That is why the arrangements were made for the specie to travel aboard the Indiaman and not a warship, why Callan was reluctant to admit he had a large sum in case I was jealous and insisted on carrying it for my percentage.'

'*Our* arrival threatened Morris's plan but *my* arrival gave him an opportunity for personal vengeance. He knew the point at which the convoy would be attacked, it was only necessary to detach us from it to accomplish both his basic plan and my own professional ruin.' He looked round, watching their faces for acceptance of his theory. 'And very soon,' he added, 'I expect an attack.'

'Who by, sir? asked Fraser, still unconvinced. 'And who are these allies you speak of?'

'Sea-Dyaks,' snapped Quilhampton with a sharp air of impatience at the first lieutenant's obtuseness.

'As the hoplites,' agreed Mount with greater perception, 'but by what power does this Morris bend them to his will?'

'Sir, look!'

Mount's rhetorical question went unanswered, for Quilhampton was pointing excitedly through the stern windows to which Drinkwater had his back. He turned. Frey was standing in the bow of the barge, waving his arms above his head. Even at that distance they could see his shirt was torn to the waist and the thighs of his breeches were dark with mud. Behind the barge, towing on its painter and still somewhat waterlogged, followed the red cutter.

Drinkwater pulled himself laboriously over the last of the futtock shrouds and into the main-top. He paused for a minute, unseen from the deck, and caught his breath. He was exposed fully to the noonday glare of the sun, and the heat and exertion made him dizzy. The heavy cross timbers of the semi-circular fighting top were warm to the touch, the iron eyebolts and fittings that secured the dark hemp rigging burnt his fingers when he touched them. Across the after side of the platform ran a low barricade terminating in mountings for two small swivel guns. He pulled the telescope from his belt, levelled it along a swivel crutch and painstakingly surveyed the surroundings.

Beyond the indentation of the coast, the sea was vast and empty, reflecting the blue of the sky and rippled here and there by catspaws of wind. To the west the prominence of Tanjong Sirik lay blue on the horizon, its distal point curled upwards as if shrivelling in the heat, a blue tongue shimmering below it – the effect of refraction, a mirage, giving the illusion of the cape being elevated above the horizon.

To the north-east the coast continued, jungle lapping the ocean with its scalloped edge of swamp. To the east and south the horizon was bounded by a spine of hills and mountains above which white coils of cloud drifted lazily upwards. Here and there spurs ran off this distant range, light green and with intervening blue furrows where, Drinkwater presumed, hidden rivers poured from the uplands. These streams with their suggestions of plashing waterfalls and cool, silver torrents sliding over smooth pebbles brought a sudden longing to him. But his shirt stuck clammily to his skin and the rivers vanished below the dark mantle of the jungle. It was not all mangroves. He could see some five miles away the different foliage of higher, more majestic species: banyan, tamarind and peepul trees, and the fronded heads of nipah palms. But in the end the mangrove swallowed everything, obscuring the streams, now become sluggish rivers that capitulated to inlets of the salt sea, to mix in the creeks and islets below Tanjong Sirik in a complex tangle of nature that defied penetration.

But Morris *had* penetrated it. Somewhere in that green desert Morris waited expectantly with Tregembo as his prisoner. Drinkwater knew with the clarity of absolute certainty that Tregembo had been taken not merely as an oarsman, but as a lure. Morris had cut loose and sunk the boats simply to delay Drinkwater, for he knew Drinkwater's character well enough to depend upon him following, just as he had worked upon old Tregembo with subtle cunning. Drinkwater could not guess with what ploy Morris had tempted Tregembo, but he knew that the Cornishman would have gone with Morris and his catamite, not in fear of Morris's pistol at his brain, but in the foolish conviction that he could save Drinkwater and that he could turn the tables on Morris before Drinkwater himself was lured to his death. But Tregembo could not have known that the rain and the squall would have covered the approach of Morris's Dyak allies and aided their retreat with all the boats so that the presence of an oarsman was barely necessary.

And now Drinkwater scanned the jungle, aware that angry pursuit would be a trap, that his seamen would flounder up every blind alley of a creek, hot, tired, bitten and, in a day or so, utterly demoralised, easy targets for the deadly blow-pipes of the Dyaks.

He was aware of a quickening feeling of panic and forced his mind to concentrate on other matters, matters that might legitimately justify him in sending his boats into that hostile and unfamiliar wilderness. But there was no sign of *Guilford*. Carefully, fighting down the impatient urge to be impotently active, he rescanned the jungle, systematically working over it. Pausing occasionally to wipe and rest his straining eye, he studied every exposed inch of jungle . . .

Nothing . . .

He blew out air and settled back against the mast. He used to sit in *Cyclops's* top like this, learning how to make a carrick bend and a stuns'l sheet bend, and how to whip and point a rope, while Tregembo, a red-faced topman of near thirty summers, good-naturedly corrected his fumbling fingers. This had been his battle station and he had fought his first action from such a place, in Rodney's Moonlight Battle off Cape St Vincent.

January 1780.

It was all so long ago. Tregembo and then Elizabeth . . . and then Tregembo and his Susan, waspish Susan who was now cook to the Drinkwater ménage . . .

God! He had to do something! Something for Susan and something for Elizabeth. He could not sit here and let the sun burn him up, no matter what the odds Morris had stacked against him.

He drew the sleeve of his shirt across his forehead, blinked his eyes and stared again over the undulating plain of tree-tops.

Suddenly he clapped his glass to his eye. Damn! The bloody thing had become unfocused. He twisted the two tubes, muttering at his own ineptitude, his sweaty hands slipping on the warm brass.

'Yes!' He felt the sudden surge of his heart. He had been hoping, hoping for the sight of an ill-concealed mast, or the thin blue column of cooking smoke, but they were too cunning for that!

He felt like laughing, so great was his sensation of relief, but the thought of Tregembo sobered him. He lowered the glass, his head unmoving. Could he see them without the glass . . . ?

Yes.

He leaned over the edge of the top. 'Mr Dutfield! In my cabin, next to the chronometer you'll find my pocket compass . . .'

He waited, fixing his eyes upon the vague and distant shapes, so tiny, so indicative . . .

He felt the faint vibration of Dutfield's ascent.

'Here, sir.'

Drinkwater took the offered brass instrument, snapped up the vanes and sighted through the slits. Yes, he could see them quite well now . . .

'Beg pardon, sir, may I ask what you have seen?'

Carefully Drinkwater adjusted his head and made sure of the bearing.

'What I can see, Mr Dutfield, is . . . is . . .' he floundered for a phrase worthy of the occasion. 'What I'd call an intervention of nature, yes, that's it, an avifaunal intervention of nature.'

Dutfield's blank look made him grin as he threw his leg over the edge of the top and sought with his foot for the top futtock shroud.

'Steady . . . keep still, Carey . . . that's it . . . bail some more.'

The launch just floated. The slop of water in it made its motion sluggish under the influence of free-surface effect and occasionally it lurched so that water poured back in over the gunwhale. The quick righting moment exerted by the nimble Carey corrected this, restabilising the thing, and, as it rolled the other way, Carey steadied it, feet spread apart, arms outstretched, like a circus rope-walker.

Men floundered alongside, half swimming, half walking in the soft, insubstantial ooze, working the rope net beneath the launch's keel as it stirred itself an inch off the bottom.

'Pull it tight!' Frey held a corner and waved to the barge,

lying ten yards away. 'Let's have those kegs, and lively, before we're stuck in this shit!'

They lashed the kegs, already haltered, as low as they could force them, fighting their buoyancy until at last the thing was done. The waterlogged launch lay within the net which in turn was buoyed up by the hard-bunged kegs.

'Right. All aboard!'

They floundered back to the barge where they clambered in over the transom. Frey was last aboard. He took the launch's painter from his teeth and handed it to Belchambers. The midshipman took a turn round the barge's after thwart.

'Very well . . . give way!'

It was a hard slog. The weight of the launch was terrific and, unless they maintained a steady drag, the water in the launch slopped into her stern, reducing her after freeboard.

Leaves brushed them, dead branches tore at them as they dragged their burden out into the wider stream. Already the sun was dropping fast.

'Back by sunset, lads, come on,' Frey urged. 'A steady pull.'

There was a sudden clatter forward. Frey leant over the side and tried to grab the oar that slid past them.

'Carey! What the fucking hell . . . ?'

'He's dead, sir! Got a fuckin' arrer stuck in 'im!'

But only Belchambers saw the gleam of brown flesh as an arm was withdrawn, and a sudden fear chilled him to silence.

The Gates of the Fortress

'Yes, I know what it is . . . do not touch the point, it may still bear poison. It is a dart from a *sumpitan*, a blow-pipe.'

'Thank you, Mr Ballantyne,' said Drinkwater.

'It is very effective, sir, and dangerous. The Dyaks use them. This man Carey was killed by Dyaks. They also carry the *parang*, a sword with which they are able to inflict a terrible wound, and they are famed for their skill with the *kris*, a knife with an undulating blade.'

'Have you fought them before, Mr Ballantyne?'

'In a hand-to-hand action only once, though I have been attacked by them more often. They will not press an attack if met with resolution, but resort to cover and strategies.'

'Stratagems, Mr Ballantyne,' corrected Mount with military punctiliousness.

'Stratagems then,' said Ballantyne, petulant at this humiliation.

'We are indebted to you, Mr Ballantyne,' Drinkwater soothed. He looked down at the chart spread before him and the pencilled line of his bearing: it petered out in a vast blank area. 'Now oblige me by listening carefully . . .'

It was that period of the crepuscular hour that nautical astronomists call 'nautical twilight', when the sun is twelve degrees below the horizon, rising to 'civil twilight' at six degrees and the full splendour of the dawn. Already the world had lost its monotones, the first shades of green were emerging from the variant greys, dull as slate still, but discernible to the acutely trained sailor's eye. Drinkwater reached the main-top.

'Morning, sir.' Belchambers greeted him with a whisper and his damp party stirred, three seamen and four marines who had slept at their action stations.

'Mornin', Mr Belchambers. Pray let me rest my glass . . .'

The whole ship's company had slept on their arms. Below, the boats were hoisted out of the water, though ready provisioned and prepared after their adventure of the previous day. Boarding nettings stretched upwards from the rail triced out to the yard-arms ready to catch any attempts to sneak aboard *Patrician* while the ship herself, her guns loaded though withdrawn behind closed ports, lay with her broadside facing the land, a spring tensioned upon her anchor cable.

Drinkwater peered southwards in the direction of his bearing. The landscape was shrouded by thin veils of mist that lay more densely in long, pale tendrils, winding across the lower parts of the swamps. In this light they seemed to stretch into infinity. Somewhere in the jungle a tribe of monkeys stirred with a sudden chattering.

'Morning, Belchambers.' Frey clambered up after Drinkwater who was already busy with his compass. Frey produced his drawing block and conferred with the captain. Drinkwater pointed out the wider streaks of fog that lay in definite lines over the mangroves.

'Those fog-banks,' Drinkwater explained, 'lie most densely over the channels of the waterways through this morass. See there,' he pointed, 'how that one leads south, then swings slightly east, bends sharply and runs to . . . here, look . . .'

Frey bent to stare through the vanes of the pocket compass.

'Runs to intersect with a bearing of south-east a-quarter south . . .'

'Got it, sir.'

'Then sketch it!'

Only the scratch of Frey's pencil could be heard. Drinkwater, holding the compass so that Frey could see it, put out his free hand to lean on the mast. Where yesterday the iron-work had burned his hand, it was now cold with condensation.

'Sir . . .'

'Pray be quiet, Mr Belchambers, and allow . . .' Drinkwater broke off and followed Belchambers's pointing hand. He could see the dark shapes detach from the jungle, see the faint white rings along their sides where the Dyaks plied their paddles.

'I'll go, sir!' The topman had reached out for the backstay even before Drinkwater had opened his mouth. Silently he lowered himself hand-over-hand to the deck. Looking down, Drinkwater saw him alert Fraser and the news galvanised the first lieutenant. He saw men radiate outwards to warn the ship, heard the low, urgent voice of the Scotsman and someone below shush another into silence.

'In the event of an alarm I want absolute silence preserved,' Drinkwater had ordered. He wondered how much of his own idle chatter the Dyaks had heard, for sound carried for miles over still water.

As if to echo his thoughts another burst of chattering came from the distant jungle. More Dyaks, or the cries of wakening monkeys?

'Finished, sir . . .'

Frey straightened up. Drinkwater shut his compass with an over-loud snap. He pointed at the approaching *praus*. Frey nodded and Drinkwater jerked his head. Frey swung himself over the edge of the top.

'Good luck, Mr Belchambers,' Drinkwater hissed, and followed Frey.

'Thank you, sir,' replied the boy. He was thinking of Carey slumped forward in the barge and the smooth muscled flesh of the brown arm that had dealt the stealthy blow.

Drinkwater reached the deck and turned. He was almost certain his movements would have been seen and had been conscious, in his descent, that his body offered a target for the deadly *sumpitan*.

'Here, sir . . .'

Mullender held out sword and pistols.

'Thank you,' he muttered; it had been Tregembo's duty. The thought filled him with a fierce desire for action. He joined Fraser by the hammock nettings.

All along the barricade the dull white shapes of men in breeches and shirts told where Mount's marines stood to, their loaded muskets presented. They were to fire the fusillade that gave the signal for fire at will.

'Your privilege, Mount,' Drinkwater hissed.

'Sir . . . they seem to be hesitating . . .' Mount's head was raised, watching the boats as they stilled and gathered together. Then Drinkwater saw the sudden flurry of energy. White whirled along their sides as, after a brief pause, the Dyaks dug their paddles into the water and their boats seemed to leap forward.

At the same moment there burst forth an ululating chant as each man wailed simultaneously, the sharp exhalation adding power to his effort. In addition to this outburst of noise, shrieks and the crashing reverberations of gongs disturbed the tranquillity of the anchorage. The air was filled too with brief whirring sounds and the clatter of darts as a battery of blow-pipes were employed. Most struck the rigging and fell harmlessly to the deck with a rattle.

'Fire!'

Mount's voice exploded with pent-up force. The spluttering crackle of musketry illuminated the rail. Above their heads the vicious roar of the swivel guns in the tops spat langridge at the attackers and then the wildly aimed, depressed muzzles of *Patrician*'s main batteries trundled out through their ports and added their smoke and fire and iron to the horrendous noise.

The air was filled with the sharp smell of powder and white columns of water rose a short distance off the ship, but Drinkwater was aware that the boats still came on. He could see details clearly now in the swiftly growing light; the red jackets of the warriors, the men at the paddles and the faces of men with blow-pipes to their mouths. Others stood, whirling slings about their heads, and he was assailed by a foul, acrid stench as the stink-pots flew aboard. They were lobbed over the rail and came to rest, giving off choking fumes of dense, sulphureous gases which stung eyes and skin.

The *praus* were closing in now and the marines were standing, leaning outboard to fire down into them.

'Drop shot into 'em!' roared Drinkwater, hefting heavy carronade balls out of the adjacent garlands and hoping to sink the *praus* as their occupants sought a foothold on *Patrician*'s side.

'Won't press an attack, eh?' Mount called, turning to snap orders at Corporal Grice. A marine fell back with a dart protruding from his throat. The poor man's hand tried to tear it free but its venom acted quickly and he fell, twitching on the deck. 'Don't expose your men, Grice,' Mount bellowed above the shrieks and gongs. 'You too, Blixoe.'

A fire party ran aft attempting to deal with the noxious stink-pots; a second marine fell back, crashing into Drinkwater. He caught the man, then laid him gently on the deck. A short spear protruded from his chest. Drinkwater took up the man's musket and tried, through the smoke, to take stock of the situation.

Below, their cannon now useless, the Patricians stabbed at the Dyaks with boarding pikes, rammers and worms. One by one Quilhampton got his guns inboard and the ports closed. But something was wrong.

'Mr Ballantyne!'

'Sir?'

The master's eyes were wild with excitement, the whites contrasting vividly with his dusky skin.

'We're swinging. They've cut the spring. And look!'

The Dyaks were swarming over the bow, where the ship was easiest to board.

'Reinforce the fo'c's'le!'

'I understand, sir!'

God! Did the man have to be prolix at a moment like this? Drinkwater tugged at Mount's shoulder, but Mount was already swinging some men into line and Fraser had seen them too.

Drinkwater was still holding the dead marine's musket. The thing was unloaded, but its weight and the wickedly gleaming bayonet recommended it. He ran forward.

'Come on!'

The party defending the fo'c's'le had been beaten back. They were in disarray and retiring along the gangways. Drinkwater, Fraser and Mount rushed forward yelling, as though the noise itself formed some counter-attack to the awful hubbub of the Dyaks.

Their enemy were lithe and strong, men with short, powerful limbs and gracefully muscled bodies who swung their terrible *parangs* to deadly effect. This was no fencing match but a hacking, stabbing game and Drinkwater was grateful for the heavy musket as he leaned forward, stamping his leading foot and lunging.

There was blood on his arm from somewhere and he felt a blow strike his shoulder, but the glimpse of a bared chest received the full power of his driving body and he felt the terrible jar as the bayonet struck bone, scraped downwards and entered the Dyak's belly. Drinkwater wrenched free with the prescribed twist, stamped back, swung half right and thrust again. This time the musket met the heavy weight of a long *parang*. The sword struck it a second time and forced it down. Drinkwater had a sudden glimpse of the *parang* withdrawn, pulled back over the assailant's head as the man prepared for a mighty cut, a curving slash . . .

Drinkwater slewed to the left, following the fall of the musket. But his right arm straightened, the twisted muscles in his shoulder cracking with the speed and strain of the effort. The butt of the musket rose as its muzzle dropped, the heavy wooden club flying up to catch the Dyak's elbow as he cut, forcing the bent arm into its owner's face and crushing the delicate articulation of the joint. The Dyak retreated a little, and Drinkwater swung, swivelling his body as fast as he could, withdrawing his arms parallel to his right flank and then driving the musket forward again. The bayonet entered beneath the Dyak's ribs so that it pierced the heart at its junction with the aorta.

Drinkwater was snarling now, howling with the awful savagery of the business. He stepped forward. He wanted more of this, more to assuage the guilt he felt at Tregembo's disappearance, more to vent the pent-up anger of months, more to remove the obloquy of humiliation he had felt at losing two ships, more to cleanse his soul of the taint of Morris . . .

'They're in full flight now!' It was Ballantyne's voice, Ballantyne covered in blood, his sword-arm sodden with red gore, his face streaked with it where he had wiped his forehead.

Drinkwater leaned on the breech of a chase gun and panted. Turning, he could see the *praus* paddling away from them. A few Dyaks swam, shouting after them. Looking back along *Patrician*'s deck he could see his own dead. Already the wounded were being carried below.

Only on the fo'c's'le had the enemy lodged a footing and now they had gone. He wanted a drink badly.

'You're going to follow 'em, aren't you, sir?' Mount came running up. 'Fraser's already getting the boats down.'

'Yes, of course, Mount. No victory's complete without pursuit.'

They grinned at each other and Mount blew his cheeks out. 'Quite, sir.'

'Very well, Mr Fraser, you know what to do.'

'Aye, sir, but I still think . . .'

'I know you do, and I appreciate it, but I am resolved. We would not be here had not a personal element been involved. Good luck.'

'And you, sir.'

'James . . .' He nodded farewell to Quilhampton who was even more furious than Fraser at being left behind. But with Tregembo gone and he himself thrusting his impetuous head into the lion's den there had to be someone to go home to Hampshire.

'Sir.'

He slid down the man-ropes, found the launch's gunwhale with his feet and made his way aft. Acting Lieutenant Frey looked expectantly from the barge.

'Lead the way!'

The two boats lowered their vertical oars and gave chase after the blue cutter. Drinkwater settled the tiller under his arm and sat back against the transom. Fraser had every right to complain; as first lieutenant any detached operation was his by right to command. It provided him with a chance to distinguish himself, to obtain that step in rank to master and commander and then, if he were lucky, to post-captain. Well, Drinkwater had denied him that right and this was not going to be one of those glorious events that made the pages of the *Gazette* glow with refulgent patriotism. It was going to be a nasty, bloody assault and Drinkwater knew he would be damned lucky to get back at all, let alone unscathed.

That was why he had also left Quilhampton behind. Quilhampton would have followed him and risked himself unnecessarily just as Tregembo had done. If he was killed Drinkwater wanted James Quilhampton to stand protector to Elizabeth and his children, not to mention Susan Tregembo and the legless boy Billy who also formed a part of his private establishment. Besides, Fraser needed adequate support in case he was attacked separately.

In any case Ballantyne seemed eager enough for glory. Let the coxcomb bear the brunt of the attack. Drinkwater stared ahead; it was too soon to see the stern of Ballantyne's cutter, but he did not want the master rushing ahead on his own. He had sent Ballantyne on to try and keep contact with the Dyaks, delaying only long enough to get the boat carronade rigged on its slide in the bow of the launch. Midshipman Dutfield was sorting out cartridges for it at that moment.

Drinkwater tried to calculate how many men he had with him. He had left Mount in support of the ship, but a handful of marines in each boat, their oarsmen and the carronade crew . . .

Perhaps fifty, at the most. He would be limited to a reconnaissance . . . a reconnaissance in force.

The mangroves had closed round them now and he had lost sight of the ship. Ahead of him the barrier of jungle seemed impenetrable. They passed the spot where Frey had recovered the lost boats. Branches snapped astern. The men struggled at the oars as the channel petered out, then they were through. A large white-painted tree reared a huge and twisted bole at an angle out of the ooze. A block hung from it, through which a rope, old and festooned with slimy growth, sagged into the water and lay across perhaps three fathoms of its surface like a snake, then fastened itself to the branches through which they had just forced their way. A cunningly hidden contrivance, thought Drinkwater.

'I think we have just forced the gates of the fortress,' Drinkwater said for the benefit of his toiling boat's crew.

Pursuit

Drinkwater tried to calculate the distance they were travelling, but found it difficult. Though he had a compass he had no watch and therefore, though his men pulled with a steady stroke, no accurate means of charting the seemingly endless corridors of smooth water which led deeper into the jungle. At a rough estimate, he guessed, they must be some four or five miles from *Patrician*, and should be overhauling Ballantyne's boat.

He was increasingly concerned about the master, a feeling that was heightened by the sense of entrapment caused by the surrounding jungle. The white-painted tree and the concealed entrance told him they were on the right trail, confirming, if he glanced at his compass, his observations from the main-top. But the oppressive silence of the vegetation, the increasing density of the mangroves and the brazen heat which increased as the sun climbed into the sky, weighed on him.

Only once had he seen a sign of life. A bright-eyed monkey had peered suddenly and shockingly at him and his cry of alarm was only stifled by the chattering retreat made by the animal. Instead he coughed, to cover his confusion.

Occasionally he stood, peering ahead and seeking evidence of Ballantyne, but the oily water ran on through the overhanging foliage, trailing creepers and burping gently from the unseen activities of the trumpet fish. The sense of oppression,

of being watched, was omnipresent. The men pulled obedi-
ently, but their eyes were downcast or stared apprehensively at
the passing blur of leaves and shadows. If their eyes met
Drinkwater's they looked quickly away. He knew they were as
nervous as kittens. In a little while they would rest on their
oars and he would stoke up their courage from the spirits keg.

Drinkwater was certain now that he would not find *Guilford*
or *Hindoostan* hidden here. They had probably been burnt and
were lying beneath the waters of the anchorage, stripped of
whatever this nest of devils could find useful. He did not like to
contemplate what reserves of powder and shot the Dyaks
might have accrued by such means. The question was, did
they need it for their attacks, for the manufacture of stink-pots
and so on, or had they fortified their stronghold? And if they
had access to powder, they also had access to firearms, for
Guilford had had an arms chest and all her officers had had
sporting guns. The sense of being lured into the mangrove
jungle fastened more firmly on Drinkwater's imagination. The
morning's attack, though it *might* have succeeded and delivered
him a prisoner to Morris, was a feint, a further stratagem
designed to draw Drinkwater in pursuit.

Should he go on?

He could not now abandon Ballantyne.

'Is your gun loaded, Mr Dutfield?' he asked, breaking the
almost intolerable silence at last.

'Yes, sir. Langridge shot.'

'Very well, pull a little harder, my lads, I want to come up
with the other boat.'

Frey saw his intention, pulled to one side and rested his men
at their oars. Drinkwater's launch drew alongside, and as both
crews refreshed themselves and the two boats glided onwards
under their own momentum, he and Frey conferred.

'He's got a long way ahead, sir.'

'My own thoughts exactly. I think we may have lost him . . .'

'I've seen no other channels, sir . . .'

'No; I don't mean in that way, Mr Frey . . .' Drinkwater left
the sentence unfinished. Frey grasped his meaning and

nodded glumly. But they could not abandon the master, although Drinkwater's instincts told him to return to the ship, to work out a better strategy and recruit his strength. He looked at the sky. He could see what he was looking for now in the almost white heat above the jungle.

'We'll continue a little further, Mr Frey. Give way.'

Grunting and sullen, the boats' crews pushed out their oars and bent once more to their task. Fifteen minutes later they discovered Ballantyne.

The creek had opened out into a wide pool into which three other inlets appeared to debouch. Ballantyne's cutter was at the far end, adrift, its oars oddly disposed, some trailing, others sticking upwards, as though their looms were jammed in the bottom boards.

The oarsmen appeared exhausted, slumped over their bristling oars while Ballantyne sat upright in the stern. As the barge and launch came into line abreast, spreading over the greater width of the pool, Drinkwater and Frey both urged their men to greater efforts. Something about the attitude of the cutter's crew combined with the oppressive silence of their surroundings to restrain joyous shouts of recognition. That, and the realisation that it was pointless.

The cutter's crew were dead, dead from a volley of air-blown darts that had silently struck them in their pursuit. Ballantyne's body had endured the added mutilation of throat-slitting; a distinction reserved for the officer whose implication was not lost on Drinkwater.

Horror-struck, the gasping crews of barge and launch lay across their own oar looms, white-faced. Someone threw up, the yellow vomit coiling viscously in the water. For a long moment Drinkwater too fought down the gall rising in his throat, a bilious reaction compounded of revulsion and fear.

'We can't go on, sir,' said Frey, with a sense of relief, 'we don't know which channel to take.' He nodded at the three creeks that wound out of the pool and lost themselves in a tangle of trailing vegetation.

Drinkwater looked up. He could still see that fortuitous

manifestation he had first spotted from *Patrician*. It was less than a long cannon shot away and it was not difficult to guess which creek led to it.

'I wonder how long they towed Ballantyne's boat after they ambushed it?' he said. 'A long way . . . long enough to lure us here, and then they released it when we were confronted with a confusing choice . . .'

'Yes, sir,' Frey agreed hastily, staring round, wondering how many unseen eyes were watching them, waiting to employ their deadly blow-pipes. His eagerness to be off was obvious, as was that of all the others.

With what he knew would be infuriating deliberation, Drinkwater picked up his glass and, focusing it, raked the shadows beneath the overhanging trees for any sign of an enemy. He did not expect to see very much, but a hidden boat or canoe would signal extreme danger. The silence of the jungle remained impenetrable. He closed the glass with a click.

'I believe we are supposed to be scared off, Mr Frey . . . but that channel there', he pointed to a gap in the grey-green tangle of leaves, 'leads to . . .'

To what?

He did not know, had no means of knowing beyond the simple and obvious deduction that somewhere beyond that opening in the dense vegetation lay the answer to the riddle of Morris and the whereabouts of Tregembo.

'To the bastards that did *this*!'

His vehemence raised a grunting response from a few of the more impetuous men.

'How d'you know, sir?'

Frey was ashen-faced, aware that he was, for the first time in his life, confronting authority. Fear had made him suddenly bold, fear and the revelation that Captain Drinkwater was not here the gold-laced and puissant figure whose will directed the *Patrician* and her company. To his keen and artistically respon- sive intelligence, Drinkwater's sharp, vehement outburst only underlined the captain's weakness. To young Frey, Drinkwater at that moment was a rather pathetic man driven on by guilt at the loss of a faithful servant and an obsession with their peculiar passenger. He had learned about Morris from Quilhampton and, as he challenged Drinkwater, he fancied the captain's wounded shoulder sagged more than usual, as though, divested of coat and bullion epaulettes, it was unequal to the weight it bore.

Just as Drinkwater's outburst had stirred a response, so too did Frey's, a buzz of agreement from men who could see no point in going on. Drinkwater's eyes met those of his lieutenant. He knew Frey was no coward, but he also knew that Frey's confrontation was deliberate. For a moment he sat in an almost detached contemplation, his eyes remaining locked on to those of his subordinate. Frey was sweating, the sheen of it curiously obvious on his pale face. Drinkwater grinned suddenly and he was gratified at Frey's astonishment.

'How do I know, Mr Frey? Look!' Drinkwater pointed at the sky. 'An intervention of nature,' he said, deliberately self-mocking.

'Those . . . birds?' The crews of both boats were staring after Drinkwater's pointing arm and Drinkwater could sense the incredulity in all their minds, voiced for them by Acting Lieutenant Frey.

'Yes, Mr Frey, those birds . . . D'you perceive what they are, sir? Eh?' There were nine of them, large, dark birds with wide wings that terminated in splayed pinions and broad, forked tails. They wheeled effortlessly round and round so limited an axis that they betrayed the Dyak stronghold, even from the distance of *Patrician*'s anchorage.

'They're kites, sir,' answered Frey with dawning comprehension.

'Yes, Mr Frey, that's exactly what they are, kites giving away the position of our enemy.' The silence that followed was filled only with the hum of flies that were already blackening the bodies in the adjacent cutter.

'We've got our own, sir,' said one of the launch crew. They looked directly above their heads.

A single kite soared in a tightening spiral, seeing and scenting the mortifying carrion in the drifting cutter.

'Very well,' said Drinkwater with sudden resolution. 'I want six volunteers to take the oars; five marines, also volunteers, with ten muskets. I will exchange these men into the cutter as being handier upstream. You, Mr Frey, will take the launch and tow the barge back to the ship. You will put the bodies of our shipmates into the barge. Mr Dutfield, I'd be obliged of your company, but I want only volunteers.'

'Of course, sir, I'll come.'

'Obliged. Now, the rest of you. Who's with me?'

'I'll come with you, sir!'

They lashed the three boats together and, rocking madly, gunwhale banging against gunwhale, effected the transfers. When they had sorted themselves out and he had disposed the marines as he wanted them in the cutter, each with two muskets and a double supply of powder and shot, Drinkwater looked at Frey.

'Well, Mr Frey, we've left you a little water, and you take our best wishes back to the ship. Be off with you.'

Frey seemed to hesitate. 'I'll exchange with Dutfield, sir,' he said.

'No you won't,' replied Drinkwater, 'give way, lads.'

'And then he disappeared?' Quilhampton asked.

'Leaving no orders?' added Fraser.

Frey nodded unhappily at Quilhampton and answered the first lieutenant upon whom the imminent burden of command was settling like a sentence of death. 'No, none.'

'Bluidy hell!' Fraser ran the fingers of his right hand through his sandy hair with a gesture of despair. 'Has the man taken leave of his senses?' He sought consolation in the faces of Frey, Quilhampton and the silent Mount. 'This is taking a vendetta too bluidy far . . .'

'No,' Mount broke in sharply, his tone cautionary and his eye catching that of Fraser. 'No. I understand your feelings, Fraser, but Captain Drinkwater is not a fool. There is the matter of two captured ships and thirty thousand sterling.'

'And Tregembo,' said Quilhampton.

The four officers were silent for a moment, then Mount went on. 'If Captain Drinkwater issued no orders, then he wants nothing done. Nothing, that is, beyond maintaining our vigilance here.'

Drinkwater stirred and sat up. He was stiff and bruised from the hard thwarts, aware that he had dozed off. His movement rocked the boat and other men stirred, groaning faintly.

'Shhh . . .'

Those awake pressed their shipmates into silence and Drinkwater looked enquiringly at Dutfield. The midshipman, left with half the cutter's crew on watch, shook his head. Both 'halves' of the volunteer crew had dossed down in the boat as best they could for an hour or so each. Now the afternoon was far advanced and Drinkwater meditated taking them back into the stream, out of the cover of the mangroves that hung close overhead. They had heard and seen nothing in the period they had rested.

'Splice the mainbrace,' Drinkwater whispered. The raw spirits animated the men and he watched them as they drank or impatiently awaited their turn. Most of the men were members of his own barge crew, strong hefty fellows with some sense of identification with himself. He was glad to see, too, Corporal Grice among the marines. Grice had a wife and family to whom he was said to be devoted and Drinkwater had not expected him to volunteer. He smiled bitterly to himself; he also had a wife and family. Not for the first time he thought that war made fools of men . . .

'Muffle your oars now . . . perfect silence from now on . . .'

They pulled out into the stream. The kites had gone, forsaking their aerial vantage point as the air cooled a little. Or perhaps they had settled themselves on whatever it was that attracted them.

The narrow corridor of green seemed interminable. From time to time the foliage met overhead, shutting out the sky and filtering the increasingly slanting sunlight so that well-defined shafts of it formed illuminated patches, contrasting with the shadowed gloom of the leafy tunnel.

There was a difference in the vegetation now, Drinkwater noticed. No longer was the mangrove ubiquitous; there were an increasing number of nipah palms and heavy trunked trees like beeches, he thought, suggesting a firmer foundation for their roots. His theory found confirmation almost immediately as a low clearing came into view, a semi-circle of ferns and grass that surrounded a low slab of rock. He noticed, too, that about the broken branches that lay in the shallows, the creek ran with a perceptible stream, indicating a faster current than lower down. This was not merely an indented coast, it was indeed, as he had guessed from his masthead observations, fed by rivers. He strained his eyes ahead. Judging by his last sighting of the kites they could not have far to go now. His heart beat crazily in his chest. They had seen no sign, no indication of hostility, of being watched, if one discounted the creeping feeling along the spine.

A bend lay ahead. There was a break in the trees . . .

'Oars!' he hissed urgently. The blades rose dripping from the water and waited motionless, the men craned anxiously round. In the bow, muskets ready, two marines nervously fingered their triggers.

Through the break in the trees, brief though it was, he could just see, not more trees as he had expected, but a rising green bluff and the grey, sunlit outcrops of rock. What appeared to be too straight a line for nature ran across the summit of the eminence. This line was nicked by small gaps: an embrasured rampart, its guns commanding the creek up which they now glided.

Had they been seen?

He thought he detected a man's head above the line of the parapet. Then he was sure of it. As the boat silently advanced out of the shadows with the setting sun behind it, the light fell upon the stronghold of the Sea-Dyaks.

Above a wooden jetty, alongside which a number of the heavy *praus* were moored, numerous huts dotted the hillside and stretched higher upstream in a veritable township. More huts stood out over the river on stilts with another group of *praus* tied to stakes and smaller dugouts bobbing alongside them. Men and, he guessed, women moved about, the colours of their sarongs a brilliant contrast to the unrelieved green of the jungle. Here and there he spotted the scarlet jackets that he had observed on the attackers of that dawn. The lazy blue of cooking smoke rose from a single fire and a low, mellifluous song was being sung somewhere.

The whole scene was one of tranquil and arresting beauty. The still evening air was now filled with the stridulations of cicadas and the faint scent of roasting meat came to them, stirring the pangs of hunger in their empty, deprived bellies.

'Hold water!'

Jerked from meditation the oars bit the water, arresting the gentle forward motion of the cutter. It slowed to a stop under the last overhanging branches of a gigantic peepul tree, concealed in the growing pool of shadow. Drinkwater could see the place was cunningly fortified. Several batteries of cannon covered the approach, and a palisade of stakes seemed to be arranged in some way that protected the hill itself. Off the river bank he could see the water streaming past the pointed spikes of an estacade. He would need more than a boat gun to force a landing, unless he could take the place by subterfuge.

As he stood making his reconnaissance he was aware of the dull mutters of men being eaten by insects, and the sudden flutter of a giant fruit-bat made him jerk involuntarily. For a moment the boat rocked and Drinkwater expected a shout and the roar of a cannon to signal they had been seen, but nothing happened. He raked the parapet with his telescope and then stopped, feeling his heart leap with shock.

A yellow-robed figure stood against the sky staring through a glass directly at him. They were observed!

For a moment he seemed paralysed, the realisation that the man was Morris slowly dawning on him. As he lowered his glass Drinkwater saw Morris turn and move an arm, giving an obvious signal.

Drinkwater's guts contracted, expecting the well-aimed shot to smash the boat and end his life in a sudden bone-crushing impact. But instead there came a scream, a scream of such intense agony that it made their flesh creep and their very blood run cold.

PART THREE

A Private Revenge

'A man does not have himself killed for a few halfpence a day . . . you must speak to the soul in order to electrify the man . . .'

Napoleon

CHAPTER 19

The Tripod

It seemed to Quilhampton an act of *lèse-majesté* to be thus conferring in Drinkwater's cabin. Behind him, in silent witness, the portraits of Elizabeth and her children seemed pathetic effects. He was too stunned, too mystified to pay much attention to what Fraser and Mount were saying and he stood obedient to whatever decision they made as, with Dutfield, they bent over the chart laid on the table and the scrap of paper the midshipman had brought back. The group monopolised the candles, leaving Quilhampton and a disconsolate Frey in umbral shadow.

'And that is all?' asked Fraser, his sandy features furrowed by concern and confusion, turning the scrap of paper over and over, first looking at one side, then the other.

'Yes, sir, beyond urging me to insist that you adhered to the instruction.'

'Adhere to it! 'Tis little enough to go on . . .'

Frey had arrived back at the ship towing his grisly cargo, bringing the news that the captain had penetrated deeper into the jungle. Frey's mood had been brittle, a product of the weight of guilt he bore at not supporting Drinkwater. He now stood silently moody, his eyes downcast.

Dutfield's arrival two hours after dark had plunged the waiting officers into still deeper gloom. The sense of having been abandoned filled Fraser with an unreasonable, petulant, but understandable anger. He knew of no precedent for the captain's conduct and sensed only personal affront. Fraser lacked both imagination and initiative, competent though he was at the routine duties of a first lieutenant.

But to Quilhampton's relief, Mount regarded the matter in a different light. A more thorough professional, none of Mount's considerations were influenced by the possibility, or in this case difficulty, of advancement. It was to Drinkwater that Fraser and the sea-officers looked for the creation of their professional openings and opportunities. Drinkwater's irregular conduct had denied Fraser any discernible advantages, and yet his rank compelled him to undertake responsibilities for which he had little liking and less aptitude.

The marine officer, however, regarded the task in a different light. Perhaps fortunately, it was a military rather than a naval problem. He leaned over and with the most perfunctory 'By y'r leave, Fraser . . .' gently removed the scrap of paper from the first lieutenant's dithering hand. Meditatively he read again Drinkwater's scribbled instruction:

Storm the place at dawn. Dutfield knows. Do not fail. N.D.

'Do not fail, Nathaniel Drinkwater,' he said aloud, then turned the thing over, staring at the rough, pencilled sketch-map of the river passage. ''Tis a simple enough matter, Fraser. We shall need all the men we've got and, as 'tis now near midnight, we have not a moment to lose.'

Fraser confined himself to an unhappy grunt.

'And you were not followed?' Mount asked Dutfield.

'I . . . I am not certain . . . at first I thought we were, but no shot followed us and, after the business of the captain, we pulled like . . . like . . .'

'Devils?' prompted Mount.

'Yes, sir,' Dutfield hesitated, swallowed and then, foundering under the earnest scrutiny of the anxious faces added, 'though I will not admit to fear, sir, once the captain had gone . . .'

'It was as though the witch Nannie was after your horse's tail, eh?' Mount's literary allusion was as much to encourage

Fraser as Dutfield. But Fraser did not appear familiar with the obscure poet and Mount let the matter drop. 'Do you tell off the men, Mr Fraser. Small arms, pikes, cutlasses, as many and as much as you can spare from the ship, with water and spirits, aye, and biscuit in the boats . . .'

'And food before we go,' put in Quilhampton, stirring at last from his catalepsy.

'We?' said Fraser suddenly in the prevailing mood of coming to. 'You, sir, will stay with the ship . . .'

'But . . .'

'I command, Mr Quilhampton . . . but you may see to the boats by all means. You are to plan the assault, Mount; Frey, you will second Mr Mount . . .'

'Aye, aye, sir.' Frey brightened a little.

'Dutfield will be our guide . . .'

While Fraser grasped at straws obvious and expedient, Mount bent his attention to details. 'Now, Mr Dutfield, please be seated, help yourself to a glass there, and cast your mind back to the sight of the Dyak fortification. I want you to recollect calmly every little detail of the place . . .'

'I wish to God I knew the captain's mind,' said Fraser, voicing his thoughts out loud and earning from Mount a recriminatory glare.

'Now, Dutfield, be a good fellow and *think*.'

Drinkwater lay on his back and stared at the stars beyond the darkly indistinct shapes of the leaves overhead. Although the stridulations of cicadas rasped incessantly about him, it was the persistent echo of that terrible scream that seemed to fade and swell, fade and swell in his brain.

There was no doubt in his mind but that a man within the precincts of the fortress was undergoing torture, and that that man was Tregembo.

The absolute certainty of this fact seemed enshrined in that provocative gesture of Morris's: Tregembo had been made to scream to Morris's order, made to scream to communicate Morris's power in this terrible place.

As the cutter had been swung short-round amid a furious splashing of tugging and back-watering oars, no shot had splintered them, no *sumpitan* had spat its venomous darts after their retreat. They had been defeated by that chilling, heart-rending cry, echoed and amplified by their primitive fear.

It had been the conviction of the source of the scream that had thrust into Drinkwater's mind the impetuous notion of remaining. He had had few moments to plan beyond scribbling the urgent need for an attack in force, before ordering Dutfield, ashen-faced over the tiller, to swing the cutter into the bank, trail his oars and allow Drinkwater to leap clear. He had landed among the ferns and grass of that first low clearing they had spotted shortly before the Dyak fortress came into view. He still lay there, waiting to order his thoughts, summon his courage; waiting for the night . . .

The night had come now with the swiftness characteristic of the tropical latitudes and still he lay supine, like a dead man, fearful of the predicament his folly had led him into.

But he knew it was not simply impetuosity that had made him jump. It was something far less facile, a complex mixture of obligation, hatred and loathing, wounded pride, a ludicrous sense of justice and, God help him, that raddled whore duty. Stern, inflexible and dutiful, Drinkwater's inner self was capable of excoriating self-criticism. If that leap from the cutter had been the compound product of largely virtuous qualities, he knew inwardly such virtue was a product of deep-seated fear. And that fear now had his heart in its cold clutch, immobilising him on the damp ground.

He recalled Mount's unanswered question: what power did Morris exert over these remote and warlike people? He supposed it must lie rooted in the silver. A Dyak prince's confederation could be purchased, no doubt, and he had learned that silver was the principal currency in these waters. But Morris must have more influence than that, for he had trusted them with thirty thousand sterling! It remained a mystery, though he was no longer in doubt that it had been Morris who had abducted Tregembo, though by what means he had no idea. A message, perhaps, through the boy, a luring to his cabin, the application of a drug . . . Guiltily, Drinkwater remembered his own exhaustion that night. He had dismissed Tregembo early . . .

It was as dark as the tomb now but for the stars. He wished he had one of Ballantyne's cheroots to ward off the mosquitoes that sought his flesh in droves. Eventually it was this irritating attack that brought him to himself. He stretched, fighting off the cramp that lying on the damp earth had induced. He had no clear idea of what he was going to do, or even attempt to do. He had vague ideas of reconnoitring the fortress, or attempting a diversion when Fraser launched his attack . . .

Or freeing Tregembo.

How could a man survive the pain inherent in that scream?

He rose to his feet. He had a marine's water-bottle, a cartouche box with powder and shot, two pistols and a sword. At the last second of his hurried departure Dutfield had hurled his dirk as enhancement to Drinkwater's armoury. It was of an unfashionable design, round-hilted, a lion's head snarling up the arm of its wielder. Drinkwater picked it up and stuck it into his belt. His eyes were accustomed to the dark now and the river threw off a weird light. Cautiously he took a draught of water, corked and slung the flask. No boats had followed the retreating cutter. Morris was damnably confident . . .

He had not gone a hundred yards before he discovered his first obstacle, a secondary creek separating the clearing where he had landed from the rising ground upon which the Dyak stronghold was located. Some trick of the twists of the creeks obscured the point at which he came upon it from the main landing, though he could see clearly the hard line of the parapet set dimly against the velvet sky.

It took him half an hour to work his way slowly and as silently as possible upstream over the tangle of roots, fallen trees and hanging vines that strung themselves like malevolent ropes across his path. The night was filled with the steaming of the rain forest, the stink of rich blooms, of humus and decay, of fungus and the rancidly sharp stench of excrement. Rustlings and sudden, startling flappings marked his disturbance of the unseen denizens of this foliated habitat. He thrust his mind away from thoughts of serpents. Ballantyne had spoken of the hamadryad cobra, of enormous lizards, of bats that drew blood from men . . .

But the second scream turned his thoughts to Morris waiting for him on the hill beyond the creek.

He made the crossing at a spot where overhanging branches obscured him from all but an observer opposite. The slime of the muddy banks covered the white linen of his shirt and the calico of his breeches. Taking his shoes from between his teeth and rearranging the parcel of powder and arms he had held above his head, he found his bearings and moved slowly uphill.

In the direction of Morris.

Ever since his boyhood when his father had been thrown from a bolting horse and killed, Nathaniel Drinkwater had believed in fate. His thirty years' service as a sea-officer, subject to the vicissitudes of wind and weather, of action, of orders, of disaster, victory and defeat, had only confirmed his belief. Although paying formal respect to the Established Church and owning a vague acknowledgement of God, he privately considered fate to be the arbiter of men's destinies. Fate was the Almighty's agent, prescribing the interlocking paths which formed the lives of the men and women he had known. These men and women had marked him for better and for worse: the gentle constancy of Elizabeth, the friendship of Quilhampton, the haunting loveliness of the Spanish beauty at San Francisco, the patronage of Lord Dungarth and the devoted loyalty of Tregembo who now endured God knew what horrors on his behalf . . .

And the enmity of Morris . . .

Drinkwater only half acknowledged that it was perverse love that bound him to Morris. The passion, unrequited by himself, had twisted the heartless young Morris into a cruel, vicious and domineering character whose forbidden vice gained greater satisfaction from the infliction of pain upon those who came under his influence. Unresolved emotions, unsatiated lusts, lay like unseen strands of circumstance between them, exerting their own ineluctable influence like lunar gravity upon the sea.

A third scream froze the sweat on Drinkwater's back as he stumbled suddenly into the edge of a small, steeply inclined plantation. It was Tregembo's fate to have drawn these men together.

Drinkwater moved with infinite caution now. Hunger sharpened his awareness and he dug from his body the reserves that the sea-service had laid there. Movement stimulated an irrational, feral thrill, a compound of fear and nervous reaction that acted on his spirit like a drug.

Making his way round the perimeter of the standing crops, he knew himself to be climbing, climbing up the northern or left flank of the stronghold as viewed from the river. It was the shoulder of the hill and he guessed, from the rising vastness of the sky ahead of him, that he was nearing the summit. Somewhere hidden beyond the crops and the shoulder of the hill, the rampart projected. Behind and below him, the dense jungle stretched in a monotonous grey, partly hidden under its nocturnal mantle of mist.

On the hillside a faint breeze stirred, striking his damp body with a chill, and bearing too the bark of a dog, suddenly near, and the sound of men's voices.

The small cultivated patch gave way to a steepening of the gradient where an outcrop of rock thrust through the soil. He edged under its cover and took stock. If there were guards they watched the river, for below him rolled the jungle running north to the sea, south and east interminably, a grey, mist-streaked wilderness under the stars, impassable to all but the Malay Dyaks who were bred to its secrets.

Cautiously he edged round the rock.

The elevation he had achieved surprised him. He had supposed the rampart was constructed on the hill's highest point and knew now that this was incorrect. The rampart was formed on a natural level commanding the river; the summit, hidden from the observation of an attacker, was set back a little.

But there was someone on the rampart below him, a long figure, dark against the lighter tone of the river. The man moved, a leisurely, unhurried gesture like a stretch. Drinkwater considered the wisdom of attempting his murder and decided so positive a proof of his presence would do him little good. Instead he was distracted by laughter, a rising cadence of voices and then again, only much louder now, loud enough for him to hear it start with a series of sobs and end in the terrible gasps of a man fighting for air, came the scream.

Withdrawing behind the summit Drinkwater wriggled backwards then moved to his left, eastwards and upstream so that when he next crossed the skyline he should, he estimated, have a view of the native village, for the scent of wood smoke was strong in his nostrils, mixing with the subtle-sweet reek of humanity.

He had not miscalculated. The flattening of the hill that had formed a narrow terrace behind the rampart before rising to the rocky summit, was here wider and further widened by the artifice of man. Beyond his sight the *atap* roofs of the huts stepped down the hillside to the landing place he had seen earlier. But immediately below him, on the flattened area, the low wooden *istana* stood, the palace of the chieftain, thatched with the *atap* leaves of the nipah palm. Before the *istana* extended an area of beaten earth illuminated by four blazing fires. Men wearing sarongs hitched like breech clouts squatted around the flames, eating and drinking. Some wore short, red jackets and head-dresses of bright cloth. The flickering light reflected from the sweat on their brown bodies and glanced off the rings they wore in their ears. Outside the gaping entrance of the *istana* were three chairs. In these sat the leaders of these men: a native chieftain dressed in yellow silk; a lesser Dyak conspicuous, even at fifty yards, by the quantity and size of the rings in the pendant lobes of his ears; and Morris.

Morris too wore yellow silk, and sat like the jade and soap-stone images of the Buddha Drinkwater had seen offered for sale at Whampoa. So vivid was the firelight and so animated the scene below him that it was some seconds before Drinkwater noticed the three timbers of the tripod that rose above the area, its apex in the dark.

As he directed his attention to this central contrivance, allowing his pupils to adjust, he saw something square hanging from a heavy block. It seemed to sway slightly of its own volition, though the light from below made it hard for his tired eyes to see . . .

A wave of excited chatter rose and Drinkwater was distracted from his speculation by a group of women emerging from the *istana*. Their arrival was accompanied by a sudden drumming and they moved amongst the men in an undisciplined but arousing dance that induced the warriors to stamp their feet in time with the pounding rhythm. One or two leapt to their feet and joined the women, others did the same and a jostling throng of wild and lasciviously abandoned Dyaks was soon dancing to the insistent drum. Cries and whoops came from the mob and Drinkwater was aware that this was no native ritual and that many of the men below him were not Sea-Dyaks, but half-breeds, Tamils and Chinese, Mestizo Spaniards from Manila, miscegenate Portuguese from Macao, bastard Batavians and degenerate Britons from God knew where.

Morris had his own Praetorian guard amongst the sea-pirates of the Borneo coast, deserters, escaped prisoners, drunks and opium-eaters, a rag-bag of riff-raff and scum that the lapping tide of European civilisation had cast up like flotsam on this remote shore. Here were the means to attack Company and Country ships, here were the means to work them, to infiltrate their crews, to rise in co-ordinated piracy that needed only the Dyaks for cover and the expertise of their skills in handling their *praus*. The cleverness of the thing astonished Drinkwater; how perfectly they had been fooled, he thought.

His deductions were confirmed by shouts of abuse in recognisable English and Spanish. Several men were arguing over women, and the drum beats died away as, aroused to an erotic frenzy, the purpose of the Bacchanalia reached its climax. Frantic coupling was already in progress, less uninhibited pairs melting into the shadows or seeking privacy in the huts lower down the slopes.

A rustling in the undergrowth below him impelled Drinkwater to retreat, moving sideways into brush and ferns as a libidinous couple burst over the ridge, flinging themselves on to the ground vacated by himself. Within seconds they were engrossed in an urgent and grunting embrace; Drinkwater took advantage of their preoccupation and shifted his position.

When he again looked down on to the beaten earth before the *istana* he was closer to the seated leaders. They remained after the departure of their men, seemingly impassive to the arousing frenzy of the dance. A few guards stayed in attendance on the triumvirate, who appeared to be puffing on pipes.

Suddenly Morris heaved himself to his feet and, like a crouching familiar, Drinkwater saw the turbanned boy scuttle from the shadow of his robe. In the dying flames of the now neglected fires the yellow silk seemed to shimmer and the guards cringed as Morris shot out an imperative arm. The Dyaks seemed galvanised, moving to the tripod. The dark square was lowered, revealing itself as a small cage of bamboo. A prescient cramp seized Drinkwater's gut, contracting it sharply. His heart thundered in his chest. The Dyaks opened a rickety door and dragged out a bundle which they quickly hitched to the lowered rope.

In a trice they were dancing back, tallying on to the rope and hoisting the bundle up again, leaving the cage dragged to one side.

Drinkwater could see what it was now, though there was something oddly liquid about its movement as it left the ground feet first. Suspended upside down was the naked body of a man. As he rose he emitted a low gurgling moan.

Still standing, Morris shouted: '*Arria-a-ah!*'

With the gorge rising uncontrollably in his throat Drink-water could hear the anticipatory pleasure in those last attenu-ated syllables. The Dyaks released the rope. The low moan rose to a brief and awful shriek which stopped as the body struck the hard earth beneath the tripod.

It was Tregembo.

CHAPTER 20

A Forlorn Hope

Tregembo, or what had once been Tregembo, lay oddly crumpled and without form. The earlier liquidity of the body was clear to Drinkwater now, clear as the piercing of those agonised shrieks, for the tripod had done its terrible work. Tregembo, though still living, had been broken into pieces, his bones fractured by repeated impact with the ground.

Drinkwater vomited, his empty stomach producing little but the slimy discharge of bodily disgust.

'There, sir!'

Dutfield's arm was outstretched, a pale line of rigidity above the swaying grey shapes of the oarsmen.

'Hold water!' hissed Fraser, and the gentle knock-knock of the rag-muffled oars ceased, the turgid water swirled with dull stirrings of phosphorescence and the boats slewed to a stop.

Dutfield's keen eye had detected the only landmark within the creek, the captain's landing place. They lay on their oars and gathered themselves for the final assault. Mount was aware that they were already late, for the edges of the over-hanging trees were darker against the lightening sky. But a canopy of vapour hung above them, cold on their skin and dampening the priming powder in the pans.

'Cold steel,' he whispered, 'if your firelocks fail, cold steel . . .'

He heard the words passed along, the sibilant consonant thrilling Mount with its menace. The slide of steel from scabbards, the last tiny clicks and rattles of men turning pistols in their hands and thumbing hammers and frizzens, an occasional grunt, the papist whisper of a prayer, passed like a breeze over dry grass.

'Ready, Mount?' Fraser's voice came low over the flat water that was assuming a faint yellow in response to the dawn sky.

'Aye,' the marine officer replied.

'Frey?'

'Aye, sir.'

'Pater?'

'Yes . . .'

Even the purser, Mount thought, the warrant officer's unusual presence indicative of just how desperate a hope rested with them. *Patrician*'s officers were spread very thinly indeed, and if their assault failed, if it was bloodily repulsed as, Mount privately thought, by all the laws of military science it should be, the ship would inevitably fall.

'Take station then . . .'

There was a back-watering, a twisting of the boats' alignments. Oars became briefly entangled in the narrow channel. A man cursed, stung beyond toleration by yet one more mosquito.

'Silence!'

'*Vestigia nulla retrorsum*,' muttered Mount, 'no retreat from the lion's den,' and in a louder voice, 'Cold steel and a steady arm, my lads . . .'

'Stand by!' commanded Fraser, and the oarsmen leaned forward, their blades hovering above the water.

'Give way!'

'Thank the Lord for this mist,' muttered Mount as the stern thwart of the launch pressed his calf with the impetus of acceleration.

Taking station on the launch, the *Patrician*'s boats swept forward to the attack.

Morris passed the pipe to the boy, exhaling the last fumes of the drug. An utter peace descended upon him, his mind swimming in a pool of the most perfect tranquillity. His body seemed to float, satiated as it was by the most exquisite of lusts. No Celestial Emperor had ever enjoyed more perfect a sequence of sensations and now his mind rolled clear of every earthly inhibition, filling with a light more intense than the yellow dawn that flooded the eastern sky. He seemed elevated, lifted to the eminence of a god. Far, far below him lay the broken, used body of Tregembo. After so many years, revenge was infinitely sweet . . .

And there was yet one pleasure to enjoy . . .

His hearing, tuned to an unnatural acuity by the opium, detected the approaching boats. Swaying slightly he looked down at the upturned face of his catamite.

'Here they come!' he said, and the boy ran from the *istana* with the news while Morris waited for the moment of consummation he had first thought of when he saw Nathaniel Drinkwater from the curtained secrecy of his palanquin beside the Pearl River.

Drinkwater woke with a start. He had no idea how long he had passed out, but a lemon yellow light already flooded the eastern sky. With quickening anxiety he lifted his head, half expecting to have been discovered, but the lovers had vanished and he was suddenly cold and lonely. The sharp stink of his spew stung his nostrils and, in a sudden wave of self-recrimination, he recalled the events of the night. It had been no nightmare that he had witnessed, though when he sought Tregembo's smashed body it was no longer there.

As he gathered his thoughts, the hill below him erupted in an explosion of fire and smoke. Hesitating only long enough to gather his arms he was up and running at a low lope, gaining height and flinging himself down in the shelter of the rocky outcrop at the summit of the hill. Here, not daring to look below before he was ready, he drew the charges from his pistols and, with shaking hands, poured fresh powder into the barrels and pans.

224

He had come here to reconnoitre and create a diversion and what had he done? Thrown up like a greenhorn midshipman and fainted! Now Fraser was launching his attack, Mount would be storming ashore at the head of his boot-necked lobsters in sure and certain faith of some diversion carried out by the ever resourceful Captain Drinkwater – and he was cowering behind a rock . . .

Christ, he had even abandoned Tregembo!

The thought brought him to his feet. He drew in a great gulp of air, filling his lungs with the sharpness and scent of the morning. Beyond the rock, on the hillside, the rattle of musketry had augmented the desultory thunder of artillery. Devoid of plans but filled with a desperate determination, Drinkwater emerged from cover.

He stood against the sky looking down upon the scene below. Heavy wraiths of mist lay over the creek and it was clear the gunners had no better a view of the approaching boats than he had, but they were working the six cannon with a regular determination that argued they had predetermined the trajectory of their shots. Drinkwater dropped below the skyline and ran to the right, towards the plantation through which he had laboriously climbed. Before he reached it he dodged down and worked his way round the hill. He had a better view here, although he was slightly below the level of the rampart. Gun-smoke hung in a dense pall over the palisade, but the plumed spouts rose from the mist where the plunging shot fell in the creek.

Below the six-gun battery on the summit the hill was terraced with earthworks, parallels of defence behind which Morris's polyglot army levelled their muskets at the pool before the landing place.

Drinkwater tried to gauge numbers. Perhaps two hundred men, perhaps two hundred and fifty, and they were supported by more cannon, smaller pieces but quite capable of decimating any assault force that stormed the hill.

There was the sudden reverberating bark and flash of a wide-muzzled gun that showed through the low veil of mist. A carronade! Fraser's boat gun, by God! The hot cloud that it belched seemed to burn a hole in the mist, though the small shot it fired did little damage beyond peppering a *prau* and cutting up the ground around the landing.

To Drinkwater's left came a shout and he looked round. A man, the yellow-robed chieftain, stood on the parapet of the upper battery and drew his gunners' attention to the presence of the launch's gun.

Quickly Drinkwater levelled his pistol. It was a long shot, too long for a man in his condition but . . .

He squeezed the trigger, then quickly rolled away beyond the edge of the escarpment, out of sight. He did not wait to reload but climbed quickly, returning to the overhang nearer the stone outcrop of the summit. Here he reloaded, then edged forward. The chieftain appeared unscathed, but he no longer leapt gesticulating on the parapet. Resting his hand on the ground and propping the heavy barrel of the pistol on a stone, Drinkwater laid the weapon on the same man. As the ragged discharge of the battery ripped the morning apart again, he too let fly his fire. At twenty-five yards the ball went home, spinning the Dyak to the ground. Drinkwater ducked down to reload.

He had begun to create a diversion.

Ten yards from the landing the blue cutter struck the stakes of the estacade. Such was the pace of her advance that the bow was stove in by the impact. Frey was equal to the moment.

'Over the bow!' he shouted and leapt from the tiller. Stepping lightly on the thwarts, he touched a toe on the stem and, waving his cutlass, plunged into the water. An outraged sense of having been misunderstood had possessed Frey from the moment he had abandoned Drinkwater. Already privately convinced the captain was dead, Frey sought to expiate his guilt. With a foolish gallantry his men followed him, cutlass-bearing seamen, half a dozen with boarding pikes, few of whom could swim in the deep water. They floundered, found the oars they had so precipitately abandoned and, wrenching them free of their thole-pins, kicked their legs as they supported their bodies on the ash looms.

The mist mercifully covered their confusion. Virtually unopposed, they dragged their way gasping ashore.

Fraser's launch had by good fortune forced the gap left in the estacade. Dutfield, in command of the carronade, wrenched clear the wedges as his crew plied sponge and rammer.

'Fire!'

The boat bucked and the short, smoking black cannon snapped taut its breechings as it recoiled on the greased slide.

'In my wake!' Fraser screamed at the other boats, seeing the fate of Frey's cutter. 'Come on!' He was waving as Mount leaned on the tiller of the red cutter and led Pater's boat past the launch that stood off and pounded the landing. Fraser's men were trailing their oars, making room for Mount and Pater whose boats were almost gunwhale under with their load of armed men. The pale glint of bayonets showed purposefully and then a plunging shot dropped on the launch. The sudden dark swirl of water ran red with the blood of an oarsman whose leg was shattered by the iron ball.

'Cease fire and give way! Don't shoot our fellows in the back!'

Tearing off his hat Fraser thrust it into the hole and then felt the boat's bow rise as it grounded.

The sun emerged above the eastern tree-line, its slanting rays striking through the swirling vapour. Both attackers and defenders had, as yet, no very clear view of the opposition. The upper battery continued to fire, blindly dropping its shot beyond the boats where the plunging balls threw fountains of mud and water harmlessly into the air. As Mount and Frey stumbled gasping ashore, they forced their men into a rough line and peered about them. The hill rose upwards, scarred by the barred lines of the earthworks and palisades, while to their right the higgledy-piggledy gables of the *atap*-roofed houses tumbled down the hillside.

The brief flashes and eruptions of smoke lining the lower defences marked their objective. The musketry fire struck its

227

first victims and Mount sensed his men waver. He shook his sword and took a deep breath.

'Forward!'

The ragged line of sodden men began to advance: seamen in the centre with boarding pikes in their hands, cutlasses swinging on their hips from canvas baldrics; on the flanks the steadying influence of Mount's marines, stripped of their red coats, but in close order. Bayonets and cutlasses caught the rays of sunlight and gleamed wickedly as, with every foot of elevation, the attackers came clear of the clinging river-mist.

Above, Drinkwater saw them clearly, recognised Mount and Frey, caught the evil sparkle of the light on the weapons. Directly below him two of the gunners were bent over the wounded chieftain. They did not seem to have considered the possibility that the shot had come from behind them, for the noise of gongs and the war-shrieks of the Dyaks, the heavy powder smoke and their own high excitement dulled their wits to this unlikely event. Despite the fact that their shot was now useless, the boats having passed the fixed line of its fall, they continued to load and fire, unable to depress their guns to command the slope of the hill. Emboldened, Drinkwater struck two of them with pistol balls, rolling backwards to reload.

The sunlight cleared his head of the cataleptic horrors seen in the night. His nerve was sharply steady, his brain functioned with that cool clarity that operated beyond the threshold of fear, when desperation summoned up the most primitive of instincts, that of the aggressive survivor.

When he looked at the battery again, he was aware of some confusion; a debate seemed to be in progress, some of the gunners favouring joining their brethren in the defences below, two pointing to their right, clearly considering some attack was coming up from the plantation. They had not yet realised that those shots had come directly from their rear. He saw the gunners split their forces. Suddenly the battery was empty!

Drinkwater hesitated only long enough to see that the wavering line of the attackers seemed to have reached the first line of earthworks, then he was bounding down the hill, his sword bouncing on his hip, Dutfield's dirk digging into the small of his back.

At the rear of the gun platform lay half a dozen powder kegs. An astonished man, a Portuguese or Spaniard by the look of him, sat quietly filling cartridges with a scoop, hidden from view by the angle of the slope above him. Drinkwater was no more than three yards from him, and only the indrawn breath of surprise alerted Drinkwater to the man's existence. For a split second the two stared at each other, then Drinkwater discharged the pistol in his right hand. The impact of the ball smashed the man's skull hard against the rock behind him. Copper scoop and cotton cartridge bag fell with a surreal slowness from his grip. Powder cascaded in a tiny stream off the man's saronged lap.

Grabbing an already filled bag, Drinkwater split it and continued the trail, scuffling backwards and drawing the grey line in the direction of the plantation. Running back to the sagging body of the cartridge-filler he overturned the broached powder cask with his foot, then ran to the battery. Piles of shot lay by the guns. Bending, he lobbed them, bowl-like, back under the overhang, aiming them at the stack of powder kegs.

Picking up a linstock carelessly thrown down by the departing gunners, he blew on the foot of slow match that smouldered in its end, walking smartly to the end of his powder trail and stepping over the body of the chieftain.

He was about to touch the slow match to the powder when he heard voices, the shouts of the searching gunners returning from the plantation. Somewhere below the rampart the gongs rose to a crescendo and shouts, screams and cheers told of savage hand-to-hand fighting. Drinkwater touched the slow match to the powder and flung himself into the upright crops in the plantation.

The voices were quite near, raised in some urgent expectation. Had they seen him? Had they seen the powder train sputtering away? He lifted his head. Someone crashed through the stems a yard away, turned and saw the prone Drinkwater. The pistol misfired, too hurriedly loaded . . . The gunner shouted something and raised a *parang*. Drinkwater gathered his legs, tossed the useless pistol aside and drew Dutfield's dirk. The *parang* swung, biting earth, its owner staggered back with the dirk buried in his loin, Drinkwater's shoulder thrust into his chest. They crashed into the gunner's confederate, the three of them falling. Drinkwater struggled to withdraw the dirk; his sword hilt dug painfully into his side, both the men were on top of him now, one vomiting blood and bile, the other yelling with rage, recovering himself and preparing to retaliate.

There was a sudden roar, blasting hot air out of the hillside in a hellish, roasting exhalation. Drinkwater heard, or fancied he heard, the crinkle of frizzing hair and skin as the gunner's yell turned to an agonised shriek. The searing force of the explosion rolled over them, pounding them with shards of rock and gobbets of earth. Only their position in the plantation saved them from the falling shot and the landslip as the rampart exploded outwards, cascading rock, stones, earth, cannon shot and two dislodged guns over the parapet on to the third defensive line immediately below it.

Badly shaken, quivering like a wounded animal, Drinkwater dragged himself from beneath the two gunners. Both were near death and he turned his head sharply from the horror of the sight. To his right as he stood facing uphill, a dense cloud of dust still hung over the site of the explosion, but a great scar of exposed earth and rock was gradually emerging beneath it.

The muscles in his thighs still shuddering, Drinkwater moved forward.

Shot, debris, rock and, quite recognisable, a man's leg, fell on the launch in which Fraser and his oarsmen, and Dutfield and his carronade crew, were theoretically covering the landing. Fraser's main preoccupation had been in stemming the leak with something more effective than his hat and, at the moment of the explosion, he had just succeeded. His coat, stretched underneath the boat by its arms and tails on light ropes, had reduced the inflow. Further insertions of shirts made it possible to reduce the amount to a trickle. As the launch crew found themselves afloat amid widening circles of disturbed water, they looked up at the brown cloud still hanging over the hillside.

'Sir!' shouted Dutfield, pointing excitedly, 'It's the captain!'

He stood at the edge of the great scar, staring down on the brief hiatus in the savage fight below. Then he turned and vanished from their sight.

'Thank God . . .' breathed Fraser with a heartfelt blasphemy.

Mount caught a sight of Drinkwater while he fought to keep his footing. As the explosion had rolled rock, cannon shot and earth down on them Mount had roared his anger, meeting a *parang* thrust and riposting before turning on a second assailant. The indiscriminate avalanche bore down on them, though the wild trajectory of the heavier debris flew over their heads. Mount was already aware of losing many of his men. Muskets the enemy might possess, but they did not disdain the deadly *sumpitan*. The struggle uphill had cost them dear, for forty of the hundred and twenty men committed to it were lying behind them killed or wounded.

But the sliding earth had caused more havoc to the defenders, unnerving them, shaking their already fragile discipline and raining debris on their backs, filling their entrenchments. The hardened Patricians recovered first. Waving his sword Mount thrust forward, shouting a manic encouragement to his men.

On the flank Frey was also rallying the attack. He had not seen the captain, and the strength of the fortification and the determination of the enemy had surprised him. His sense of having betrayed Drinkwater lay heavily upon him and he fought with a sullen, dogged and careless energy.

'Look out, sir!' He heard Corporal Grice's warning and turned, his cutlass half-raised to parry, but Grice had spotted a new movement by the enemy. To their right, along the lower slope from the direction of the village, red jackets bright and the light gleaming on their *parangs* and blow-pipes, advanced a column of Dyaks.

'Right face, Corporal!'

But Fraser had seen them from the launch.

'Mr Dutfield . . .' Fraser pointed at the ragged column threatening Frey's flank. Dutfield nodded his comprehension and busied himself round the carronade.

'Hold water starboard, one stroke larboard.' Fraser swung the launch. 'Hold water all . . . a short pull larboard bow.' The bow oarsman dabbed at the water and Dutfield, sighting along the stubby barrel, held up his hand, then stood back and jerked his lanyard. The carronade roared and a swathe of langridge cut into the Dyaks, sending them reeling. The counter-attack broke and fled.

Looking again at the hill, Fraser was aware that the resistance was crumbling. His men were everywhere triumphant, putting to death the last fragmented pockets of opposition.

'By heaven,' he said, his voice almost reverential, 'I believe we've done it!'

CHAPTER 21

A Private Revenge

Drinkwater left the struggle for the hill in the balance. What-ever the outcome he had unfinished business to attend to and he wanted it over with, even if afterwards he had to tumble ignominiously into a retreating boat.

Half sliding, half scrambling, he descended to the area before the *istana*. The high framework of the tripod dominated the place and the smell of ashes mixed here with the tang of powder smoke. Despite the raucous noise of battle, it was deserted, the Dyaks involved in their attack on Frey's men. Pausing only to check his weapons, Drinkwater ran up the steps into the wooden *istana*.

It was dark inside and it took his eyes a moment to adjust. The entrance chamber was floored with intricately woven mat-ting, and hung with bright-coloured cloth. Beyond, a partition with a door led to the inner *balai*, or audience hall. A pale shape lay in the centre of the matting and Drinkwater knelt beside it.

'Tregembo . . . Tregembo, forgive me . . . I was too late . . .'

There was the faintest respiration in the thing, for it was no longer a body, but a shapeless mass, blotched with pale areas from which the broken blood vessels had emptied themselves, and dark with suggilations where, like some foul and swollen bladder, it spread upon the flooring. Uncontrolled, the bowels wept.

Shaking with disgust and rage, Drinkwater pressed the barrel of his pistol against Tregembo's skull and pulled the trigger. The swollen body subsided as a red and white mass fanned out across the matting.

'Goodbye, old friend . . .'

'What a touching sight . . .'

His eyes blurred with tears, Drinkwater looked up. Morris stood before him, a pair of heavy pistols in his hands.

'The faithful retainer . . .'

'Hold your tongue, you bastard.' Drinkwater made to rise.

'Stay where you are!' Morris commanded sharply. 'Your kneeling posture is, how shall we say, most appropriate, eh?'

'You do not approve of the pursuit of pleasure, my dear Nathaniel, do you? You cannot understand it, can you? You and your ridiculous preference for *duty!*' Morris spat the word contemptuously. 'You are a fool, a willing tool of your masters, an instrument of policy, hiding yourself under your epaulettes and trumpery nonsense, knowing *nothing!*'

'Damn you . . .'

'Oh, damnation, my dear Nathaniel, is a condition figuring largely in *your* calendar. There is nothing after death and in life we are free to pursue pleasure. It is a more acceptable way of employing power than your own and I imagine I have caused less deaths than you . . .'

'You . . .'

'Disarm yourself . . .' Morris jerked his head and the turbanned catamite emerged from the inner chamber. 'Don't lecture me on the perversity of my philosophy, Nathaniel, surrender your weapons to Budrudeen.' Morris moved the pistols, emphasising Drinkwater's weakness.

Drinkwater threw his own on the matting, pulled the second from his waist and dropped that, the boy skipping as the heavy pistol skidded towards his bare toes. Budrudeen bent to recover them and Drinkwater jerked the sword free from his scabbard and offered the hilt to him.

Budrudeen took it. The red stub of his tongue clacked in his wet mouth. Drinkwater felt the comforting hardness of

Dutfield's dirk nestling in the small of his back. Budrudeen retreated with his trophies.

'No, don't lecture me . . . I have waited a long time for this moment. Ever since you took a dislike to me . . .'

'Damn you, Morris, you wanted buggery . . .'

'Among other things, yes. Do you know a Sikh fortune-teller in Calcutta told me I was blessed among men, that I should have everything I desired and when he asked what was it I desired most, he put his hands upon my head then wrote your name on a paper.' Morris smiled. 'Most remarkable, eh?' He chuckled. The noise of gongs had ceased and screams and shouts came from somewhere below them.

'I had planned to take the specie, of course. That had long been in my mind, but seeing you in that foolish demonstration at Canton . . .'

The noise of retreat was now obvious. Morris's composure began to waver.

'Stand up!'

Drinkwater obeyed.

'Precede me into the inner chamber . . .'

Drinkwater met Morris's eyes and as the other made way he stepped forward, gauging the distance . . .

'No tricks.'

Throwing his full weight behind his left shoulder, Drinkwater charged.

'Dog's turd!'

Morris fired. A searing heat burnt across Drinkwater's left forearm, the ball grazed his thigh and struck harmlessly into the wooden floor. The other shot went wide as Morris fell back, stumbling on his robe, his mind still under the residual effect of opium, his reactions slowed. He crashed into the partition and made to jab one pistol into his assailant's ribs. Drinkwater's fist had already closed round the hilt of Dutfield's dirk. He slashed Morris's wrist.

In a reflex of pain, Morris dropped both weapons. Drinkwater drove the foot-long blade hard into Morris's gut.

'Bastard!' he roared, wrenching the blade upwards so

that his wounded muscles cracked.

Morris crashed to his knees as Drinkwater withdrew the blade. He was red to the wrist. Morris looked down, his hands going to his belly. Something blue and shiny slipped through his fumbling fingers.

'Drinkwater . . .' Morris looked up, his voice reaching a crescendo of agony, his mouth twisting, his veiled eyes now wide with disbelief.

Drinkwater stood back horrified. Morris fell forward, caught his weight on his right hand. His eviscerated entrails slithered on to the matting. A faintly offensive smell rose from them on waves of vapour. Morris raised his slashed wrist in a terrible gesture of supplication.

'Nathaniel . . . !'

Drinkwater felt a terrible pity rising like vomit in his throat.

'Nathaniel . . .'

'Christ damn you!' Drinkwater screamed, slashing the dirk across Morris's face. His frenzy ebbing, Drinkwater stepped backwards, gasping. Morris remained supported by one hand. His lower jaw and cheek showed white through the fallen flesh, but his eyes remained on Drinkwater. Then suddenly a dark hole appeared in his forehead. It was a small hole, Drinkwater noted; though the impact of it threw Morris rearing backwards. Drinkwater had not heard the pistol and it was only gradually that he turned his head and saw the smoking muzzle in the hands of the boy Budrudeen.

With the assistance of the boy, Drinkwater found a lamp and spilled its oil, setting it on fire with powder and a spark. It caught quickly, flames racing across the dry matting of the *istana*. Still dazed, Drinkwater backed out into the sunshine. Within the *istana* the flames were already licking up the columns, curling the cloth hangings. He caught a last glimpse of Morris stretched under his robe of yellow silk in a pool of gore. He lay beside Tregembo's poor bruised and bloated corpse. Then thick coils of smoke and the racing flames hid them from his view. The boy was tugging at him, clacking urgently and indicating that they should run. Something in his face set Drinkwater in motion, releasing him from his archarnement.

He began to run, to run and run, leaving the foul place far behind him in a blind panic. The hot blast of the explosion thrust him in the back. He fell skidding forward, aware of earth and filth in his mouth and the tumbling form of the boy whirling through the air, some trick of the blast tossing him high. A force seemed to squeeze behind Drinkwater's eyeballs; all he could see was a lake of blood.

And then it was raining!

The silvery droplets fell about him. He looked round for Elizabeth and the children. They would get wet, for the rain was heavy, beating down, striking his bare flesh.

'Sir? Sir? Can you hear me, sir? Are you all right, sir?'

'Elizabeth . . . ?'

'It's Frey, sir . . . Frey . . . It's all over, sir . . .'

And he opened his eyes to see silver coins falling from the sky.

Penang

It was ironic that he should have been saved by the boy Budrudeen. In that final confrontation with Morris the boy might have saved his master instead, but mutilation and degradation had, in the end, turned him against his persecutor. The shot was probably the only act Budrudeen had performed uncoerced in his short life. It was, too, a refutation of Morris's appalling creed.

The boy had not survived long, expiring soon after they brought his abused body back to *Patrician* in the flotilla of boats pulled by exhausted oarsmen. The losses they had sustained had been fearful and they had burnt the *kampong* as an act of corporate vengeance while the Dyaks melted into the jungle. And yet they returned with an air of triumph, for they had discovered a hoard of silver, much of it picked up on the hillside by men induced to be honest on the promise of legitimate reward, though there were undoubtedly private sums hidden about *Patrician*. Over forty thousand pounds worth, by the best calculations, the proceeds of years of depradations against the merchant trade in the South China Sea. Some of this booty had been held near the powder magazine below the *istana* and so had been blown spectacularly into the air.

But even this justification, satisfactory though it seemed to the profit-mesmerised survivors, failed to gratify Drinkwater. He was seized by the most profound doubts about his conduct, plunged into the blackest of depressions as *Patrician*, under the easy sail manageable by her depleted company, rounded Tumasek Island and headed north-west into the Strait of Malacca.

'All men murder their own innocence, sir,' said Derrick as he sat, pen poised, awaiting the captain's dictation. Drinkwater looked at the Quaker; it was the first time Derrick had called him 'sir'.

'Why do you say that?' he asked guiltily, as though caught in a culpable act.

'It is part of the human condition.'

'That is damned cold comfort.'

'The truth is rarely comfortable, especially when it touches ourselves.'

Drinkwater opened his mouth to damn the canting and sanctimonious prattler, but acknowledged the other as an equal. 'Does your creed prohibit you rendering assistance?'

'My creed tells me to be guided by the inner spirit . . .'

'I had no time for such deep considerations,' said Drinkwater with a hint of returning spirit. 'A course of events initiated and guided by an amoral hand will find little to inhibit it. The most outrageous evil can be perpetrated with bewildering ease, especially if directed by a cool mind . . .' And Morris had possessed that, he thought morosely. He stared fixedly at Derrick who lowered his eyes to the paper.

'It has not been my lot, sir, to come face to face with such things.'

The ghost of a smile crept across Drinkwater's mouth. 'No; you have been fortunate,' he hesitated, 'or wise . . .'

Had he had innocence left to murder? Yet something had died in him as he slashed Morris in his frenzy, and the realisation robbed him of all sense of having avenged Tregembo.

'Perhaps that is why the Almighty reserved the right to vengeance,' said Derrick with disarming prescience.

'Damn it, don't preach at me,' snapped Drinkwater, 'bend your attention to my report,' and he began to dictate.

'Penang, sir.'

Quilhampton was smiling as Drinkwater came on deck and they exchanged salutes. The high-peaked island was still distant, still remote and blue. Beyond it and stretching away on the starboard beam lay the line of the Malay coast.

'We shall be at anchor by noon, sir.'

'Yes.'

'How is the wound, sir?'

'The wound is nothing, James. Lallo's curettage removed the morbid tissue and there is no inflamation. I assure you I am quite well. It is not yet time for you to step into my shoes.'

'Sir, I never . . .'

'No, of course you didn't. You are certainly more cheerful than you have been, no, hear me out. It was a bloody business, James, not an affair of much honour. To be candid I did not expect to survive it and, damn me, considered you owed me obligation enough to attend to Elizabeth and the children . . .'

'Sir, of course . . .'

'Well, sir, enough said about the matter then. I apprehend,' went on Drinkwater, diverting the conversation with an obvious hand, 'you will be disappointed again today.'

'Why so, sir?'

'Your high spirits are evidence of expectations, ain't they?'

'Er, well, I, er . . .'

'You will receive no word from Mistress MacEwan, James, because, despite the foolish inventions of your imaginations, no one in England knows where we are, beyond the fact that we were last ordered to the Pacific.'

'But we are homeward bound, sir, are we not?'

Drinkwater turned, lifted his glass and scrutinised the island as it loomed over the horizon.

'God and Admiral Sir Ed'd Pellew permitting.'

'Captain Drinkwater, pray take a seat . . . a glass, sir?'

'Your servant, Sir Ed'd.'

'I collect we've met before, sir?'

'In ninety-four, sir, a night action on the French coast with the flying squadron. I was in *Kestrel* . . .'

'Ah, yes, the cutter . . . a gallant scrap, eh?'

'Indeed, sir.'

'May I present Captain Frederick Torrington of the *Polyphemus*, the latest teak frigate from the Parsee yard at Bombay.'

Drinkwater recalled the elegant, over-painted thirty-six-gun cruiser his boat had passed pulling to the flagship.

'Sir. A fine-looking ship, a credit to the Service . . .'

Drinkwater nodded to the thin-lipped boy who wore the single epaulette of a junior post-captain, then turned again to the pock-marked, balding admiral whose tall frame still seemed to possess the energy of a young man.

'Sir, my report . . .' he handed over the papers. 'May I enquire, Sir Ed'd, if those two ships in the roads are from Canton or Calcutta?'

'You refer to the Indiaman and the Country-wallah?' drawled Torrington.

'I do, yes . . .' Drinkwater was aware of an amused glance passing between Pellew and Torrington.

'Why do you ask, Captain Drinkwater?'

'The Indiaman seemed familiar, sir . . .'

'She should do, sir, she was part of your convoy.' It was Torrington who spoke, the tone of his voice impertinent, even insolent.

'Is she *Guilford*?'

'Yes . . . I took her . . .'

'Torrington had the good fortune, Captain Drinkwater, to be sent on a cruise by myself . . .'

'Hoisted Dutch colours and lay to in the Gaspar Strait. Took those two fellows two days later . . . damndest piece of luck. Taken by pirates don't you know; got 'em back without a shot being fired.'

'Damndest luck, sir. I congratulate you. Captain Callan is in health?'

'Positively so, sir, *absolument* . . .'

'Leadenhall Street will be most gratified, Captain Torrington. I had despaired of ever finding them again.'

'*Nil desperandum*, Captain Drinkwater.'

'It is difficult to avoid it sometimes, sir,' said Drinkwater ruefully, 'but doubtless the experience will affect you one day . . .'

Pellew coughed, a trifle pointedly. 'I expect Captain Torrington will be rewarded by the Court of Directors with a present of plate,' he said.

'I do most assuredly hope so, Sir Ed'd,' Drinkwater stood.

'Sit down, sit down. Captain Torrington was just leaving . . .'

There was a twinkle in Pellew's eyes as the door closed behind Torrington. 'Forgive him, Drinkwater, he's a bear cub.'

'That is the trouble, sir.' Drinkwater stopped, thinking he had gone too far with such a shameless nepotist as Pellew, for all his reputation as the finest seaman of his age.

'Now tell me, when will Drury be back? Did you see my son Fleetwood? I am damnably weary of this station and long to follow you home.'

'Sir?' Drinkwater looked sharply at the admiral.

'You are a person of some standing, Captain Drinkwater, though I admit the fact is not known to Captain Torrington.'

'How so, sir?'

Pellew shuffled his papers on his desk, failed to find what he was looking for and tinkled a hand-bell. While they waited for his secretary he added, 'I have received specific instructions about you if, as the Admiralty has it, you "appear in these seas", a quaint turn of phrase, you'll allow.'

'Indeed, sir.' Drinkwater suppressed his revivifying curiosity. Somehow it was enormously stimulating to find that life went on.

'His Lordship requires you in England.'

'His Lordship?'

'Lord Dungarth who, as we both know, attends to matters of some delicacy.'

'He is not dead, Sir Ed'd?'

'I think, sir, it was intended that his enemies should think he was.'

'It deceived his friends . . . then he is quite well?'

'He is hulled, but serviceable. He lost a leg, but his reasoning parts are unaffected.'

'I am sorry for his leg, but that is good news.'

'Now your report . . . the matter of the silver is serious.' Pellew dropped his avuncular attitude and was, remorselessly, the Commander-in-Chief, East Indies Station. 'Those damned *traders* in Calcutta have a powerful lobby . . .'

'The silver is safe, sir. I recovered it. And a little more besides.'

'Ahhh, that *is* good news . . .' And Pellew's well-known cupidity was interrupted by the arrival of his secretary. 'Have the goodness to find the Admiralty's instructions regarding Captain Drinkwater, if you please.'

'And so, sir, after consultations with Sir Edward's physician I am persuaded they offer no threat and that my regime of salt-bathing has been efficacious. I apprehend that there will be no further outbreaks of button-scurvy, sir.'

Drinkwater nodded at the surgeon indulgently. 'Ah, Mr Lallo, I am delighted to hear it. Your remedy', he said, with a touch of irony, 'does you credit.'

'Thank you, sir. I also learned from Sir Edward's man that Captain Rakitin lately succumbed to a quotidian fever induced by a carcinoma.'

'I am sorry to hear that, Mr Lallo, indeed I am. I do not believe the Russians will long bear arms against us.'

'Let us hope you are right, sir. We have few friends in the world.' Lallo rose to take his leave, then seemed to hesitate.

'There is something else, Mr Lallo?'

'Sir . . . there is wild talk of a duel, sir.'

'A duel?' snapped Drinkwater incredulously. 'By God, is the appetite for blood insatiable? Between whom pray?'

'Between young Midshipman Chirkov who is still here in Penang and . . .'

'Go on, sir, go on, I demand to know!'

'Frey, sir.'

'God's bones, has the young jackanapes lost his reason, send for him upon the instant.'

Drinkwater sat immobilised while he waited for Frey. What the deuce was the matter with the lad?

'You sent for me, sir?'

'Indeed, Mr Frey, I did. I hear you are engaged to meet Midshipman Chirkov upon a matter of . . . of . . .'

'Honour, sir.'

'Have you any explanation to offer me? You know the practice to be forbidden, a rule I most strictly enforce.'

'You forbid me to meet Midshipman Chirkov, sir, even in our capacities as private gentlemen?' Frey's manner was prickly.

'I most certainly do, Mr Frey.'

'But my honour, sir?'

'Damn your honour, sir! You will oblige me by your obedience.'

'Sir, I protest!'

'Hold your tongue, sir! I have just obtained for you ratification of your commission as lieutenant from the Commander-in-Chief! I have just persuaded Admiral Pellew that it is unnecessary for you to take the formal examination. I have just descanted upon your abilities, praised your steadiness, recommended your proficiency as a watercolourist, as being an officer ideally fitted for surveying. I have, in short, Mr Frey, enlarged on every segment of your character that I might adduce in your favour to procure this preferment. You will therefore attend to my own orders in preference to your foolish notion to demand satisfaction.'

'Sir,' said Frey unhappily, 'I had no idea of your high opinion.'

'Mr Frey,' said Drinkwater grimly, 'I have lost too many friends to allow you to put your life to the hazard for a trifling notion of honour.'

'But, sir . . .'

'I forbid it!'

Drinkwater's voice cracked with anger. He paused, then

244

added in a quieter tone, 'Your talk of honour and the compulsive need for satisfaction are foolish principles . . .' The captain lapsed into an introspective silence. An awkwardness hung in the air, broken in the end by Frey.

'Very well, sir, I submit. And thank you for your efforts on my behalf.'

'Eh? Oh, yes . . . yes, very well.' Drinkwater recovered himself, coughing to clear his throat. 'You will be glad to know', he seated himself, 'that we are ordered home. The rigours of your duty will demand more courage than facing Mr Chirkov's pistols, a thing quickly done, but it's courage of a different sort, Mr Frey.'

Frey left the cabin. For a moment Drinkwater stared after the young man, then he buried his head in his hands.

Author's Note

The British occupation of Macao and Admiral Drury's extra-ordinary demonstration before Canton are a sideshow of the Napoleonic War largely ignored by standard histories. Drury, the first of several British naval officers to appear in the Pearl River during the nineteenth century, was unique for his sympathetic attitude to the Chinese. I have largely used his own words to express his sentiments. The Chinese regarded his 'humane treatment' as a victory of their own. Pellew too, though a shameless nepotist, was no imperialist, and Drinkwater's view of British policy in India was also expressed by Sir Edward. Both Pellew and Drury were harassed by Company and Country mercantile interests who considered the convoy arrangements of the former inadequate, and said so publicly. To some extent their criticisms of the Navy's preference for seeking prizes were justified.

Few, if any, merchant ships got out of the Pearl River during the 1808 season, but Drury did send a frigate up to Whampoa to secure a quantity of specie owed by the Chinese merchants. Rumours of a French overland expedition via Persia were current at the time (and considered by Napoleon), while the depredations of French corsairs continued in the Indian Ocean. I am chiefly indebted to Captain Eastwick's memoirs for a contemporary picture of the Canton trading scene and in particular the Country ships.

Piracy in the South China Sea continues to be a problem in the present century. Raffles's acquisition of the island of Tumasek broke much of the power of the pirates when he founded Singapore in 1819, but at that time, as his own Malay tutor, Abdullah bin Abdul Kadir, wrote: 'no mortal dared to pass through the Straits . . . Jinns and satans even were afraid, for that was the place the pirates made use of . . . There also they put to death their captives . . . All along the beach there were hundreds of human skulls, some of them old, some fresh . . . in various stages of decay.' Shortly after the end of the Napoleonic War the British Admiralty sent Captain Henry Keppel to extirpate these nests of pirates. Doubtless they were influenced by Drinkwater's report on the subject. Nor were naval vessels immune from what Raffles called 'an evil of ancient date', for in 1807 the Dutch warship *De Vrede* was captured and her officers and crew treated with characteristic barbarism.

Although unseasonal, typhoons are not unknown as late in the year as November. Finally, the origin of the enmity between Drinkwater and Morris may be found detailed in *An Eye of the Fleet* and *A Brig of War*; the presence of the Russian prisoners in *In Distant Waters*.

Sphere now offers an exciting range of quality fiction and non-fiction by both established and new authors. All of the books in this series are available from good bookshops, or can be ordered from the following address:

Sphere Books
Cash Sales Department
P.O. Box 11
Falmouth
Cornwall TR10 9EN.

Please send cheque or postal order (no currency), and allow 60p for postage and packing for the first book plus 25p for the second book and 15p for each additional book ordered up to a maximum charge of £1.90 in U.K.

B.F.P.O. customers please allow 60p for the first book, 25p for the second book plus 15p per copy for the next 7 books, thereafter 9p per book.

Overseas customers including Eire please allow £1.25 for postage and packing for the first book, 75p for the second book and 28p for each subsequent title ordered.